MY
Funny Old
SOUL MATE

MY

Funny Old

SOUL MATE

STEVEN HARTMAN

iUniverse, Inc.
Bloomington

My Funny Old Soul Mate

iUniverse books may be ordered through booksellers or by contacting:

iUniverse
1663 Liberty Drive
Bloomington, IN 47403
www.iuniverse.com
1-800-Authors (1-800-288-4677)

ISBN: 978-1-4759-5237-7 (sc)
ISBN: 978-1-4759-5239-1 (hc)
ISBN: 978-1-4759-5238-4 (ebk)

Library of Congress Control Number: 2012918476

Printed in the United States of America

iUniverse rev. date: 10/04/2012

For Caitlin
My Soul Mate

1

She wore her hair in a ponytail; a blonde rope hanging off of the back of her head. She had a handful of earrings poking out of her earlobes; there were six total. These didn't draw the attention to Annie. She had a bubbly personality. Her mouth had a tendency to shift upwards in an almost permanent, slight smile. It was charming and sweet.

She was eager to please in spite of getting walked on by friends and strangers alike. Some men noticed this, and through the course of her life, some men took advantage of this. Sometimes they got away with it and sometimes Annie deflected their advances.

Her optimism rarely wavered, her happiness never seemed to wane and her dreams were out-of-reach and had been crushed constantly by negative feedback and quick changes of the subject.

"Really? That's cute," was a response she had received from her boyfriend who shunned her aspirations as ridiculous. She studied event planning in college and had barely used the degree a single day after graduation.

That's why Annie was thirty years old and working at a diner in the Boston metro neighborhood of Brookline. Just off of Beacon Street it was considered a "greasy spoon"; an unintended adjective for a once booming establishment. The backdoor led to an alley that smelled as if the garbage piled and was rarely picked up. The cooks were unmotivated, overweight and looked ten years older than they actually were. They smoked cigarettes on their breaks next to the unfriendly odors of rotting heads of lettuce and discarded pancakes and waffles. They dropped their butts on the ground. They were friendly to Annie.

The coffee wasn't premium but it was cheap. Men from a different era who shunned flavored coffees congregated and discussed politics, current events and the Red Sox. Kids in their twenties sought the hash browns, eggs and coffee to combat a hangover on an idle Sunday morning. It did a decent business.

Every morning Bill Dooley sat with a copy of *The Boston Globe* and scanned the articles until one piqued his interest. He read through a pair of thin reading glasses and moved his finger along with each line he read. He had gray-white hair that was easily blown around in the wind. His eyes were blue and the wrinkles around them were carved deeply with age. He was young in spirit and enthusiasm while in his comfort zone but his age was just north of seventy.

When he ordered there appeared to be no logic. He never looked at the menu but simply order what he desired. There was never an occasion in which he ordered an item that wasn't available and he changed his order every single day.

"Good morning, Aldo." He said with a smile to the owner who sat at the counter always keeping an eye on his staff. Aldo spoke with an accent so faint he passed as a man that had lived in the country his entire life. He just about had. Aldo moved to New York at twelve with his family from the north of Italy and opened the diner in Brookline at thirty-two. His silver-fox hair created a harsh contrast of black and white.

"Good morning, Bill." Aldo responded turning his head as Bill took an open booth at the window where he could slight his gaze to passing cars or a couple, hand-in-hand, heading towards the T-stop on Beacon Street. "Did you catch the Sox game last night?"

"There was no game," Bill would respond sitting down. "A game would mean that the other team had a chance."

"Kansas City got two hits," Aldo responded.

Bill tossed the newspaper down on the table. "Every fisherman gets a bite every once in a while . . . even with a piece of string and a hook."

Annie approached Bill with a filled cup of black coffee and placed it in front of him.

"Thank you, honey," he said with a courteous smile and he put on his reading glasses. He rarely made chit-chat. He was friendly and quiet and when asked if he had plans for the weekend, he simply answered, "No," followed with a smile and then down-cast his eyes back to the newspaper.

Annie left the diner around one in the afternoon after working through a breakfast and lunch shift. She walked down to Beacon Street and watched as the train cars continued westward in the median. The mid-April sun felt warm against her skin and she walked the half-mile to her apartment building. She said hello to a fellow resident as they were opening the mailbox. "Mailman didn't come yet," the woman replied bitterly and continued walking towards the exit.

Annie cheerfully entered the elevator and rode to the sixth floor. She stepped out into the vacant, cream colored hallway with faded khaki-green carpeting and made her way to the apartment.

Her thoughts gravitated towards the idea of wanting a cuddle buddy to greet her upon entering but Andre wouldn't hear of it, not in his apartment. He declined her request with a story of when he visited his grandmother how the house always smelled of cat piss and day-old tuna fish. "There was fur everywhere. I had to throw away a shirt because duct tape wouldn't get all of it out."

"We could get a short-hair kitty, that way . . ." But she was cut off.

"No cats in my apartment. End of discussion."

She closed the door and entered the empty apartment. A light breeze floated inside from the cracked window on the opposite side of the room.

They had been dating for five years, four of those years spent living together in the Brookline apartment and she never considered asking Andre a second time about adopting a kitten.

Steven Hartman

Annie placed her purse onto the kitchen counter and used the bathroom. Moments later she stepped out of the bathroom with little trickles of water she neglected to dry on her fingertips. She grabbed her copy of *John Adams* from the bedroom night stand and collapsed onto the dark-gray leather sofa. *John Adams* was a book which Andre insisted she read as oppose to the chick-lit drivel she craved. He felt that reading can enhance brain function, however reading crap is equivalent to watching reality programming, another vice that Annie secretly enjoyed.

She didn't want to offend her boyfriend of half-a-decade so she dove into the best-selling biography on America's second president. She had spent two weeks reading it thus far having to put it down frequently and barely able to retain its words. She simply couldn't wrap her head around a topic that didn't hold her interest to begin with. When Andre insisted she read the same books he enjoyed she would argue that they weren't very enticing. He always insisted though and so she found it was easier to just drive through the pages than face the anger that boiled to the surface. His usual self-confidence seemed to nearly fade as he questioned her respect for him. "Just because I'm not interested in the same books as you does not mean I'm not interested in you!" She argued when his confusion-based temper flared.

After reading a few pages restlessness caught up with her. She closed the biography and sighed at her boredom. With a breath inward she could smell the sweet scents of spring in Boston and decided to take a stroll.

She wasn't hungry but the odor of baked, high-caloric treats at every Dunkin' Donuts she passed was causing her stomach to insist that she stop and give in to temptation.

She continued and finally entered an Italian bakery. Annie purchased two large cookies: chocolate chunk and butterscotch/chocolate chip. She opened the bag and smelled its pleasuring contents. She would hold off eating the cookie now for the joy of eating it later after dinner with Andre.

2

Annie checked her watch. It was eleven in the morning and an old couple, barely speaking to one another sat at the booth that Bill had occupied the day before; his favorite booth, he told the servers. It hadn't quite crossed her mind that Bill hadn't come in for his daily breakfast until Aldo looked at the clock above the tin Coca-Cola sign behind the register and mentioned it.

At noon there was a sense of worry emanating throughout the diner.

"Maybe he's just out-of-town," Annie mentioned with hope.

"Out-of-town where? Where would he go?"

At twelve-thirty, Aldo smacked his hand on the counter. His frustration was overwhelming and he called Annie over.

"Check on Bill!" He ordered.

"What?"

"Go to his apartment and check on him."

"What?" She wanted to make sure she heard her boss correctly. "I don't know where he lives."

Aldo moved towards the register opening a drawer just underneath the counter. He started sifting through a stack of papers until he found an address book.

"People still use those?" Annie teased.

"Yes, they do. Not all of us have those stupid little . . ." he motioned with his thumbs ". . . smartphones." He looked at Annie. "Stop smiling like that."

His insistence only caused her smile to widen.

Aldo shook his head and continued searching for Bill's address. When he found it he wrote it down on the back of a receipt slip and handed it to Annie.

"Why do you have this?"

"We used to play cards and I mail him a Christmas card every year." Aldo decided to tease back, "Does your generation know about mail? You know stamps and envelopes."

Annie pointed at him with a warning; he pointed back mocking her play at seriousness.

Annie studied the address. "You should try calling him."

"Oh gee, why didn't I think about calling him?" Aldo smacked his forehead. "Of course I called him, Annie! Go." He motioned his hands for her to get going.

"I'm not clocking out," she responded taking off her apron and tossing it under the counter. She grabbed her purse.

"Go!"

She knew the street and located the apartment building. Her finger followed the call box until she saw the apartment number. Annie buzzed up once and waited turning her back to the door and looking out onto the street. A bus flew by sending a flurry of street dust and dirt in the air. She turned back around.

A moment after pressing the button a second time she was flustered and felt silly standing idly outside an apartment awaiting a response from Bill. A woman, busy on her cell phone, exited, powering through the door with no courtesy to hold it for Annie.

"Thank you," Annie muttered and slipped into the building.

She took the elevator to the ninth, and top, floor.

She knocked on the door with the same results as the buzzer however she could hear a television blaring, the audience of trash TV encouraged a fight and hollered and cheered as the brawl ensued.

She pounded on the door with her fists then cradled the door knob finding that it was locked.

"Bill?"

No reply.

"Bill?" She said louder.

Nothing.

Annie rode the elevator down to the lobby and reviewed the names above the mailbox finding the landlord's apartment. She sought out the apartment and knocked on the door. It flung open as if the woman was anticipating a visitor and was standing by the door.

"Hello?" She said with a confused look upon her face. She was old, very old, in her mid-eighties, and looked exhausted like the act of walking caused her to become winded. She was taller than Annie with dyed light brown hair. How did she get to the door so fast? Annie wondered.

"Hi. I'm checking on a friend of mine and I'm getting worried. I'm wondering if you could help me out."

"Who's your friend?"

"Bill." She realized she didn't know his name. "Bill in apartment 901."

The landlord nodded. "Have you tried calling?"

"And knocking."

"How did you get in the building?"

"Some very nice lady let me in," she lied. "I'm worried about my friend."

"Hm," the landlord grunted upset that one of her tenants had allowed a stranger on the premises. Annie took a quick peek inside her apartment, she looked like a hoarder. Boxes were piled up against a wall and newspapers were stacked to the point of tipping.

Annie's trusting smile allowed the landlord's skepticism to wane just enough to travel to the top floor and check on her tenant. "I'll be back in a moment, Alan," she shouted and they both made their way to the elevator.

The landlord waddled side-to-side advancing down the hall at a snail's pace looking straight ahead.

"Is Alan your husband?" Annie asked as she pressed the up button. The door chimed and opened up instantly.

"My pussy cat," the landlord replied.

Annie didn't ask any further questions and the silence was awkward. They reached the ninth floor and exited. The landlord went through the same knocking motions as Annie had previously. She sighed and pulled the master key outward from her key ring and unlocked the door knocking as she entered the apartment.

"Bill?" She asked announcing her presence.

It was immediately clear that the television noise was coming from inside his apartment.

"Bill?" Annie said stepping in behind the landlord.

They both saw a hand lying motionless on the floor of the bathroom.

Annie gasped pushing her hand to her mouth as if she were trying to keep the air inside her body. The moment of pause passed and she pushed past the landlord.

She saw Bill, khaki pants around his ankles and a light blue shirt on his body, unconscious. His exposed buttocks became an image she would never be able to shake.

"Bill!" She shouted but he didn't move. An odor crossed her nose and she squeezed her face in disgust. Looking into the toilet, she found a mess of water and broken up pieces of poo; the result of it sitting in the bowl for an undisclosed amount of time.

She whipped her cell phone from her purse to call for an ambulance and flushed the toilet.

3

The doctor was tired, or his eyelids naturally hung low looking as if he was in a permanent state of calm. He had a young face and in spite of his exhausted demeanor he looked more like a primetime television doctor than a real medical professional.

"He's awake now."

"Oh thank god," Annie replied allowing her breath to move in and out with ease. She tilted backwards into the hard plastic chair with its weak blue back and butt pad. "What happened?"

"His back gave out as he was . . ." The doctor appeared embarrassed to say any words indicating using the toilet. ". . . and he collapsed to the floor. He couldn't reach a telephone and no one heard his call for help. He needed to take his heart medicine but couldn't so his blood pressure dipped and he became unconscious."

Annie rolled her eyes thinking that this doctor was acting like a child. "Okay. How old are you?"

"Thirty-three."

"Is he going to be fine?"

"You two will be back to performing your sexual deviancies in no time. Just go easy for a bit."

Annie's eyes bugged and she was taken aback at the unprofessional nature of the doctor. "We're not . . ." It was a cringe-worthy thought. "He's not my . . ."

"Oh, of course not," the doctor said without the hint of embarrassment at his error. "Are you single?"

She smiled kindly and shook her head. "I have a boyfriend."

His demeanor had not altered away from confidence. "Well, you can see him now." The doctor turned and shuffled down the hallway stopping at the nurse's station.

Annie stood up and began her walk down towards Bill's room. Did he really think I could have been Bill's lover? She asked herself and thought it more appropriate that she be considered his granddaughter.

As she approached the room, she felt a sudden fear of being alone take root in her mind. She pondered Bill's fate and wondered how long he would've lay on the white bathroom floor until he simply perished, how many others are yet to be found.

But Bill didn't seem fazed. He was smiling and enthusiastic when Annie entered.

"My guardian angel," he announced with open arms. Annie raced to them feeling his hands meet upon her back.

"I'm so glad you're okay."

"No one more than me."

"I don't know what would've happened if Aldo didn't order me to check on you."

"Oh, pshhh," he waved it off. "You're crying, Annie. Let me see that pretty smile."

She wiped the tears away and smiled at being called out on her crying.

"It sounds like I should start taking my cordless into the bathroom." He was still grinning with delight.

Maybe he was just so happy to be alive, maybe he wasn't honing up to the reality of the situation or maybe he was just on muscle relaxants. He refused to let it bother him though and it was forcing Annie to be calm. This was bewildering; she wanted him to be troubled by his near-death experience.

"How are you not . . ." She shook her head backing away.

Bill's response was a shrug of his shoulders. "When it's time it's time. I kind of know how Elvis felt when he died though." He chuckled and Annie shook her head in disbelief at Bill's comparison. He dismissed her reaction. "It was my back. I would have been conscious and screaming again in no time. Someone would've heard me."

"No you wouldn't have! Your blood pressure dropped, you could have . . ." She didn't want to say the word.

Bill allowed his happiness to fade briefly and responded with calm. "I know but I want to celebrate the fact that I didn't."

"Do you have anyone you want me to call?"

Bill pursed his lips and shook his head.

"No one?" Annie wanted to confirm.

"No."

She contemplated why there was no one in his life and, out of courtesy, refused to question further. She was used to his short answers with little information.

"Would you like me to get you a newspaper?"

"That would be lovely. You don't by any chance have my reading glasses on you, do you?"

"I forgot them as the EMTs were placing your unconscious body on a gurney."

"That's fair. I'd still like the newspaper though. I'll just hold it close to my face."

By the time Annie found her way to the lobby, bought a newspaper out of the stand and entered Bill's room, he was getting dressed. He buttoned his last button and took in a deep breath.

"They gave me an eviction notice." Bill shrugged his shoulders. "Something to read on the T then." He grabbed the newspaper.

"Don't you think we should take a cab."

"No."

"You don't have to follow me home," Bill said opening the lobby door to the apartment complex.

"I don't mind." She backtracked thinking maybe he was hinting that he didn't want her around. "Unless you don't want me to."

"Come on."

They rode the elevator in silence.

Bill opened his apartment door and tossed his keys and filled prescription on the stand.

"Excuse me," he said and went into the bathroom.

"Don't fall!" Annie shouted.

She looked around the apartment. She barely remembered being in here earlier. Waiting for the ambulance, the paramedics, and seeing Bill's ass in the air offered no chances to take in the environment.

It was small but perfect for an old man who lived alone, which she gathered he did. A box-television was plugged in on the far side of the room and the couches were brown and old. Mail was piled on the kitchen table that hadn't been dusted in the past year. He wasn't one for décor.

There were pictures of him as a younger man standing next to a woman that she assumed was his wife. There were pictures of children from different time spans. Three kids, some when they were really young and others of them older standing by their family.

Annie picked up the picture frame that held a photo of Bill possibly fifty years younger standing in a tuxedo next to a bride. They smiled like they had been taking pictures all day and were ready to move to their wedding reception.

The toilet flushed and Annie replaced the photograph. She heard the sink run and moments later the door opened.

Bill opened his arms like a magician at the end of the trick. "Disaster averted. There's a sense of accomplishment when you fail at something then succeed the next time around."

"You've been going to the bathroom your whole life, Bill, it's not like you just figured it out."

"Don't rain on my parade."

"I should get going," Annie said. "Andre is going to be home soon and I should get dinner started."

"Andre's your boyfriend?"

She nodded.

"I think you should break up with him." Bill let out a loud sigh as he plopped onto the couch and provided nothing further.

"That's a bold opinion to present." Annie moved to the side of the couch and crossed her arms. "Are you going to follow that up with any particular reasons?"

"I've heard you complain about him a lot."

"People complain about their loved ones all the time. When did you hear this?"

"Annie," Bill said finally looking at her, "you talk to Bethany and you talk to . . ." he struggled to remember some of the other waitresses' names. "You talk to all of them about the way he treats you. It's not like you have these conversations in private; half the diner can hear you."

"It's not that bad," Annie defended. She was upset that he would suddenly confront her like this.

"It doesn't sound that good."

"Every relationship has its problems."

"I absolutely cannot argue that."

"It doesn't mean that you just leave them."

"Agreed."

"Okay." She stated ending the debate.

"Okay." Bill responded nodding his head.

Annie wanted more though. "Anything else?"

"Thank you for rescuing me. I appreciate it," he said kindly affixing his reading glasses on the bridge of his nose. He unfolded the newspaper he had carried from the hospital and started scanning the front page.

"Of course, you're welcome." It meant to sound pleasant but it came out with a hint of hostility.

Bill offered a charming half-smile.

Annie made her way to the door. "I'll see you tomorrow."

As Annie walked home she tried but couldn't shake Bill's bluntness about his thoughts on Andre. Sure, Bethany had offered a similar suggestion but Bill's statement swirled around in her mind longer.

Annie spent twenty minutes preparing a vegetable dish with a little lightly sea-salted salmon. With a glass of red wine she leaned over the counter and continued reading *John Adams* waiting for Andre to come home from work.

Minutes passed and she took a seat on the couch. The minutes accumulated into a half-hour. Annie checked the clock on the oven and wondered where her boyfriend could be.

She checked her cell phone and saw no messages. She sent a text message inquiring on his whereabouts, refilled her wine glass and continued reading. The meal was room temperature.

He was expected home at 6:30 and it was nearing a quarter-after-seven with no word on his expected arrival time. She checked her cell phone as it vibrated with an incoming message.

At work

She sighed and responded asking when he expected to be home. It was five minutes of reading and a half-glass of wine before his response came through.

IDK

Annie tossed her cell phone onto the counter and sighed, frustrated. Her stomach grumbled as she continued through her second glass of wine. She placed a piece of the salmon on a plate along with the mixed veggies and tossed it in the microwave.

She sat down on the couch and ate while watching an entertainment news program and followed it with a reality dating show.

Close to 8:30 she heard the door unlock and quickly changed the station to a sitcom that was low on comedy and high on canned laughter. A commercial was starting as Andre shuffled in. Wet spots stained the shoulders of his suit jacket.

"Hi," she said looking over the couch. "Is it raining?"

"Yep." He sniffled into the air. "Smells good. They brought in food so I'm not hungry."

"It should reheat well."

Andre stepped into the kitchen area without making eye contact. He looked at the pink salmon on the tray. "You know I don't take food to work," he replied in a snide tone.

"I meant tomorrow night."

"Seriously?" He said staring right through Annie as if he was surprised at the idea of leftovers. "You can have it."

He picked a small piece of salmon off and popped it in his mouth.

"I'm going to have a shower. I'm beat."

When Annie heard the shower start she lifted off of the couch and packed the remainder of the food away. She crawled into bed before Andre presented himself from the bathroom.

The wine swirled in her head making her lust for her boyfriend. She continued to read while eager for Andre to come to bed. She kept eyeing the page numbers and occasionally flipped to the last page prior to the *Notes* to see how much more remained.

Andre exited the bathroom completely nude. He was in great shape often waking up early and going to the gym two blocks away before getting ready for work. Below the waist he had been smaller than average but could get the job done. She stared at his butt when he turned towards the dresser. Opening the dresser drawer he pulled out a pair of blue and maize colored flannel bottoms and a gray T-shirt with a faded M on the front. He slipped into his sleepwear.

"It's good, eh?" He said nodding to the book on Annie's lap.

She smiled. "Yes. Very interesting."

He chuckled at her response as he collapsed onto the bed.

"What?" Annie asked.

He lifted himself up on his arm and looked at her. "You have a stunning way with words." She furled her eyebrows, confused. He repeated her criticism. "Very interesting." He lifted up and kissed her on the lips; a short meaningless kiss. "You're cute."

"Are you mocking me?" She asked as her sexual urge faded in lieu of anger.

Andre sighed not interested in a conflict before shutting his eyes. "I thought you could come up with something a little less arbitrary than 'very interesting'. It's David McCullough, for Christ's sake, not a hokey rom-com that they turn into movies that star that one blonde chick."

"People like those books, you know."

"Sorry," Andre said with no true sincerity. He turned over to his side and ruffled the pillow to reach his desired comfort level. "Are you going to keep that light on all night?"

"I was going to read for a bit." She felt disappointed at his lack of passion.

He answered with an exaggerated sigh and said, "Don't fall asleep without turning it off."

"I won't."

She could hardly concentrate on the words she was reading. She could only think of the evening she wanted with her boyfriend, a night that would revolve around a healthy, tasty meal to his liking and a glass or two of red wine and then they would make love in the bedroom.

Maybe it was the five-year relationship or his demanding work schedule but they hadn't even fooled around in more than a month. She could only think that he was getting his kicks elsewhere. For sanity's sake, she dismissed the idea.

There was a similar time many years ago when she had the discussion with her mother that her sex life was far from ideal.

"Men go through certain phases in their lives. Call it sickness or work, but, believe it or not, they don't crave sex." She always had a very open relationship with her mother and could speak to her about almost anything. The details of her parent's sex life were off limits and she was happy to have never accidentally walked in on them. "Your father once had a really bad bout of bronchitis. Remember when he was home for a month and coughed all the time? We didn't make love for more than six weeks. He just didn't have it in him."

"What did you do?"

"I had other ways."

The thought grossed her out and her mother confirmed that it was a battery-operated device used and not another man.

As Annie looked at her boyfriend's rising and falling body, his back facing her side of the bed, she considered that they would be back to their usual escapades in a matter of days. She hoped.

Annie continued reading but her mind drifted to Bill's words earlier in the day and his nonchalant comment about leaving Andre.

What did he really know? Annie told herself convinced that you just don't throw away five years because of a rough patch.

Her eyelids grew heavy and the words she was attempted to read blurred together. Her head eventually swayed and she fell asleep.

The light remained illuminated.

4

"And it was gone?"

"Gone." Annie replied to Bethany. "He took the lamp. I couldn't find it anywhere!"

"Wow." Bethany was seven years younger than Annie, lived at the end of the green line off of Cleveland Circle with her parents and occasionally attended Roxbury Community College. When she took classes it was usually only one or two. She was pretty with short bleach-blonde hair with a hint of her original brunette peeking out of the base of her scalp. She drank cup after cup of coffee throughout the morning but never appeared to be over-caffeinated. She ate horrendously but never gained a pound.

"Cherish those eating habits," Annie would advise her, "because sometime in your mid-twenties you have to start eating healthy and working out every day."

Bethany couldn't wait to leave her parent's house and desperately filled her savings account with as much money as possible. Her father provided her with money for school, books, and expenses yet she dreamed of living with a roommate away from her parents—she dreamed of freedom.

"I can't believe you're just eating a piece of bacon like celery."

Bethany shrugged her shoulders and snapped off a chunk of the crispy bacon that the cooks prepped for the rush. "He didn't say anything." Bethany wanted to confirm.

"I woke up in the middle of the night, the light was off, it was dark so I didn't even realize it was gone until this morning."

"Weird."

"He's upset."

The door opened and both waitresses looked at Bill as he entered. He waved to both of them.

"How ya doing, Aldo?"

Aldo turned from his stool and lifted his body upwards. "Glad to see you're doing well."

"You were just worried I found a new place."

Annie filled a cup of coffee and walked it over to Bill as he sat down in his usual booth. "Here you go."

"Thank you, angel. How about a tuna melt but spare me the onions."

"I think I can do that for you."

They held smiles with one another for a beat before she took the order to the kitchen.

"So, it's your back?" Aldo inquired.

"Funny thing is I felt fine the moment I woke up but that probably has everything to do with muscle relaxants. Doctor said maybe it was a spasm or something. I'm fine though. The main problem was my inability to take my medicine. The joys of aging," Bill replied opening up the *Boston Globe*. "Thank you, Aldo."

"What are friends for?"

"Free meals."

"No. Friends are not for free meals," he replied sternly then revealed his smile. "Nice try, cheapskate."

Bill dug into the articles of the newspaper until his food arrived.

"Annie," he started, "I've procured a pair of tickets to the Sox game against Cleveland Thursday night and I would very much like to take you. The seats are bottom-tier pricing and it's supposed to rain but it's the least I could do for you." He smiled innocently, warmly. Then seeing the concern in her eyes he sucked in a breath and his eyes bugged. "It's not a date," he assured her and was oddly aware of the possibility of coming off as a creepy old man. "I promise."

"Umm . . ." She hesitated and pondered Andre's reaction to her asking his permission to attend a baseball game with another man. She wanted to believe that he wouldn't be jealous but knew that he was apt to throw a temper tantrum and question her fidelity as well as her taste in men. "What does that say about me?" She imagined him shouting.

"You know I'll be here tomorrow if you want to tell me tomorrow."

"I'll tell you tomorrow." She started backing away.

"You tell me tomorrow."

"Would you like some more coffee?"

"Please."

"Oh, you're here," Andre said when he walked into the apartment and saw Bethany on the couch. He immediately started sifting through the small amount of mail sitting on the counter.

Andre didn't hide his dislike for Bethany. Annie was well aware of the earful that she would get about Bethany's presence in the apartment. His dislike was traced back to the first night that Annie and Andre had Bethany, Annie's new and only friend in Boston at the time, over for dinner and drinks. Andre kept joking about a three-way and always backtracking on his insistence when Annie would get upset. "I was just kidding, jeez, Annie, lighten up!" He would say. Bethany had called him out saying he was a pig and their dislike grew from there.

Bethany and Annie had taken in a late-afternoon movie, stopped to pick up dinner at a local, fast-food Mexican restaurant, then headed to the apartment where they were now sipping on red wine.

Annie shared Bill's invitation with Bethany who used it as another platform for insisting that Annie end her relationship with Andre. Always the small details, it was months of listening to

Annie's malcontent that pushed Bethany to insist there were better men out there.

Annie's rebuttal was always the same. She couldn't afford to live in the city on her own if she wanted to end the relationship. Also, many older couples told tales of ruts that lasted months in their own long-term relationships. Annie simply believed that things would turn around and that happy days were just around the corner. It was normal, she told herself, not realizing she was too afraid to leave. After the five-year investment into the relationship she couldn't convince herself to search for something new. She was, after all, thirty-years-old.

"What's for dinner?" Andre asked without looking up.

"We brought in food from the Taqueria."

He opened up the bag to find a container with a burrito bowl with extra mixed veggies meant for him.

Andre sat on the single chair opposite the couch and turned on the Red Sox game.

Annie and Bethany eyed the game for a moment then each other.

"I'm going to go. I have stuff to do before tomorrow."

"I bet you do," Andre replied sarcastically with a disdainful, quiet chuckle.

Annie shook her head signaling Bethany to let it go but the frustration burned beneath her.

Annie and Bethany stood up, walked to the door and hugged.

"If I don't see you before then, have fun at the game on Thursday," Bethany said loud enough to get Andre's attention.

Annie sighed and lowered her eyes. Bethany mimicked an apology reinforcing her determination to push Annie into the conversation about Bill's invitation.

The moment the door closed, Andre asked, "What game?"

"I was invited to the Red Sox game on Thursday." She folded her arms.

"Who invited you?"

"Someone at the restaurant," she replied, her voice catching on a swallow.

"Enough of the short, vague answers, Annie. A man?"

"It's not like that."

He stood up not caring that the food that was situated on his lap had fallen to the floor.

"So, yes! A man!" He shouted.

"Let me explain."

"Oh, you better start explaining."

"Andre, please just sit back down."

He continued to approach. "Don't order me around. If it's 'not like that' then what are you worried about?"

"There's this customer that comes in every day, he's old, like seventy, and he didn't come in one day . . ." she sped through her words hoping that if she could get out the full situation then Andre would back down. "Aldo knew where he lived and asked that I check on him and I went there and the landlord let me in and he was on the floor and had to go to the hospital. He's old, he wanted to thank me and he said that he had an extra ticket. That's all."

Andre stood inches from her. She could feel his clenched teeth, his burning eyes and heavy, labored breathing. "That's quite a story." He placed a hand on her arm. She felt a chill run through her body. "I don't think you should go."

"I thought it would have been strange," she falsely admitted. "What am I going to talk about with someone who could be my grandfather?"

"He just wants eye candy and maybe feel you up."

She wanted to reject the remark but abstained. "I'll just tell him no."

"That's a good idea." His voice wasn't pleasant, it was domineering.

Andre gave her a small peck on the forehead and turned around. "I'm going to have a shower. Would you mind being a sweetheart and cleaning that up?" He waved a finger in the direction of his spilled food. "I've lost my appetite."

5

"It's a shame. I really wish you could have joined me."

"Sorry, I appreciate the gesture," Annie replied.

"Oh please, it's the least I could for you." He looked beyond Annie's shoulder. "Hey Aldo, what are you doing Thursday night?"

Annie walked away as Bill extended the invitation to Aldo. She grabbed the coffee pot off of the warmer and did another round refilling the drinks of the patrons with half-empty mugs on their table. She felt saddened and a little angered because there was no reason why she couldn't go. She wanted to rush back over to Bill and renege on her response.

Thursday night was spent watching the game next to Andre. He had arrived home from work around 6:30 and, after looking at the meal she prepared, he sprung on his spontaneous idea of eating at a bar and watching the game.

"You know, I feel a little bad about my reaction. It probably would have been okay if you went to the game. Let's go out and watch it, okay?" He looked at the clock on the stove. "We can throw on some Sox gear and hit up the Cask N' Flagon."

"Sounds nice," she responded. Andre rushed into the bedroom to change while Annie placed the chicken dish she had prepared into small containers.

They reached the bar outside Fenway Park as the game-attendees were heading inside the ballpark for the start of the game. With the crowd clearing out they easily found a table and Andre proceeded to order both of them a Sam Adams.

His eyes shifted towards one of the televisions over the bar until the waitress approached with their drinks. Annie caught his wandering eye towards the cleavage of the twenty-one-year-old bubbly brunette who strove for additional energy after battling the pre-game mega rush.

Andre ordered unconventionally: a cheeseburger with bacon and onion rings under the bun and a side order of fries.

Annie asked for a Caesar salad.

"No longer on a diet?" Annie asked jokingly.

"What?" He responded harshly.

"Just a joke. I said 'no longer on a diet'." She shrugged with a smile and Andre smiled back.

"Sweetie, it's a lifestyle. Diets are for fat people always trying to lose fifty pounds but can't seem to." He looked outside to the street between the bar and the ballpark and spotted two hefty men at a hot dog stand ordering. The stand was so close to the restaurant he could spot the condiments on the dog. "Like them. They'll always wonder why they have to struggle to sit in normal people chairs. They order like I just did every day."

Annie shook her head but still held a smile, "Don't be mean." She looked at the men sympathetically.

"I'm not being mean," he defended. "They did it to themselves." He looked at Annie and saw her eyes looking at the men as they bit into a hot dog with all the fixings, a dab of ketchup slipped out at the end of the bun and fell to the street. The two men laughed it off as the spiller grabbed a napkin. They were content with who they were. "Oh, come on." Annie looked at Andre and he took her hands. "I'm sorry, you're right, that was mean."

"I just don't like when you make comments like that."

He patted her hands. "You're a sweetheart." He took a drink from the bottle. "I don't have the empathy." He pulled out his smart phone and began scrolling through emails. He clicked on one and read it.

Annie focused her attention outside on the slim chance that she would see Bill and Aldo strolling into Fenway.

Andre typed something on his phone and looked up to Annie. He opened his mouth to say something and then closed it realizing there was nothing he cared to say.

"Tell me about your day," Annie insisted.

Andre grunted a chuckle. "What do you want to know? Some old lady fell outside a Dunkin' Donuts so we're working on a lawsuit to the business, the building and the city."

"Oh no, is she okay?"

"Everyone who falls gets hurt."

"How bad?"

"Wrist, back, shoulder, emotional distress."

"Broken?"

Andre shook his head with a grin. "No. Not broken."

"Who's at fault though?"

"Whoever we get to settle first is at fault."

He looked down at his phone. "Raj and Jessica are coming."

"You invited them? I thought this was a you-and-me thing." She wasn't very interested in seeing his two friends. She always felt excluded and they had the habit of turning the night into a loud and obnoxious drink-fest that lasted until the bar closed. Her shift started at six the next morning and she wanted desperately to be in bed by eleven.

"I wanted to have some fun tonight."

"It's not fun with just me?"

"Don't twist my words, Annie." He turned his head to watch the start of the game but watched a local Chevy commercial. He refused to turn back around and shook his head.

Twenty minutes later they were working their way through dinner and Raj and Jessica appeared through the door. Raj was an asshole. He was smart and unafraid to show off his prepared sound bites to the point of degrading the person's intelligence he was debating with. Jessica was a popular girl in high school and continued to believe she was the most popular girl in the room. She was smart, narcissistic, like her boyfriend Raj, and she loved interrupting to bring the focus of attention onto herself.

Jessica gave Annie a hug and asked how she was doing.

"I'm doing just fine." She got the last word out before Jessica jumped in.

"Oh my god, you will not believe this!" Jessica started looking at Raj and Andre, "Game 1. Celtics. Playoff tickets." She beamed holding up a finger to keep the final point in suspense. "Courtside."

"No shit!" Andre screamed. He punched a smiling and nodding Raj then looked at Jessica. "Who'd you blow to get that?"

They laughed.

"There's a ladder, I had to work my way up it." Jessica joked but Annie wasn't entirely sure it was all facetious.

"The perks of having tits and lips," Andre responded setting a second round of chuckles around for himself and Raj.

"Andre, you're such a douche bag," Jessica said back then turned towards Annie and continued. "One of our clients is a corporate sponsor and they have tickets. My boss received a pair but it just so happens he will be in Buffalo for his nephew's bar mitzvah so he passed them along to *moi*."

"That's great, Jessica. I'm happy for you."

The topic turned to fashion which was always a sore spot for Annie. She had a few nice pieces but more often than not liked to hold on to her older, more favorite items until they were completely un-wearable. One of the high points of Boston, for Annie, was its lax ways. Jessica frequently went on shopping excursions but, unlike Annie, she could afford it. As an assistant to a marketing coordinator at one of the Northeast's most elite agencies her paychecks were hefty and bonuses and perks were plentiful whereas a waitress in the city brought in minimum wage and some change.

Annie preferred comfortable and cute over hip and trendy.

Jessica told of her new $100 pair of blue jeans that matched a $65 mint-green halter-top on sale at Filene's Basement.

Andre was in his own conversation with Raj but Annie knew he would be taking note and would respond later with something like, "Why can't you dress classier? I'll give you the money!" But she didn't want handouts from him even though he was the rent and bill payer. He would beg of her to take his money and buy something new insisting that if they were to ever have a future than they would be sharing more than their lives.

New clothes bought by Andre were often flashy and never worn. They were too stylish for day-to-day wear and only worn when Andre insisted upon it.

Her eyes darted upwards to the screens and watched the game go into the top of the seventh tied at five runs apiece. A Boston Red Sox fan for the previous four years, Annie would cheer for the team to make the winning run, but as she looked at her watch, her thoughts gravitated to the sleep she desired. Somehow, being at the game with Bill would have been different than enduring the bar across from Fenway with Andre and his friends.

The eighth inning brought no runs. In the top of the ninth, Cleveland's center fielder knocked a line drive into deep center allowing one run. It was just past ten o'clock. Quietly, Annie cheered the run.

In the bottom of the ninth, to Annie's chagrin, the Red Sox pinch hitter with two outs on his conscience nailed a solo run into right-center tying the game back up. A pop-out ended the inning and she was stuck at Cask N' Flagon for another twenty minutes, minimum.

"Get Annie-Malaise here another one!" Raj shouted. "She's passing out."

"No, I'm okay."

"Bah! What are you drinking?"

"I'm not."

"Double vodka tonic," Andre answered for Annie.

"No. I have to work tomorrow."

"We all have to work tomorrow," Raj replied. "But it's Friday, who cares!"

"Not a double then."

"Triple?" Raj said throwing a thumbs-up her way. "Get you all good and lubricated." His eyebrows bounced up-and-down suggestively.

"I don't want another drink," she pleaded to Andre. "I'm tired."

"Why are you being so fucking lame?" Andre shouted back. "It's one. More. Drink." He looked at her shaking his head in disapproval and she caved lowering her shoulders. Andre looked at Raj, "Vodka tonic for the lady," pointing to himself, "Sam Adams."

The tenth inning turned into the eleventh and at the top of the twelfth Cleveland's first baseman knocked a three-run homer into the centerfield stands. A collective groan overtook the bar. All eyes were glued to the screen now as the bottom of the twelfth started.

Annie had drunk the liquor a little too quickly and was feeling it swirl around in her stomach causing her to become woozy and fatigued. She feared a hangover headache the next morning.

After two walks followed by a stand up double the game was back to being dangerously close. The Indian's third baseman picked off a shot almost guaranteed to be another base hit and he launched the ball to first. It was too hard though and it sailed over the first baseman's head. The man who had been on base rounded third and headed home against the line coach's insistence as the ball was recovered. He slid safely and the game was tied.

It was 11:30 as Cleveland brought up a new pitcher. Annie's head pounded as the bar continued to fill up with Bostonians catching the great comeback of the night. Cheers and unified claps grew increasingly louder.

Andre was a part of the cheering as Annie rested her forehead on the tips of her fingers closing her eyes. She felt anger and a desperate urge to tear out of the bar. She begged for the Sox to get one more run and end the damn game. She thought of Bill in the stands and how much more fun he was probably having amid the excitement.

The first pitch was a 95 m.p.h. fastball that connected with the right-handed batter. He launched it higher and higher as it barely shot above the Big Green Monster. His two-run homer ended the game and Annie sighed with relief.

The roar of the bar was deafening.

The waitress approached the table smiling. "Are we all done here?"

"Mind Erasers for us," Raj ordered pointing to himself and Andre. "Red Headed Sluts for the ladies." He chuckled.

"No!" Annie jumped in. The waitress was off though and the drinks would be arriving momentarily. "I'm leaving," she announced standing up.

"Sit down, Annie." Andre said waving off her drama. "Quit with the theatrics and sit your ass down." His speech slurred. "We're having fun. Don't ruin our fun."

"Andre, I have to work at six. That means by the time I get home I'll only get five hours of sleep. I've been accommodating all damn night and now I'm leaving," she said instantly wishing her voice hadn't held on to the last word so long. She felt like she lost any gained sympathy by the final word sounding like a whine. She bit her lip.

Raj and Jessica held their looks waiting for Annie's continued insistence or Andre's refusal to leave.

"Come on," Jessica pushed.

"Yeah, Annie. You have all afternoon to sleep," Raj added.

She stood her ground. "Good night, it was nice seeing you." She looked at Andre whose look turned sour. "Are you coming with me or are you going to make me walk home alone?"

He lifted a hand and lowered his fingers three times waving her on without him.

She nodded, not surprised by the rude gesture and walked towards the front door.

When Annie stepped into the night air she felt the chill that a warm April day can spring on you when the sun dropped. The nice day transformed into a cold night and she zipped up her jacket and shoved her hands in her pockets.

She allowed a few seconds to pass before she accepted that Andre wasn't interested in following and reconciling.

Crowds of fans were exiting the park and she knew the T would be jammed. She braced herself for a walk home through light drizzle and started down the street.

She made it only a few steps before she heard her name called.

"Annie!" Andre said as she spun around. He wasn't worried about her or sad that she left him, he was angry. "You're a real bitch, you know that?" She popped her mouth open to defend herself but Andre cut her off. "No, you don't have the right to talk yet. Raj ordered you a shot. He bought a drink thinking that you would be nice enough to actually accept his gesture and spend some more time amongst friends. Now he's out seven dollars!"

"That's not a seven dollar shot," she remarked.

"Whatever. The point is that you just don't leave like that when you have a drink coming. You're embarrassing yourself and, more importantly, you're embarrassing me in front of my friends!"

"*I* didn't ask for a drink. *I* didn't order a drink."

"Well then you say something if you don't want a drink. You don't storm out of the bar like a psycho-bitch!"

"I'm sure Jessica has no problem with shooting two Red Headed Sluts."

"You're missing the point. What's the matter with you? Think!"

"Right, this is all on me. It's just so fucking unfortunate that I have to wake up at the ass-crack of dawn to work. Excuuuuuse me!" Tears were forming in her eyes. She hated when her emotions in such a situation led to her crying. She swallowed hard. "Why can't you see that I just want to go home?"

"I wanted to show you a good time," Andre said shaking his head feigning disappointment and confusion. "You like going out and we're out. It was an exciting game and you sulk and complain and cry and run out. I don't get it." He started backing away. "I work hard, I like to have fun. So, I'm going to have fun knowing full well that I can sleep all fucking night tomorrow night! All fucking Saturday! And sleep all fucking day Sunday!"

"Andre," she said hoping he wasn't going to turn away before she could continue. She began to feel bad for not seeing it his way.

"Nope. I'm not going to have this discussion right now. I have friends waiting for me. I'm not going to be selfish and keep them waiting." He spun around and slid back into the bar.

She stood outside for a moment more and felt her eyelids dip. It was enough persuasion for her to go home. So with a yawn and a steady, quick gait, Annie walked westward.

6

It wasn't that she disliked coffee. She just never acquired the need to have the caffeine flow through her system.

This day was different and Annie found herself looking at the clock above the register with the small hand barely touching the nine as she was forcing down her third cup of coffee. Her eyes were in constant tears as she felt she was yawning deeply every thirty seconds. The small headache didn't help the time go by either.

"Late night, eh?" Bethany said passing by Annie and heading into the kitchen then into the break room. Annie followed as Bethany peeled off her yellow raincoat and hung it up. Outside was a mess of gray soup hanging in the air. Rain was forecasted again and the air was thick with it. "It was a good game. I lost sleep."

"I barely got any."

Bethany paused, turned towards Annie and raised a curious eyebrow. "Go on."

Annie shook off the comment. "Not like that."

"It was a good game though?" Bethany restated.

"I didn't go."

Bethany shook her head in disappointment. "You bitch."

"Andre didn't want me to go."

Bethany mimicked Annie silently.

Annie took the playful insult in stride and replied, "What could I have done?"

"Five years. You can take a night off to go to a Sox game with a friend."

"Bill's not a friend. He's a customer."

"Bullshit defense!" Bethany shot back. "Do you know how much tickets are? You could have taken a night off from Andre the Asshole." Bethany punched her code into the time clock to start her shift. "So, what did you do?" They bee-lined through the kitchen.

"Don't call him that," Annie defended defiantly.

"What did you do?"

"Sweetheart, order's up," Omar said to Annie pointing to a plate filled with scrambled eggs, hash browns, bacon and sausage on the counter. He was goofy and heavy and could get away with comments that less confident men would never say. "Babe, I'll be here waiting for you," he winked at Bethany.

"Oh Omar, you couldn't handle my eggs."

"You couldn't handle my sausage."

Bethany and Annie stepped into the dining area. Annie placed the warm plate in front of a scruffy older man at the corner booth. He didn't look up from his tablet.

Bethany took an order and met up with Annie behind the counter.

"You better be tired due to animalistic sex." Bethany faked a shudder of disgust at the thought of Andre in bed. "Better yet, you better be tired from getting shit-faced."

"Eh! Language!" Aldo shot back holding a hand up then waving it over the restaurant.

"We went to the Cask," Annie replied to Bethany.

"Oh, so you were allowed ten feet from the park, you just couldn't enter. That's a bunch of bull . . ." Bethany caught Aldo's eye, ". . . honky. Bull-honky."

"Bethany!" Annie barked holding her colleague at bay. "Let it go."

Annie turned and approached another table with a smile asking if they needed anything prior to her placing the check on their table.

She was frustrated but didn't quite know if it was due to the reality that Bethany was trying to show coming into focus or if she was tired of defending her life choices or if she was just tired. Everyone seemed dead-set against her relationship with Andre yet their relationship outlasted many marriages.

Bethany took one final shot before letting the matter drop. "Did he at least return the lamp?"

Bill entered around noon taking up a booth at the far end of the restaurant.

"Aldo, I should've called to let you know I would be tardy today. I wouldn't want you sending another server to check on me." He was all smiles.

Annie asked that Bethany take the table and she agreed.

"Is she avoiding me?" Bill asked when Bethany approached the table.

"Why on earth would she avoid you, Bill?"

"She's a woman."

Bethany placed a fist on her hip and asked with attitude, "What's that supposed to mean?"

He smiled coyly opening his mouth slightly prior to speaking. "Bethany, it means I've been on this planet seventy-one years and I still can't figure any of you out."

Bethany placed a hand on Bill's shoulder. "She's not avoiding you."

"Turkey club, mayonnaise on only half the sandwich. French fries."

"Bottom half or top half?" She joked and left to place the order.

Bethany went behind the counter and placed the order on the rack. Annie refilled a Diet Coke for a customer who was eyeing her eagerly awaiting their drink.

"Bill's seventy-one." Bethany said to Annie. "I thought he was much older."

Annie took a quick glance over to Bill and analyzed his appearance. She shrugged her shoulders.

Bethany continued, "You're avoiding Bill for what reason?"

"I'm not avoiding him."

"It's one of your tables."

"I feel bad. That's all."

Annie spun around to evade further questioning.

7

It had been an exhausting morning and Annie had dreamt of collapsing into her pillows and blanket. The air was cool enough that an open bedroom window would aid in her attempt to get as comfy as possible.

She entered the apartment building and headed into the mail room. She opened the mailbox and took the single envelope inside.

She stepped into the elevator and pressed the number six.

"Hold it. Hold it. Hold it!" A hand sliced between the closing doors. "Ah, shit." They opened back up and a tall, cute man entered with a messenger bag over his shoulder. He clutched the strap nervously.

Jon was another Boston transplant. With a smile that often looked like he was recanting on something he shouldn't have said and a mop of brown hair that appeared constantly in a state of disarray, he was the perfect guy for a girl looking for a boyfriend. She didn't know of his relationship status, or anything really about him, but thought him perfect for someone she could set up with Bethany.

Annie couldn't recall where he originated or what he did for a living. Their banal conversations had lasted no longer than two minutes though he moved in across the hall months ago.

"Crazy weather," he said. "Pretty gray out there."

They didn't look at one another. Both watched the glowing numbers rise as the elevator neared the sixth floor.

"Yeah. It's supposed to rain all weekend, I heard," Annie replied.

The elevator chimed and the door opened. Jon held out a hand and Annie stepped out in front and walked down the hallway. She wondered if he was looking at her butt; it made her uncomfortable. She didn't think there was much to be attracted to in a waitress that worked a breakfast and lunch shift on little sleep. The thought of the massive bags under her eyes made her dread being in public.

Annie reached her door and looked up as Jon passed to the second door on the opposite side of the hallway.

"Have a great day."

"You too," she smiled back.

Annie entered the apartment and slipped off her shoes tossing them next to the door. She pulled off her shirt that reeked of grease and coffee and dropped it on the floor. When she was in the bedroom she dropped her pants and snuggled into bed embracing the fluffiness of the comforter. She wrapped her arms around a pillow and lifted the comforter to her shoulders.

Her eyes closed but her body refused to fall asleep. Minutes passed, grueling minutes that she wished she would be unconscious for. It upset her, frustrated her. All she wanted was to nap.

There was a knock at the door. A knock that filtered into her dreams even though she knew that it was occurring outside of her mind. "Don't go." Someone said in her dream. The rapping happened one more time and she grunted as her eyelids slid open realizing she had been asleep for three hours. She pulled herself out of bed and trudged to the door.

Looking through the peephole she saw Jon on the other side avoiding eye contact with the peephole on the opposite side of the door. There would be a certain amount of creepiness if someone was staring you down from the hallway.

She leaned towards a mirror next to the door. It was decorated with a black and green frame and purposely placed for those last looks prior to stepping out into the real world.

"Ooh." She murmured not impressed with what was looking back. Her hair was in tatters, it was every which way like she spent the entire time in bed moving her head back and forth on the pillow. She had gunk in the corner of her eyes which she properly wiped away and intended to flicker on her shirt when she realized she was wearing only a dark blue bra and flower-patterned panties.

"I think I can hear you moving around in there," a voice from the hallway said.

"Shit," she whispered looking down at her apparel.

"Bad timing?" Jon called.

She felt a deep desire for him to not leave. "No!"

"Ah, there is someone on the other side. You called my bluff."

She was impressed by his manipulation.

"Give me a minute, will ya?" She shouted and raced for the bedroom without waiting for a reply.

"Shit. Shit. Shit." She said, her hands flailing desperately figuring out something to throw on. She ran into the closet and pulled on a pair of dark blue jeans and a dark gray Boston Bruins T-shirt with a faded logo. "Oh good lord," she said as she took another look in the bathroom mirror. She returned to the closet and put on an Irish green Red Sox ball cap. She settled on her somewhat presentable look.

As she crossed the threshold into the living room her bladder was calling for release. "Son of a bitch. Really?" She ran towards the door. "Still there?"

"I've got nowhere else to be."

"One minute!" She held up a finger to a person who couldn't even see her and rushed into the bathroom.

By the time she opened the door no one was there.

"I figured I should set up camp."

She looked down and Jon was on the ground with his hands on his chest looking up at her. He smiled and she reciprocated.

"Sex toys or dead body?"

"What?" Her eyebrows furled inward in confusion.

"I figured you were hiding one or the other. Unless it was sex toys being used on a dead body." He stood noticing that her reaction leaned more towards discomfort than enjoyment at his remark. "That was a joke and I bet I sound like a major creep."

She nodded without comment.

"I'm really not creepy, I promise. I spend a lot of time alone in my apartment. Wow, I'm not helping my cause in the slightest bit."

"Not in the slightest." She wasn't put off by his remarks yet. He was endearing in his awkwardness. "Can I help you with something?"

He sighed. "I'm bored and I've had a half-a-bottle of wine and I mustered the courage to come over and talk to you."

She offered a friendly smile and suddenly noticed the smell of Merlot emanating from his breath and a rosier hue to his lips, slightly stained with red wine. "I'm sorry, I have a boyfriend."

"Oh, I have a girlfriend."

"I'm not into that."

His eyes widened. "No, me neither, unless it's in movies." He chuckled nervously and then grew serious. "I'm kind of new to the city and I don't have any friends and you seem friendly, neighborly even." He shoved his hands in his pockets and shrugged his shoulders. "I have half-a-bottle of wine."

She weighed the scenario of Andre walking in to see a man drunk on wine sitting with his girlfriend against her own loneliness and sympathy for Jon. She wanted to pause time and contemplate her options but that was impossible so she offered an idea. "Let's get some coffee."

"I kind of really want to drink."

She bit her lip. "For someone looking for friends you're being awfully demanding."

"It's been one of those days."

"Okay. Stay." She held up her hands and backed into the apartment. In the kitchen she found a flask and presented it Jon. "Fill 'er up."

*   *   *

They sat inside a coffee café three blocks away.

Jon sipped from his cup and pursed his lips then let them go with a soothing "Ah."

"Good coffee?" She asked with a smile.

"You're a genius." He took another sip. "A grande Merlot."

"It's not a bad marketing concept. Wine in a paper cup."

"Paper sleeve is a little too much though," he responded pulling the sleeve that surrounded the cup off. "My wine isn't heated."

"You have to sell it."

He tipped his head and placed the sleeve back on the cup.

There was a brief moment of silence in the conversation.

Annie finally asked, "You said you were new to the city. How long have you been here?"

"About seven months."

"And no friends?"

Jon shrugged his shoulders innocently.

Annie asked, "What brought you to Beantown?"

"Do you know the reason behind the name Beantown?"

"I assume it has something to do with beans. Why do you think it's called Beantown?"

"I have no idea. I thought you might." Jon sipped some more wine. "So, my reason for moving here . . . Well, I'm originally from Detroit, not the city, one of the suburbs. I worked as a sales person at a local TV station. I was pretty much the guy who tried to get advertising on the station so let's say a grocery store wants to have their commercial play during the five o'clock news then I was their guy."

"Interesting."

"Not really." He sipped more wine and continued, "My girlfriend and I grew up in Detroit, went to school near Detroit, we pretty much never left our 25 miles of safety. I got laid-off. She has a B.A. in Marketing. The degree is like fancy toilet paper. She works part-time at the mall and lives with her parents. The first one to get a job in a new city is where we were going to relocate. Hence, Boston."

"What's her name?"

"Jonie. Joanne. I call her Jonie. You can call her Jonie too. She's adorable, I'm crazy about her. Did you know that people gravitate to something close to their names? There are a shit load of dentists named Dennis. My parent's names are William and Wendy."

Annie instantly thought about her name and its similarity to Andre. "Interesting."

"You say that a lot."

"I find a lot of things interesting." She slurped the remainder of her iced coffee and placed the cup on the table. "Continue."

"Laid off again but this time from a Boston television station. That killed the plans on Jonie moving out here, and I'm stuck with five months remaining on a one-year lease." He gave two thumbs to sarcastically portray his predicament. "So the job search continues. I'm hoping I can get laid off from a television station in Chicago next."

"How can you afford that?"

Jon lowered his head. "I have a little savings and my parents are very generous."

"How old are you?"

"Let's continue this embarrassment. I'm twenty-eight."

"Me too!"

"Liar!" Jon jokingly accused.

"Nope." Annie said with a wide, open smile. "When's your birthday?"

"June sixth."

"No way!"

"You too?" Jon asked fascinated by the coincidence.

"Not even close!" Annie said chuckling. "I'm messing with you."

Jon faked disappointment at falling for her little joke and crossed his arms. "Okay seriously, when's your birthday?"

"December seventh."

"Wow that means I was born on D-Day, you were born on Pearl Harbor. That is interesting."

"Maybe we can find someone born on February 19th to become our friend too."

"What's the significance of that date?" Jon inquired taking a sip from his drink.

"That's the day we stormed the beaches of Iwo Jima."

"Are you a history buff?"

"No. My grandfather was there and when I learned the date in high school it stuck." There was a brief pause in the conversation and Annie blurted out. "I'm thirty. I don't know why I told I was twenty-eight."

"Do you lie often?"

"Occasionally."

"Well, at least you're honest about lying." Jon smiled and stood up. "On that note, I'm going to break the seal."

"Charming."

As Jon made his way towards the unisex bathroom Annie found herself smiling and happier than she could recently remember. They had an instant connection and she found herself enjoying the time spent with her new friend.

Jon returned and immediately went for the wine. "I didn't do it but I'm warning you to not go into the unisex bathroom."

"Warning heeded. You're drunk."

"I'm never this blunt on dirty humor."

"It's quite all right. It reminds me of my brother."

"Yeah? Where does he live?"

"Africa."

"Really?" Jon seemed intrigued and leaned in.

"As far as I know." Annie twisted her head towards the window and looked outside.

Jon leaned back as if he knew not to inquire any further. "So, tell me Annie, what are your dreams in life?"

Annie took notice of the handful of pedestrians strolling by, some with their babies in strollers, others with lattes in hand, and older members of society in conversation.

"Annie?"

She looked back at Jon briefly and lowered her eyes. "I guess I'm not sure what my dreams are anymore."

Annie's mind raced scanning her life and where she wanted to be when she was this age. She felt a strange tightening in her chest as she lightly scratched the side of her face; a reflex in an attempt to create a fictitious dream if only to change the subject.

When Annie looked back at Jon she shook her head. "That's funny. I can't think of a single dream I have."

"Really?" He was taken aback and blew a long-winded breath like the air was being sucked from his lungs.

"That's sad." She looked back outside.

"You ever wanted to be a rock star? Ever wanted to be part of the Bangles? Walk like an Egyptian?"

"Everybody wants to be a rock star and everybody wanted to walk like an Egyptian when they were eight. In hindsight, do you think that song was a little . . . racist? Maybe not racist but could you imagine a song that was called *Walk like an American* in which a bunch of foreigners did goofy dances?"

"It was a different time," Jon offered.

"The 1980s were a different time?"

Jon and Annie walked to the front of their apartment building. He opened the door for her then pressed the button for the elevator.

"This was fun."

"What are you going to do with the rest of your night and weekend?" Jon asked.

"I'll see what the boyfriend has in mind."

It was a silent ride up to the sixth floor and when the doors opened he allowed her to exit first.

Annie stood at her door and Jon rocked back on his feet. It was an awkward silence.

"What do we do? Hug? Shake hands?" Jon asked.

"We can hug, I think. I mean, you live right there and I don't think one hug would get us in the habit of hugging." Annie replied.

"Right. It's not like we won't see each other for five months."

They hugged and Jon lifted her off her feet and spun her in a full circle as she giggled playfully. He placed her down.

"If you want to hang out," Jon started backing away towards his door, "you know . . . just knock."

"Have a good night, Jon."

8

"More coffee, Bill?" Annie asked as she yawned deeply. It was just after ten and the morning slow down revealed how tired she was.

"Please," he replied, "and thank you." He didn't look up. Time was all that was needed for their unsaid awkwardness to fade.

"What's new in the world?"

"There's a fascinating article on the upgraded security systems at the airport." He looked beyond Annie and saw the many vacant booths and tables. "Have a seat."

"I'm still working."

"I think you know Aldo will be okay with it."

She placed the pot of coffee on the edge of the table and took a seat opposite of Bill.

There was silence as Bill continued reading the article. Annie felt the vibrating sensations on the bottom of her feet move up her leg as she rested. She knew that this signaled relief from nearly four hours on her feet.

"And done." Bill placed his hands on the newspaper and looked at Annie. "Where are you from, Annie?"

"Grand Rapids, Michigan."

"I've never been."

"The winters are cold," she replied then continued sarcastically, "but at least it stays cold for months and months on end."

"We have Nor'easters."

"We have lake effect snow."

"What's worse?"

Annie lifted her eyes upwards. "Lake effect. A Nor'easter hits and it's done. Lake effect can go on and on, every day for days."

"It's supposed to be seventy-five tomorrow. Are you working?"

Annie nodded.

Bill continued, "You'll at least be able to enjoy the better part of the afternoon. Maybe go up to the Commons."

Annie looked at Bill and wondered who he truly was. Even the brief moments of being inside his apartment brought forth more questions. She blurted out a question that was floating idly on her mind.

"What was your dream?"

"My what?" He was confused by the sudden shift in conversation.

"Your dreams. When you were . . ."

"Young?"

"My age."

"Young," he verified. "Annie, by your age I was married with a couple kids."

"Does that mean your dreams fade with wedded bliss and rugrats?"

"They change. My dream in life was to become a pilot."

"Were you ever a pilot?"

"Never, but it wasn't for a lack of trying. I got as far as the medical examination and they told me my eyesight disqualified me."

"So what did you do?"

"I got a job as a salesman. I sold luggage."

"In a store?"

"At first. I was the top salesman for five years in a row. Corporate was here in Boston and they offered me a position as a regional manager and then I oversaw regional managers for the entire country."

"Wow. You never think about a job like that. You never think retail manager at a luggage company."

"Tell me about it." Bill took a sip of his coffee. "But luggage has to come from somewhere."

Annie was silent for a moment, "Someone asked me yesterday what my dream was and I couldn't think of one. That's sad, isn't it? I should have a dream."

"Absolutely."

"But I don't."

"That's a shame." Bill sipped his coffee again. "Have you ever had a dream?"

"Sure. I wanted to be an event planner. Not big corporate events though; events like weddings or bar mitzvahs. Maybe local events like community fairs or something. I planned my own Sweet Sixteen party and it went over so well all my friends asked me to plan theirs."

"What happened?"

"The parties went great!" Annie beamed. "Everyone had a great time and then their sisters asked me to help plan their parties."

"What happened?"

Annie's eyebrows furrowed inward. "What do you mean?"

"Why did you stop?"

"Well, I did a few graduation parties when I graduated and then I went to school, I got a Conference and Event Planning degree from Grand Valley State and started looking for jobs."

"What happened?"

"I don't know! Life. Life happened. I was working at a banquet hall and I wasn't making very much. Everyone I talked to suddenly didn't need my services; they went with 'real' planners." Annie was increasingly becoming hyper and flustered as if she were recalling a bad decision while attempting to defend that bad decision. "When I told people what I wanted to do they all thought it was 'interesting' and a 'cute idea'. No one helped. No one took it seriously."

"And how did you end up in Boston?"

"I fell in love with Andre and he got a job here. I thought maybe I could find something better. So we moved. It took some convincing for me to join him, we were only together for a little bit, but ultimately, obviously, he complied. I couldn't find any work until I found Aldo's Restaurant."

"You just stopped looking?" Bill tried to be empathetic.

"It was frustrating getting rejected and sending out my resume to every banquet hall and catering company from here to Providence. I figured I would be married by now too."

"Marriage doesn't necessarily free you from life's dreams."

"I know. That's not what I meant. I meant I would be married, maybe raising a family. I would feel more stable. More satisfied."

"You don't feel stable?"

"Doctor Bill, I don't know how I feel."

He chuckled. "I apologize. People fascinate me. I like learning about their decisions and my wife often said I was nosier than an anteater. I probably should have been a psychologist. I always thought Doctor Dooley sounded like an accident prone cartoon character like Mr. Magoo."

"I don't know Mr. Magoo."

"That saddens me greatly." She still looked confused so he elaborated. "He was a clumsy cartoon character . . . never mind."

The door of the restaurant opened and Annie turned to see a young couple enter and look at the register then around the restaurant.

"You can sit wherever you'd like!" Annie shouted and they took the second booth against the window. Annie looked at Bill. "I guess I really do have to go." She stood up.

"It was nice having a discussion with you," Bill said.

"You're the second person in as many days that I've had a meaningful conversation with. What are the chances?"

"Good?"

She smiled and turned around grabbing a pair of menus on the way to the table.

9

"Mom, you really need to settle down about this . . . he will . . . he probably has!" She hated raising her voice to her mother especially since emphasizing never seemed to matter to begin with. "You know what, next time we're in town, you ask him why he hasn't proposed . . . Marriage isn't everything you know . . . oh stop it."

Her mother pressured her to force Andre to settle down. She too felt that the length of time of their courtship was long enough. She insisted that Annie didn't back out of the relationship without serious consideration, there simply was too much invested now and Annie was too old to try to find the next one.

"Mother! My vagina is not going to dry up." Annie poured herself another glass of Riesling as her mother's voice screeched continuously about her worry that grandchildren wouldn't be in the future, that Annie's biological clock was ticking, and that all of Annie's friends were either married or married with babies. "Yes, mom, and half those marriages are shit."

But at least their parents had grandchildren, she insisted.

Annie's mother would run into a friend who would ogle over her granddaughter or grandson's piano recital or first time swimming or pooping in the big boy toilet. It sent an obnoxious tirade of pressuring Annie to pressure Andre.

The only way to relieve the pressure from her mother was to actually be engaged to be married. She had no proof though that Andre had even begun searching for an engagement ring and she would be lying if she said she hadn't occasionally searched throughout the closet or dresser drawers for indication. There was no way to make her mother feel better about the situation so she did her best to change the conversation.

"Mom, I was thinking about getting back into event planning."

"Now, why would you do something like that?" She responded. "That's just silly."

"How is that silly?"

"Well, you always had nice ideas but there's more to it than nice ideas."

"I know, I majored in it."

"Look, honey, we all know you gave it your best shot. What does Andre think about this idea?"

"I haven't discussed it with him yet."

"Perhaps you should. Perhaps your, lord please, future husband would like to know what's stirring in that pot of yours."

Annie slowly closed her eyes as she felt a tightening in her chest. She recalled the time she contacted her parents after a series of severe thunderstorms that sprouted multiple tornadoes across the west side of Michigan just to make sure everything was okay. Indeed they were and her mother responded, "It was all south in Barry County, but I appreciate your concern. Today is a sunny, beautiful day, it's in the seventies and no humidity. Perfect May wedding day, if you ask me."

Hints were dropped like fall leaves at the end of October. Everything came back to marriage.

She reopened her eyes and replied, "I have to go. Love you."

"I love you too, sweetheart."

Annie ended the call and placed her cell phone on the kitchen counter gulping down the rest of her drink and dramatically collapsing her head into her arms with a grunt.

* * *

"I spoke with my mother today."

"Yeah?" Andre was glued to his smart phone scrolling through emails. Occasionally he would look up at the television to glance at the talk-news show. "How are your parents?"

"They're fine."

"Your mother still harping on you to get married?" He finally made eye contact with her and smiled at the jab.

"She is."

He chuckled puffs of air through his nose and shook his head looking back down at the phone. With his reaction she closed off any desire to discuss the future and hoped that his silence meant that the surprise proposal was imminent.

"I was thinking of going into event planning . . . again."

"Uh huh."

"I wanted to get your opinion."

"Go for it."

"You're okay with it?"

"Uh huh. It doesn't matter whether you're a waitress at a restaurant or at a banquet hall. In fact, I wouldn't be so embarrassed to say you work at a banquet hall."

She was taken aback by his nonchalance and instinctively placed a hand over her breaking heart. She leaned back into the chair. "You're embarrassed of me?"

"What?" He looked up. "No. Oh god, stop getting all emotional. You're thirty and working at some shit diner off of a side street that's off the main road. You should be embarrassed too. Anything to get you into a better place, go for it."

The clarification wasn't as reassuring as he meant it to be and she showed it.

Andre sighed and tried again. "I'm not embarrassed of YOU. Look at you; I have nothing to be embarrassed about but again, thirty, waitress. It would be different if you were at Radius or even Ruth's Chris. That would be killer." He looked back down at the phone and tapped his finger on an email. "Shit," he muttered and then finalized the conversation. "But really, go for it. Get a new waitress thing at a better place."

Annie stabbed her fork into the lettuce of her salad and brought it to her mouth. "I don't want to be a waitress. I want to be an event planner." The lettuce slipped off her fork and fell into her lap. Oily, fat-free Italian dressing left a mark on her yellow shirt. It mattered little that she grabbed it as quickly as possible and tossed it on table. She looked at the stain.

"That sucks." Andre laughed. "Bring your mouth to the fork not fork to the mouth, sweetie. Lesson learned."

"You're a jerk." Annie responded standing up and rushing into the bedroom taking her shirt off.

"Yeah, but you love me." He tossed back at her.

Annie tossed her shirt into the bathroom sink and turned the water on. She grabbed a solution that, hopefully, would get the stain out. She started wiping and looked upwards at the mirror.

She let Andre's last words about still loving him stew in her mind. She wasn't exactly sure she did anymore. The thought of not being in love with the man she had loved for years was discomforting.

The water turned scorching and jolted her back into the present.

"Silly." She said turning the cold water tab clockwise. Every couple had to feel that way. "Of course I still love him."

10

Annie was bubbly and, when Bill entered the restaurant and took his usual seat, she skipped over to his table to share with him her thoughts.

"I'm going into event planning!" She cheered. And then she saw the grim demeanor as he looked at her.

"Pancakes," he solemnly said.

She furrowed her eyebrows and asked, "Coffee too?"

He nodded and she turned around but only stepped one foot forward before spinning back around.

"Are you okay?"

"There's a certain downside to getting older," he said before breaking eye contact. "Death."

"I'm sorry," Annie said lowering her hands to her sides unsure on how to react. "Were you close to him . . . or her? Were you close to them?"

He shrugged his shoulders. "Wife's friend. I haven't seen them since her funeral."

"Let me get you that coffee."

His only reply was a nod accepting her awkward position. She returned placing the coffee mug next to his hand. The newspaper was still closed and his eyes weren't placed on the front page. He was staring off somewhere, the edge of the table, or the window sill. She wondered if he even knew that she just placed the mug by his side.

"What are you doing tomorrow?" He suddenly asked and then looked at her. "Want to go to a funeral with me?"

"Like a date?" It was a silly question and it somehow slipped out of her mouth, a strange reaction that she instinctively inherited when men who didn't interest her asked her out. It was a defense mechanism to see if they would recoil.

Bill didn't though. "Yes, a date."

"To a funeral?"

"Yes." He looked deep into her eyes.

Annie felt obligated to comply based on the circumstances alone but balanced it with the oddness of the whole situation. "You want to take me on a date to a funeral?" She enunciated each syllable.

"Yes." He let a light smile creep up.

Annie was at a loss for words.

"I'm kidding," he stated and she breathed a massive sigh of relief. "You honestly thought that I was asking you out on a date to a funeral?"

"Stranger things have happened." She giggled nervously.

"Seriously though, would you go with me?"

"If you need a companion there, I'll be your companion."

The following day Annie was dressed in her only black skirt and black blouse. She cradled her small purse in her arms standing outside the restaurant.

Bethany stood by her side donning the standard waitress attire. She bit her nails, a nervous habit since she stopped smoking three years ago. Annie guessed that the nail biting was a habit long before she shunned cigarettes. She spit out the tiny edge of the nail she bit off.

"You make me laugh," she finally said.

"Is that so?"

"You're going to a funeral but you wouldn't go to a Sox game. And I bet you didn't even tell Andre."

"What's the point? He doesn't need to know about this."

Bethany shook her head. "What other secrets are you hiding?"

"It's not a secret."

"You just opted not to tell him."

"He didn't ask what I was doing today. There's no secrets. There's no lying."

"Honey, I didn't say a single thing about lying. That's your guilty conscience creeping out."

Bill turned the corner and was walking in their direction.

Bethany muttered under her breath, "Is he going to be the one in the casket?"

"It's a suit."

"It's an old man suit."

"He's an old man," Annie retorted then turned towards Bill. "Hi!" Annie said holding out her arms as she hugged Bill.

"Thank you, Annie. These funerals can be rough. At one point in your life you have to make time for weddings. Nowadays I have to schedule in funerals."

"At least you don't have to bring a gift, right?" Bethany said.

"There's hardly ever an open bar either," he replied.

"I'm out then." Annie said tossing her hands up in the air and starting to walk away.

"You want to go with me?" Bill asked Bethany.

"Hell yeah!" She shouted with false excitement.

Annie stopped and looked back once her dramatic turn had run its course. There was a silence that hung in the warm spring air that represented the peacefulness amid death.

"What's her name?" Bethany asked.

"Dorothy." Bill tipped his wrist and looked at his watch. "Dorothy Lippard."

"My condolences."

"Thank you." Bill looked over to Annie. "We should get going."

Annie insisted to Bethany, "Call me. I want to know how the interview goes."

Annie and Bill walked down towards T stop.

"Interview?" Bill finally inquired.

"She found a place she wants to rent. Some girl not too far from here is looking to lease a second room in her condo."

"Hmm." Bill ended his inquiry with a grunt.

The outbound train arrived within moments and both boarded the nearly vacant car.

"There is something quite strange about knowing this woman has passed away. We used to play cards. Old people card games like Canasta and Hearts but something funny happens when you lose a spouse," he paused for a second. "You start to get excluded."

"That's sad."

"It is. But when you play as couples for so long and then suddenly one of the couples becomes a single and that single represents that the person sitting next to you today may not be there tomorrow, well that can be depressing. No one wants a downer."

"So they shunned you out?"

"They didn't call as frequently. When I went over it was awkward like when everyone is afraid to address the eight-hundred-pound elephant in the room."

"This isn't meant as a joke," Annie started.

"Okay."

"No, I mean it. This is a legitimate question."

Bill changed his gaze from the outside passing by to Annie. "Shoot."

"Now that Dorothy is dead, do you get to get back in the game?"

Bill chuckled. "Maybe I'll get an invite today. Maybe we'll start a widow/widower game."

"Like a single's event."

Bill stared at Annie whose smile was cheering him up. He noticed he was looking at her for too long and quickly turned his head. "I like you, Annie. You make me feel good. We would have been great friends a long time ago."

"We can be great friends now, Bill."

"We could."

The train continued three stops before Bill announced that this was where they exit. They hopped off and Bill pointed north across the street. The sounds of street life flooded the air. Although noisy, it was a soothing urban familiarity whereas the strange quietude of a rural country would make them uncomfortable.

Bill and Annie entered the small chapel on the cemetery grounds. The pews were wooden and the walls were white. The casket was opened and displaying Dorothy Lippard. It was quiet as expected and there were nearly forty men and women of all ages sitting or congregating. Many tears. Many pieces of tissue were being stuffed in the sleeves of the older women in the beautifully simplistic chapel.

"Would you like to have a seat?" Bill whispered.

Annie nodded and sat one row behind the last row that had people in its seats. Bill walked up with his head high towards the casket. He stood above the woman, observing her as if remembering a memory from decades ago. His hands were clasped in front.

"Bill," a gruff voice said. "Billy Dooley."

He turned and saw a man in his seventies approaching the casket. His steely blue eyes and white hair popped amid his dark tan. The man donned a gold chain, watch and ring.

Bill shook his hand. "Louis. Still in Florida?"

"We migrated back north last month." Louis looked at Dorothy's body. "It's a shame."

"She was a good woman."

"You fuck her?" Louis held an open-mouthed smile as if he were getting a kick out of discussing the deceased woman's sexual proclivities and Bill, eyes bugged, felt he heard one thing and believing he should have heard something entirely different.

"Excuse me?"

Louis leaned in close lowering his voice but enunciating each word. "Did you fuck her?"

Bill instinctively moved back creeped out by the surreal, inappropriate question. "No." He was worried he was being accused of a crime he didn't commit.

Louis patted Bill on the arm. "It's okay, half of Brookline did in the seventies." Louis, still close to Bill held a thumb out towards the back of the chapel. "You bring the skirt?"

"Yes."

Louis motioned an 'OK' with his hand and winked. "Good work."

He waddled down the aisle on stiff knees. He stopped to shake the widower's hand and offer condolences.

Bill followed Louis and shook the broken-hearted man's hand. "I'm very sorry, Teddy."

The man nodded as he sniffled and reached into his pocket for his handkerchief. Bill noticed liver spots and an upward fluctuation of weight since their last encounter years ago. Bill had to double-take to ensure that this was Teddy.

"Hey Bill." Teddy's daughter leaned over and they hugged.

"Hello Peggy."

"That's not your daughter, is it?" Peggy nodded towards Annie.

Bill looked back along with Peggy and Teddy.

"Oh her. That's not Chrissy. She's just a friend."

"A friend?" Peggy asked.

It all seemed perfectly innocent to Bill but further defending of his companion might lead to suspicious glances towards Annie. Nonetheless, Bill expected scandalous gossip amongst Teddy and his relatives whether or not he explained further.

Teddy raised an eyebrow, intrigued.

Before the conversation could continue Dorothy's tear-filled sister approached Teddy and clutched onto his lapels leaning herself inward and crying into his suit. It caused a ricochet of emotions to project on to Teddy and Peggy.

"It's so sad," she moaned. "She comforted me when my cat Archie Bunker died."

Bill didn't have the sadness in him to cry so he backed away slowly and walked towards Annie.

"Excuse me." Bill motioned past Annie and sat on the inside of the pew.

"You okay?" Annie whispered. The slightest raise in volume could echo across the entire room.

"This is weird."

"Why? How?"

"That guy who approached me up there . . ."

"The sun-soaked man that keeps eyeballing me?"

"Yes, Louis. He asked if I had sex with Dorothy."

"The dead woman!"

"Yes," Bill looked at Annie. "Not while she was dead."

"I didn't suspect as much."

"Apparently half the commonwealth slept with her."

"Wow. Wait, did you?"

"No!" Bill shook his head and looked forward. "Did you really think I would?"

Before Annie could answer the service started and, fifteen minutes later, concluded. There were more tears as the pallbearers carried the casket to the car and then drove towards the allotted plot. There was another brief service before the closed casket was slowly lowered into the ground.

Bill stood towards the back with his head tilted respectively downward. Annie noticed his struggle to keep his composure through clenched teeth. She thought if he were alone in his bed at night instead of outside in front of friends then maybe he would allow himself to cry. He resisted the overwhelming of emotions.

Annie placed her hand in Bill's. It seemed big like a grandfather's would to a five year old.

He shook it away though and tilted his body away.

"Sorry, I can't," he whispered. "I won't be able to hold . . ."

"It's okay," she replied to the excuse of his rejection. She found Louis wearing large wrap-around sunglasses looking back at her. It made her uncomfortable and she refused eye contact however she couldn't help looking over to see if he was still leering at her.

There was a small gathering at Dorothy's brother's home nearby. Deli trays were brought in, liquor was being served and guests meandered and talked almost as if they didn't bury a dear friend or relative earlier that day.

Bill enjoyed a beer while looking over the bookshelf in the vacant, front sitting room.

"There you are." Annie stepped in with a drink. "You okay?"

"You keep asking me that."

Annie nestled up beside him and placed her free hand on his shoulder. "What can I say? I like all my customers to be in good moods."

"Customer, eh?" A man entered from the second opening into the living room. "What does this little honey pot charge by the hour? I have a bar mitzvah next weekend."

Bill chuckled, smiled and then knew instantly to correct the situation. "She's not like that, Winnie. She works at the restaurant I go to, the one I've wanted you to meet me at."

Winnie was a larger man with a potbelly that protruded outward with his belt lined right around the middle. His cheeks hung downward and his crown of light gray hair lined his head ear-to-ear without a single hair to be seen on the top of his head. He looked like a cross between Alfred Hitchcock and the man he was named after, Winston Churchill. He held his brandy glass appropriately but lacked a cigar to complete the picture. His voice was even low and slow like Churchill's sans the British accent.

"Quite all right, Bill. The missus would kill me but I might have to take you up on the offer to visit the restaurant if this is what awaits me." He warmly smiled at Annie.

"The missus always wants to kill you," Bill replied.

"You'd think forty-seven years of marriage she would have completed the task. She's not a follow-thru-er."

Annie smiled shyly yet endearingly; the kind of look that made men want to flirt, the kind of look that she sometimes wished she didn't project.

Bill introduced the two and held out his hand clarifying, as he had done since he was born, why his name was Winnie. "You know who Churchill was, right?"

"I do."

"You can never tell what the kids retain these days." Winnie replied and looked to Bill. "We don't see enough of you, Bill. You should come out and play more often."

"It's hard to know where to go when there isn't an invitation."

Winnie responded with a grunt, an acknowledgment of neglect.

"Let's not wait 'til the next funeral. Excuse me." Winnie looked at Annie. "Pleasure meeting you and I hope we see each other again soon."

They shook hands. Winnie turned to Bill.

Annie could see a faded friendship in each other's eyes. Both hesitantly aspired to reverse the disconnection in their relationship. They shook hands and smiled cordially and, as Winnie turned, Bill patted his old friend on the shoulder.

"Why did you want me here?" Annie asked. "I feel awkward. I'm either your gold-digging girlfriend or your paid-for escort."

"That's the same thing, semantically speaking."

"Bill."

"I thought it would make things easier."

"You thought?"

"It did." Bill's eyes were sad. They looked bluer than normal like his repressed emotions were seeping outward. "I haven't been to a funeral in six months. I missed the last two: Jonathan Palmer and Martin Wilkinson."

Annie remained quiet, listening. Her arms were crossed hugging her body for comfort and her head was tilted with concern.

Bill continued, "I couldn't. I wanted to be there but I couldn't leave my apartment. I literally couldn't leave my apartment. I sat on my couch wearing my suit. I couldn't move my legs." He shook his head slightly trying to shake away the thoughts. "I was paralyzed."

"With fear?"

"No. I don't think it was fear. It was . . ." He struggled for the answer. "It was . . ." He sipped his beer. Annie watched the liquid fall from the bottom of the bottle to neck and back. "It was . . . loneliness."

Bill looked back at the bookshelf and exhaled a long, low breath of air allowing his thoughts to linger.

His eyes shifted back to Annie; the comforting blonde waitress that listened to him and took a chance at accepting his invitation to a funeral. He swallowed hard. "Thank you."

Annie responded by placing her drink on the table and wrapping her arms around him. They hugged and he thanked her one more time.

It was only appropriate that they stopped back at Aldo's Restaurant. It was the security blanket in Bill's life, it was a place that he could go and feel accepted. He ordered a Coke and French fries. Annie drank a Diet Coke.

"You have children, right?"

Bill nodded.

"What are their names?"

"Bill Junior, my oldest. Chrissy, then Hank."

"Do they live nearby?"

"No." Bill dipped a fry in ketchup and popped it in his mouth. "I think their goal was to live as far away from me as humanly possible."

"Australia?"

"As far away in the United States."

"Hawaii?"

"Continental U.S."

"California."

"Please have some," Bill said pushing the fries towards Annie. She took two and ate them. "Bill's in Los Angeles. Chrissy's in Minnesota. Hank . . . Hank's in . . ." Bill searched the corner of his mind but couldn't find the answer. "I don't remember."

"You don't remember where your son lives?" Annie was aghast.

"He's very nomadic. I could name the city but I haven't had an accurate address from him in years."

"Does he call?"

"No."

"Never?" She was stunned as Bill shook his head.

"None of them do."

Annie opened her mouth to find out more. She wanted to know why this man's three children refused to acknowledge their father's existence. He was such a kind man. He never gave the allusion of being a bad man; quite the contrary. She hesitated though and ultimately let the matter drop.

"And your relationship?"

"Andre? We're good."

"Do you have grandparents?"

"I have grandmothers but I don't see them often. One is in a home. She has dementia."

"The other?"

"She's comfortable not being in our family's affairs."

"Understood."

"My grandfather on my mom's side passed away when I was really young. I was only seven but I remember he was the greatest. He loved taking us for ice cream and he spoiled us rotten. It was great. He insisted that he babysat whenever my parents wanted to go out. We would be there at a barbecue or family dinner and he'd say 'You two need to get out of the house'. He adored us. We adored him."

"That's a good snapshot to have."

"You kind of remind me of him," she stated with a smile. "My other grandfather was an asshole."

"Didn't spoil you?"

"No." Annie shook her slowly, remembering. "Not in the least. He didn't call on our birthdays. He was an alcoholic. My family confronted him many times and it pushed him away. That's why my grandmother probably doesn't talk to us these days. She never accepted our thoughts on him. Really, my mom's thoughts." Annie changed the pitch of her voice to imitate her grandmother, it was old and cracky. "That's Pauly. Like him or leave him, just don't try to change him." Her voice returned back to normal. "She adored him. They were party animals."

"Was he an alcoholic? Not all drinkers in their 60s are alcoholics."

"I don't know." Annie looked out the window gathering her thoughts and allowing the memories to replay. "Yes." She looked back at Bill. "He was."

"Bill, my condolences." Aldo approached the table and patted Bill on the shoulder. "How are you?"

"I'm okay, Aldo. How's business?"

"It's good. I just wanted to stop over and say hello. If you need anything . . ." Aldo held his hands outward inviting his courtesy.

"One of your wife's delicious peach pies might help me get through this troubling time."

Aldo pointed a skeptical finger towards Bill. "I don't sense this time is as troubling as you're leading on." Bill smiled at being called out. Aldo kindly continued, "But maybe I can get you a half of a pie. I will need to eat the other half myself."

"Why don't you bring the whole pie over tomorrow night for the playoff game?"

"Let me get permission from Lucetta." Aldo looked over to his employee. "Annie, how are you faring?"

"I'm faring finely."

"Good."

He turned and walked into the kitchen.

"Aldo's a good guy," Bill said.

"Yeah, he is."

11

Annie stepped into the empty apartment and headed directly into the bedroom to shed her funeral attire. It was nearing four and she contemplated the rest of the late-afternoon.

She considered a jog through the city reaching the Massachusetts Bay and back in just over an hour. The thought pleased her and thought it a nice way to clear her head. Within five minutes, she was dressed in shorts and a workout T-shirt and was stepping out in to the city air. She switched on her workout playlist and was off.

She breathed in part fresh air and part smog and dirt that floated around the urban landscape. The noise of the passing T soothed her in a strange way. It somehow indicated that everything was all right in the world like reruns of a TV show that you watched when you were in high school.

It dawned on her that she wasn't sure where her life was at or how it got there or where it was headed. She thought of the complete lives that Bill and his friends from the funeral had led. The future felt so far ahead.

The revelation made her want to turn around, head back into the apartment and cry.

Her laptop that often sat on the coffee table in front of her allowed her to easily search for a new job yet the fear of not finding one made her hesitate even going online. And what if there was that dream job available or company that was hiring? She didn't even feel qualified.

She pushed through the sidewalks of Boston heading east. She jogged past the statues that lined the median of Commonwealth Avenue where the pedestrians were minimal and the scenery was more comforting.

She loved the city and had lived here for almost five years only it all didn't quite feel real. Annie felt her dream was likely to end with an alarm buzzing and her lifting her head in some apartment just outside of Grand Rapids.

She thought of Andre and wondered how she would handle a break up. What if she was to enter the apartment and he simply said they were over. She had been dependent on him for so long that it was hard to imagine a life without him.

Annie was struck with the fear that she didn't have anything to offer Andre and she grew self-conscious about her few faults.

Annie arrived home sticky with sweat and imagined the comforting shower that was calling her name.

Her phone buzzed. Bethany's text message inquired about plans.

I'll text Andre, Annie responded.

I dont want to hang out w Andre. I want to hang out with u, Bethany replied.

Bethany didn't get it, Annie thought. She was in a relationship, a partnership, so she couldn't very well just ditch her significant other whenever she pleased. That response though would have initiated a reaction back from Bethany that Annie wasn't interested in dealing with. "Would he do that for you?" was a common question that was often posed and she shunned it, refusing to answer it.

Time crept on and Andre didn't respond to her text. Thirty minutes passed. Thirty minutes of mixed emotions causing her to wonder if she ever wrought such dramatics onto her boyfriend as her boyfriend did to her. Did she ever leave him waiting like this?

Annie was angry feeling that he was deliberately avoiding her or making her wait in some power game he enjoyed playing.

"I'm my own person," she stated aloud and responded to Bethany insisting that they make plans.

They would meet near Aldo's Restaurant and ride the T down to Haymarket opting for a quaint but price-friendly dinner in the Italian district called the North End. They would dine amongst its romantic red brick buildings overshadowing its small streets then follow it up with drinks nearby.

Annie didn't feel her cell phone vibrate in her purse and didn't see the message from Andre until she looked at her phone upon exiting the T.

"Shit," was Annie's initial reaction.

"What?" Bethany asked stopping and turning to face her friend.

"Andre got back to me. He says that he's already made plans for us with some friends." She heard the disappointment in her own voice.

"When? Where?"

"They have an affinity for Cask N' Flagon but he didn't specify."

"Are these work friends Bostonian transplants?"

Annie nodded. "Some."

"Hmm, that pokes holes in my theory . . ." Bethany said.

Annie finished her thought, ". . . that Cask is only for those not from here?" Bethany nodded in a way that shrugged with acceptance that her opinion was flawed. "You can come, I'm sure." Annie restated the response, "I mean, of course you're invited. I insist you join."

"Insist I join." Bethany was visibly upset. "So goes OUR plans in the name of the Adonis." She started walking towards the T station. "I should have expected this would happen."

"Now what the hell is this about?" Annie shouted giving chase. Bethany continued into the station. "We still have plans! We're still hanging out! What's your problem?"

Bethany shouted over her shoulder, "We don't have any plans. You're the one with the plans and now I get to tag along. And it's not my problem, it's your problem." Tears that she was attempting to suppress were coming to her eyes.

"Wait!" Annie grabbed Bethany's arm before she could scan the Charlie Card and pass through the gate to get to the platform. "I don't understand what's going on."

"We had plans, Annie. You and me. We were going to have dinner and grab a drink. Now our plan has changed because Andre has told you what he wanted to do. Why can't he just have a night to himself with his friends?"

"You don't get it," Annie responded calmly. "He's my boyfriend of five years! We're going to get married. It's a partnership."

Bostonians continued passing the two women avoiding their confrontation with one another. They scanned their cards while trying to catch a quick line so they could understand the reason for the public argument.

"It's not a partnership, Annie," Bethany said shaking her head. "A partnership implies equality. There's nothing equal."

"You're accusing me of what? Asking how high when he says jump?"

"It's not an accusation, it's an observance. You're guilty of it."

The cell phone in Annie's hand buzzed but she didn't unlock eyes with Bethany. "That's not true."

Bethany stopped herself and held up her hands defensively. "I'm criticizing, you're defending, and I don't blame you for doing so. I'm sorry that tonight has turned out this way."

"It doesn't have to."

"I'm going to go home but please consider these questions. Question one: If you were to ask Andre if it's okay for me to tag along, what would his response be? And question two: If he responded negatively, would you defend me or insist I still come or let him have the final word? Dare I pose another one?"

Annie sighed defeated. "What's to stop you?"

"What if you responded that you wanted to just hang out with me? What are the repercussions?"

Bethany scanned her card and walked through the turnstile without further discussion. She didn't turn around but desperately wanted to see the reaction of realization in Annie's face. She kept her ears open in hopes of Annie's final push to be with Bethany. She ended up waiting for a train hoping her best friend would stand tough.

Upstairs, Annie started walking westward towards the next stop. The walk offered time to reflect. She felt the same feelings of anger and sadness, of blame and defiance that she felt earlier when thinking about her decision to not wait for Andre's response.

She didn't recognize anyone's looks. She didn't see if anyone noticed the hurt blonde girl walking in their direction. She walked with a foggy cloud hurt by Bethany's display of emotions.

Those thoughts simmered in her mind. They were moments of defense and regret, the accusations were both uncalled for and they were exactly what she needed to hear.

By the time Annie reached the Government Center outbound T stop she figured Bethany's train would be ascending from underground and onto the tracks that sat on Beacon Street. There was no threat of an awkward moment of meeting on the same train.

That's all I need, Annie thought, a delay on the rails causing us to be in the same car.

Annie boarded the crowded T and listened as the announcement advised the passengers of the next stop and the final stop of the train. She was on her feet and wrapped her hand around a pole for stability. No one looked directly at her but, just like many of the passengers, they were scanning the faces of their fellow riders or avoiding the possibility of eye contact altogether.

There was a middle-aged man with a mustache that was uneven and sloppy. He looked upwards at her, stared at her for a long moment then tilted his head back down to continue playing Tetris on his smart phone. She was looking beyond him, just staring into space, not aware of how uncomfortable he was becoming.

As the train entered the station she came back into reality and looked at her phone to check on the time. She wanted out of the crowded train and wasn't happy to see a platform full of riders eager to squeeze onto an already packed car.

She smashed against the wall and kept her grip on the pole. A woman entered with an offensive amount of perfume. She was short with dyed red hair and her eyes and head shook almost instinctively at her own thoughts. The odor tickled Annie's nose. The man standing next to her smelled as if a shower wasn't a ritual he partook in on a regular basis.

Annie wanted off this train and dreaded the next ten stops before her destination.

Annie was tired when she exited the T. She felt anxiety in her heart and she couldn't figure out specifically why. There was fear and unease.

Annie entered the apartment feeling the pains in her feet. She wanted to sit down and unwind if only for a moment.

"Annie, come here." Andre ordered nonchalantly. She did and saw him standing in khaki pants, a blue shirt and sport coat. He looked like the poster child for New England, the kind of man anyone would want in their neighborhood. "Let's find you something that goes with this." He said referring to his outfit.

She smiled and followed him through the bedroom.

Andre started scanning her wardrobe.

"What about this one?" She offered holding her hand out to a blue blouse. "I can wear a white jacket over it or a shawl."

"No. Too plain for me." He continued scanning. "Is this all there is? Do you have anything stashed anywhere else?"

"This is it?"

"Hmm," he grunted in disappointment. "Then I guess the blue thing is okay."

"You mind if I invite Bethany? We were going to hang out. You know I have trouble talking to some of your friends and coworkers."

"You have trouble talking to them because you don't try." He kissed her on the top of her head. "You're not going to become good at conversation unless you let go of your anchor."

"I'm perfectly fine at conversation."

"You know what I mean," Andre left the closet, "and you know how I feel about your friend."

Annie stood scowling at the lack of an answer. She shouted back, "So, is that a yes or a no on inviting Bethany?"

"Do you really want to invite her along?" He answered back hoping his vague insistence and disregarding tone was enough of an answer to drop the question.

"Yes, I do. We were supposed to hang out tonight and I came home for this, I would like to still see her." Annie entered the bedroom as Andre was slipping on his loafers with a shoe horn.

"Well, you came home because we are going to do something more fun."

"That's not an answer."

Frustrated, Andre stood up and tossed the shoe horn onto the dresser. "No. That's my answer. I don't particularly care for her and I think you can do better. She's not a very good friend, Annie. She insults you and questions your choices. There's no support there and support is key to any relationship. I support you and you support me." He held out his hands as if finalizing his point. "And she's rude to me. So, I'm sorry if it hurts you, Annie, but I don't want her joining us."

Annie accepted Andre's decision and turned around. She paused then turned back to face him. "What do you mean, I can do better?"

Andre looked at her with confusion. "Simple, Annie, you can just do better."

"But better how?"

"I told you," Andre said facing partially towards the bedroom door hoping to avoid the fight he thought Annie was picking. "She's kind of a bitch."

"I think I'm going to wear this."

"What? Don't be silly, put on the blue thing you wanted to wear."

She remained defiant. "I wanted to wear this. It's why I'm wearing this."

Andre sighed and shook his head. "Fine," he mumbled and
opened his mouth to say something but hesitated. He left the room.
"I'll be out here when you're ready."

"I'm ready now."

Andre rolled his eyes ever so slightly and motioned towards the
living room. "I'll be out here when you're ready."

Annie didn't change clothes and was spending her time in the booth
of four-top table looking at her beer. Her fingernails flicked the
edges of the label and she worked at it as if it were a puzzle that
needed solving.

"How's everyone doing over here?"

"Another." Andre held up his empty Stella glass towards the
waitress without making eye contact. The others ordered second
rounds.

"Apple-tini." She ordered wanting something with more of a
kick than a beer.

The night trudged onward. Andre got up and mingled with
others leaving her to fend for herself. She sat, bored, finding it near
impossible to speak with anyone who came near. It was the same
looks from the same people. The women were envious and catty.
The men were frightened that speaking with Annie would bring
forth a fight with their girl. Andre's friends, the ones that knew her
better, tried to make conversation but they were mostly one-sided
and interrupted when others barged in.

She spoke to a boyfriend of one of Andre's coworkers. After less
than ten minutes of learning about one another's lives they were
approached by the co-worker.

"Michael, come with me, I want you to meet someone." The
jealous girlfriend looked at Annie and said with a sneer, "Hi."

"Pleasure meeting you," Michael said, standing up.

They went to a group of others that Annie recognized.

There were a lot of advantages of being pretty, Annie thought,
and there were a lot of unintended disadvantages that are often
overlooked. Rarely could she hold a conversation with a man
without wondering if the whole basis of their talking was merely his

desire to get into her pants. Jealous girlfriends saw her as a threat. There were women who had given her dirty looks when she was out at a bar or club because they viewed her as competition.

Michael was replaced by a heavily intoxicated, squirrelly man whose body swayed back-and-forth as if he might pass out at any moment. He had a light tattered goatee. His buttoned-shirt was open and she saw a bright-green shirt underneath with writing regarding a bar crawl on St. Patrick's Day.

Annie spotted Andre standing near the bar with two others. He was laughing and enjoying himself.

She resented it.

Chugging down a big gulp of her apple-tini she muttered to herself, "This sucks."

"We're having a party." Andre sprang out of the cool spring air of the night. Their walk home was long and awkward. Annie minded her own business as Andre talked enjoying each syllable of his own voice. Annie had blocked a lot of it out, all the drivel of that he learned that night, the gossip he took advantage of and the concerns of his colleagues he liked to possess as a way of making him feel superior.

"What?"

Andre wrapped an arm lazily around Annie's shoulder and brought her in. "We're having a party."

"What are we celebrating?" Her words were spoken solemnly and distant like her tongue was on autopilot while her mind raced around a flurry of random thoughts.

"Well, nothing."

"Then why are we having a party?"

"Oh, come on now." Andre was boisterous due to the combination of vodka/Red Bulls and his intention of getting laid in about thirty minutes. "You did good tonight."

"I sat there."

"You were charming."

"Were we at the same place?"

"Annie, give your self some credit. Do you like being depressed?"

"I'm not depressed."

"Maybe I should dance for you?" Andre hopped a few steps in front of her and tapped his feet clownishly while waving his hands.

"You're drunk," she responded walking past him as he held his arms outward signaling the end of his jig.

"But you're smiling now." He started walking beside her.

She looked over to Andre with a smile pushing forward. "Suppose I am."

"Score one point for Andre."

Annie rolled her eyes. "When's this party that we're having?"

"Saturday."

Annie stopped in her tracks. "Saturday!" Andre stopped and spun around to look at her. "This Saturday?"

"As in today's Thursday, tomorrow's Friday and after Friday comes Saturday."

"Don't be cute," she snapped.

"I can't help it." He approached her and placed his hands on her shoulders. They felt heavy. "We just need booze, mixers and snacks, babe. Nothing fancy. We'll get ten pizzas."

"How big is this party going to be?"

"Twenty, thirty people. I don't know. I'll help with it. I have a golf game Saturday morning but I can help after. You want to do the party planning crap again, right? Well, plan a party!"

"I work Saturday morning so I will need your help." Annie sighed and confirmed that he really wanted it simple yet she felt the urge to expand it. "Drinks and pizza. Can I plan a little bit more than that?"

"As long as there are drinks and pizza, sweetie, you can do whatever you want."

12

Bethany didn't speak to Annie for the first part of their shift. They served coffee and food, took orders and played nice with the customers without saying more than two words to one another. There was hidden tension behind each "Excuse me" and "Thanks".

It took Aldo's insistence for them to reconcile their differences before the dialogue began.

"You two make nice," he said. "I don't like when my employees are at odds." Aldo shifted in his seat and saw a handful of regulars sipping on coffees and talking politics. He lifted himself off of the stool and grabbed the coffee pot attending to the pair of older gentlemen discussing a western Massachusetts congressman's inability to keep his privates private. He added his two cents to their conversation.

Annie and Bethany looked at one another.

"Have you ever had two people offering advice for what they feel is best and those two pieces of advice from people who claim to know you and your life are at complete opposite ends of the spectrum?"

"What?"

"I'm sorry," Annie said.

"For what?"

"For ditching you."

"When are you going to realize he's not . . ." Annie held up her hand to cut Bethany's words off.

"Beth, stop. Both you and Andre don't think the other is good enough for me."

"He said that?"

"You said it too." Annie rubbed her own arm nervously and averted her eyes. "Sometimes I just need a pair of ears rather than a counselor."

The door of the restaurant opened and Bill entered with a smile.

"I'm sorry, Bill, we are full, please take your business elsewhere." Aldo stated.

"You haven't had a full boat since the Bush Administration." Bill tossed his paper down on his usual empty table. "The first one."

Aldo followed Bill to the table. He pulled out a five dollar bill and tossed it on the table. "What would you like my cook to spit into today . . ." Aldo threw up his hands dramatically. "Silly me! I meant to ask you what you would like for breakfast this morning."

"Don't be upset with me. It wasn't my New York team that lost."

"Damn Yankees."

"That's what you get for being a closet Yankee fan in Boston."

"What can I get you today?"

"I'm not in a breakfast mood. Let's make it a simple tuna melt."

"Coffee?"

"Coke."

"I got it!" Annie exclaimed. She filled the beverage and brought it to Bill. "Here you go."

Bethany walked behind Annie. Bill acknowledged her with a friendly greeting and Annie stopped her in her tracks.

"Both of you," Annie said stopping Bethany in her tracks. "I have a question for both of you. More of an invitation really. Tomorrow night me and Andre are having a party." She smiled at Bethany and then looked at Bill. "I would like both of you to attend."

"You want me . . . at a party?" Bill wanted to confirmation.

"Yes, of course," she responded with her usual bubbly manner.

"And did he ask you to invite me? Us?" Bethany asked suspiciously with a raised eyebrow.

Annie shook her head.

Bethany replied with excitement. "Count me in then!"

"I don't think so," Bill said and tilted his head away as a matter of changing the subject.

Bethany left the two alone.

"Bill." He ignored the first call so she spoke his name again.

"Annie, I'm seventy-one. I have no business at a social gathering like that unless you were my granddaughter. I appreciate your gesture but I'm going to decline."

"Come on." She begged.

"No."

"Pleeeeeease." She whined like a five-year-old.

"Annie."

She became serious and expelled a quick, heavy breath. "Bill, you're my friend and I want you at this party."

"I'm your friend and you want to prove something to your boyfriend."

"What?"

Bill looked into her eyes and held the gaze for a long pause. "I don't know. What I do know is that your boyfriend has no clue that I am being invited to his apartment."

"Our apartment."

"And Bethany seems very interested in attending without his approval."

"I don't need his approval to invite Bethany or anyone I damn well please to a party we're throwing."

Bill laced his fingers and placed his elbows on the table. He leaned inward resting his chin on his knuckles. He smiled and stated, "And you're sure going to prove it tomorrow night, aren't you."

Annie's shoulders slumped and she turned to walk away. But she hesitated. For a brief moment she stopped herself and decided to turn back to Bill in order to defend her actions.

"And so what? I have a shitty time hanging out with his friends. They are boring and talk about dull topics that I either don't know anything about or don't care to know and before you say anything, yes, I've tried talking to them. Bill, I'm inviting you because I like talking to you, because you're my friend."

"I'm seventy-one."

"I can have seventy-one-year-old friends! Are you having a hard time adjusting to having a thirty-year-old friend? Is that what this is about?"

"No."

"Then what is it?"

"I'm not commenting."

"You have to comment."

Bill shook his head.

"I want you there, Bill."

"Are you going to keep this up?"

"I might."

Bill tilted his head to begin reading the top of the newspaper and replied in a hoarse and serious whisper. "Then I would like to request a new waitress."

The remark froze Annie where she stood. Her reaction was an open mouth and wide eyes. She hadn't noticed she was holding her breath and the faint signs of tears were arriving.

"I'm sorry. I . . ." She turned and quietly fled. When Annie burst into the kitchen she was shaken up.

"I'm totally going to nail one of his friends, just out of spite. An ugly friend," Bethany said to Annie.

Omar overheard the remark. "Why wait, sweet pea? I can be an ugly friend."

"Omar! Not now." Bethany noticed the look in Annie's eyes. "What's wrong?"

"I . . . um, nothing."

"That doesn't look like nothing, sweetheart," Omar said. "Speak up."

Annie looked at her two co-workers and told them the situation that just took place. Omar backed off and continued making the food. Bethany swooped in and offered reassurance that it was just his way of telling her to drop the subject.

However, like the previous week's awkwardness, waiting on Bill became a challenge of dealing with thick tension.

When Annie placed the check face down on the table she offered a second apology.

"It's okay," he responded placing a warm hand on top of hers.

13

To put together a party regardless of the size wasn't just a matter of picking up a few snacks at the store and it wasn't about ordering pizza. As a newly reclaimed event planner, Annie wanted to make the Saturday evening gathering something more than just another night at a friend's apartment.

She wanted decorations and games. Even the cups she desired were to be similar in theme. She simply couldn't just have chips and dip and pizza.

Annie opted for a Red Sox theme. It was easy and fun and there was a game on. She went to the store and bought Red Sox plates, Red Sox cups, and a deck of cards with the Boston B on the front of the deck—she would try to create or find a clever drinking game that she could use them for. She would wear her Red Sox jersey and Red Sox baseball cap. Flags on a string were hung from one end of the apartment to the other and she stocked up on Boston's own Sam Adams.

She found Boston Red Sox ice cube trays with the classic Boston B. She hoped the water would be frozen in time for the party.

She figured pizza was fine and the additional selection of liquor would suffice. She found ballpark peanuts and Boston Red Sox bowls to put the chips and salsa in.

By 3:30 most things were set up and ready to go. The party still wouldn't get going for four hours.

Annie collapsed onto the couch and closed her eyes feeling the muscles in her body relax. She took a few deep breaths and felt her heart beating begin to slow down.

She moaned feeling a much needed nap take hold.

Then there was a knock at the door.

"Someone's going to get punched," Annie said standing up from the couch and heading to the door as a second rapping sounded throughout the apartment. "Calm down, I'm coming!" She playfully shouted.

After looking through the peephole she opened the door with a smile.

"I'm looking for a Miss Annie Ferguson," Jon stated holding an envelope in his hand.

She held out her hand and took the envelope, a cell phone bill. "Thank you."

"I'm going to start calling you Fergie from now on," Jon said.

"Then don't plan on talking to me very often."

"Annie it is then."

"I've been meaning to talk to you."

"Why? Do you have a crazy idea to put coffee in a wine glass?"

"No, but I'll have to remember that one," Annie looked behind her as if she were guiding Jon's eyes into the apartment. "We're having a party. Wanna come?"

"I'm busy."

"I'm sure you could record it," Annie responded trying to call him out on his lack of plans.

He laughed at her remark. "But it's a *Hogan's Heroes* marathon."

"You're lying."

Jon over-exaggerated his shock at being accused of telling tales. "I am appalled at such inflammatory accusations."

Annie wasn't impressed and, with a monotone voice, asked, "What's the lead character's name in *Hogan's Heroes*?"

"Hogan."

"Wrong."

"Really?" Jon shouted back with a crack in his voice. She called his bluff and the surprise showed.

"I have no idea but you just showed your cards. The party starts at 7:30."

"You manipulative little minx."

"7:30," she repeated and began to close the door.

"Wait!"

She stopped.

"Should I bring anything?"

"Dress appropriately. It's a Boston Red Sox party." She started to close the door once again.

"Wait, wait! Is that football?"

She shook her head chuckling. "I'll see you later." She responded closing door all the way.

Andre was home by 4:30 and he immediately headed for the shower, stripping as he went. His golf bag leaned up against the front door, his golf shoes lazily sat next to them. Annie stood in the bathroom, her butt against the counter. She was meticulously painting her nails blue with the red Boston B in the middle.

"Looks good, honey," Andre said on the other side of the shower curtain. "Thanks."

"You're welcome."

"Do you know how many people are actually going to be here?"

"No."

Annie vacated the bathroom and went into the living room switching on the television. She sat down and paged through the guide finding a movie or rerun that she could enjoy. Saturday, however, afforded little quality television.

A John Hughes movie was the only option that satisfied her so she let it play. It was a movie she watched a hundred times between the age of thirteen and sixteen, then a few more times while huddled with friends on an apartment couch throughout college delighting in a girl's night of margaritas or ice cream; occasionally both.

Unable to sit still, she popped up off the couch and went into the kitchen. Opening the freezer she was happy to find that the ice cubes were freezing nicely. Her stomach growled and she considered the dangers of opening the bag of chips fearing that half the bag would be gone by the time the first guest arrived.

She blew casually on her nails hoping they would dry quicker and stood at the kitchen counter watching the television.

Andre exited the bedroom wearing a fitted gray T-shirt and dark jeans.

"Aren't you going to wear something Boston Red Sox?"

"Sweetie," he walked over to her and placed an arm around her bringing her in closely. "I love that you went out of your way to have this theme. The banner thingy's a nice touch." He let go and looked into Annie's eyes. "I don't want to dress up."

"You're not dressing up. You can wear your Sox T-shirt."

"Then we would be matching and that would look weird. I don't want to be 'that' couple. You can dress up, it looks cute."

"Did you at least text your friends and let them know it's a Red Sox party?"

Andre pulled his phone from his pocket and started flipping through his messages as if Annie's question reminded him that he had to respond to an email. "No," he said walking away.

"Why not?"

"Because it's not a Sox party, it's just a party!"

"I did all this for you. I bought all these decorations."

Andre looked up from his phone. He stood right at the frame between the living room and the bedroom. "And they're nice and it looks really cool, but Annie, I never asked you to do any of this. I said we need drinks and pizza. So, don't get mad at me. This was your idea."

"You said I should use my party planning skills. Can you support me a little?"

"Hey, I do support. I think it's kind of strange at the last minute to tell my friends to wear costumes when it's not Halloween."

"It's not costumes," she shot back feeling insulted as if he wasn't even listening to her concerns. "Just tell them to wear something Red Sox," she murmured.

"Half of them probably will anyway so don't worry about it." Andre reentered the bedroom.

"Not now," Annie said to herself, it was barely audible on the end of a deep breath. She shook her head and closed her eyes. "It's not worth a fight." She pulled the bag of tortilla chips across the counter and opened them up. "Fuck it." She placed a full chip into her mouth and started chewing. Before she swallowed she already had another one ready to go and stuffed it into her mouth. Before she was done with the second chip there was a third in her hand.

Andre exited the bedroom once again without a word. He sat down and grabbed the remote control from the arm rest and started flipping through the guide. "Score!" One station below her movie was a Sylvester Stallone movie from the mid-nineties.

"Do I embarrass you?" Annie asked.

Andre responded with an exaggerated groan and looked over his shoulder. He barely had her in his peripheral vision. "Can we stop with the questions that are designed to get me into trouble?"

"They aren't designed to get you into trouble."

"Yeah they are, they all are. You women can ask us about the weather and turn it into something that's our fault that we have to apologize for." He had an open-mouthed smile on his face enjoying his comedic observation.

"Do you know how silly that sounds, Andre? They're thinking questions. I'm not out to get you and I'm not trying to start a fight."

Andre turned around and looked at Annie. "The problem with thinking questions is you thought about the answers all day and then ask them expecting me to give you the answer you want to hear within seconds." His eyebrows rose at the conclusion of his point.

"Okay, I won't ask you any other questions, just please answer that one."

"Which one?"

"Do I embarrass you?"

"No," he replied quickly and honestly. "Why would you think that?"

"I don't know. It's something I've been feeling."

"Well, stop it." He spun back around and turned the volume up two levels.

Annie pulled the Grey Goose from the freezer and filled an empty glass with a shot's worth. She palmed a few ice cubes and tossed them in the glass then filled it with cranberry juice.

She stared at the back of Andre's head. There was the tiniest hint of a bald spot forming. It could easily be confused for the way the back of the head was part differently than the front. But Annie knew better.

She took a big gulp of her drink and listened as the ice cubes rattled around. He was still handsome, she thought, and he had lots of charisma.

As she continued to drink and stare uninterestedly at the action movie with cheesy dialogue, she contemplated the dating world. It had been so long since she was in the game that the thought of reentering unnerved her.

Annie almost would rather stick it out with Andre with the hopes of things improving than deal with first dates and new relationships once again. She remembered the time she met a man at a friend's party. He was sweet and charming and she happily accepted a first date. They met at an Applebee's and shared a drink. He spent most of the time talking and, whenever he posed a question, they were very personal. He spoke for ten minutes about his job as a chauffer and the prominent local citizens he drove around.

"I usually don't have sex on the first date," he said segueing into a new topic, "but for you I would make that exception. What are your rules on the first date?"

Annie remained friendly and avoided his statement outright. He had an affinity for talking about ex-girlfriends. She did not want a second date and regretted meeting the man when her phone started ringing at three in the morning or ten text messages were sent when she was in a movie theater. She ran into him at the mall three weeks later after avoiding his communication efforts at all costs. He was with a girl. "This is Annie," he said introducing them, "she's an ex-girlfriend who can't take a hint, if you know what I mean." Annie stood frozen as everything he had done to 'stalk' her was now being played as if she were the aggressor. Too stunned to respond, she just walked away shaking her head.

Annie stood at the counter in the kitchen still looking at the back of Andre's head, his balding head, with an empty glass of cranberry/vodka in her hand. Maybe he wasn't so bad after all, she considered.

I'm thirty, she reminded herself, and refilled her glass.

14

If she wasn't an embarrassment to Andre before she seemed bent on becoming one now. She had knocked back two drinks prior to the start of the party nursing that second one until around seven. Having eaten very little it was hitting her like an eighteen-wheeler and she stumbled around the apartment letting her arms sway loosely like a breeze was blowing through the room.

"I need to stop," she announced.

"Or slow down, a lot," Andre said walking to the door to allow the first set of guests to enter.

"My man, my brother!" Raj said entering. "I hate coming to parties on time, it makes me look like a loser."

"You are a loser!" Andre said back.

"I arrive early this time because I have business to discuss." Raj looked over to the television. "Who's winning?"

"Tied," Annie responded.

"Check you out!" Raj beamed with delight seeing Annie decked out in a Sox shirt and ball cap.

"How adorable!" Jessica cooed looking at Annie's fingernails. She turned back to Raj and then to Andre, "I should've worn my pink shirt." She turned back to Annie. "It's so *cute*, it has the B in the middle with rhinestones around it. It's a *cute* V-neck."

"It shows her boobies quite nicely," Raj announced with a smile.

"Damn, I wish I told you about the theme," Andre responded looking directly at Jessica's chest.

"I'm wearing Red Sox boxers, would you like to see?"

Annie and Andre responded at the same time, "No!"

They laughed at the coincidence which segued beautifully into making mixed drinks and opening beers.

"Come with me into your office," Raj said putting a hand on Andre's back and leading him into the bedroom.

"What are they talking about?"

"Who cares?" Jessica responded taking a sip of her vodka/Red Bull.

There were a handful of guests arriving and starting to drink. Annie ordered the pizzas just after eight o'clock anticipating its arrival to be forty-five minutes to an hour later.

The party remained relatively dull until 8:30 when Bethany entered the apartment.

"Greetings one and all."

"Hey!" Annie shouted racing from behind the counter to give her friend a hug.

"Jesus Christ, how many have you had?" Bethany asked as she scanned the room looking for Andre. She desperately wanted to see the initial look on his face. When she found him she greeted him with a beaming smirk as he reciprocated with a smarmy look. He shook his head and continued talking to the three others that surrounded him.

Annie replied mimicking The Count from Sesame Street. "I've had four. Four drinks. Ah ah ah."

"How strong were these drinks? Maybe you should eat something before continuing."

"Whatever, mom!" Annie giggled.

"I just don't want you to have to clean vomit out of your hair."

Annie groaned but understood. "I'll wait until I have at least two pieces of pizza. And a breadstick. And some chips . . ." She took a handful of potato chips and stuffed them in her mouth. She mumbled, ". . . before I have another."

"If you eat that much maybe you should drink until you throw it up," Andre said approaching the counter. "Speaking of puke," he looked at Bethany.

"Kids, kids!" Annie held up her arms towards both Bethany and Andre stopping both from continuing further. "Are you going to take the high road and be nice?" Annie asked. "That's a question for both of you."

Andre sighed. "Fine."

"Yeah, fine."

"Shake hands."

They did as they were told.

"Can I speak to you for a minute?" Andre asked and headed towards the bedroom without waiting for a response. Annie followed.

He closed the bedroom door and folded his arms.

"I can't believe you invited her."

"She's my friend. It's a party."

"What did I tell you? She's a bitch. She shouldn't be here."

Her speech was slurred with exaggerated inflections. "I'm not a big fan of half of those people out there but I stomach them whenever you want to see them and you like to see them a lot. You invited your friends and I invited mine. You both don't like each other, but I like both of you, so y'all gonna have to do deal with each other."

Andre sighed, "Stop drinking for a little bit, you're embarrassing yourself."

"Mlah!" She responded incoherently shrugging off his rebuttal.

Andre rolled his eyes and stepped back into the living room.

"Score one for Annie," she said with a smile pumping her fist in the air.

When Annie exited the bedroom there was quiet in the living room. All eyes were on the front door. Jon stood with a six-pack of Boston Lager being judged by the handful of party guests.

"Annie invited me earlier." He was explaining to Andre.

Annie rushed up to Jon. "Happy you could make it." She took the beer and placed it on the counter. There was still silence settling in the apartment.

Andre angrily approached Jon. "She invited you?"

"Yes, Andre, I invited him. He's our neighbor, he's kind of new to the city and I wanted to introduce him to people."

"I'm Bethany," Bethany said with a seductive gaze and a hand held out.

"Pleasure." Jon shook her hand then moved it towards Andre. "And you're Andre."

Andre stood defiant refusing to shake his hands. "I want an explanation." He was staring down Jon.

Jon was confused. "From me?"

"Not from you, asshole. Annie."

"Don't mind him," Bethany started, "Andre thinks every guy he encounters wants to sleep with his girlfriend."

"I don't want to sleep with Annie," Jon tried to reassure Andre. He looked over to Annie. "Nothing personal, you know. I have a girlfriend."

"So, you would sleep with her but you have a girlfriend and don't want to cheat on her," Andre said trying to trick Jon up. "Maybe it's time for you to leave and never look at my girlfriend ever again."

"Stop it!" Annie finally shouted to Andre, she grabbed Jon's hand and led him the few feet to the kitchen counter. "Have a drink, Jon." She looked at Andre. "And you, what the hell is the matter with you? He's a guest at our party. You wouldn't say those things to any of your other guests here, would you?"

One of the guests yelled, "He was safe!" Everyone looked at him and the guy pointed to the screen using his beer almost like a pointer. The man defended his outburst mumbling, "He was safe by a mile."

"He was out," Raj said putting both his hands up before anyone could call him out. "Look, I want him to be safe with the rest of you, but watch the replay." Raj nodded towards the screen.

It was enough to get the tension to break slightly and the ten guests started talking amongst themselves once again.

Andre sighed as Annie placed her hand on his arm. "Andre, he's a friend, he's our neighbor," she said soothingly. "Is there something stressing you out?"

"Life stresses me out, that's why I wanted to have a party." Andre responded and looked at Jon. He didn't say it but his eyes offered a small apology. "Any other surprise guests I should expect?"

On cue there was a knock at the door. "The pizza guy?" Annie said shrugging her shoulders. "Although we kind of expected him."

She went to the door and swung it open, her mouth dropped open.

"Yes!" Bethany yelled. "Now it's a party."

The guests quieted down and looked back at the door to see if another dramatic scene would unfold.

What they saw was an older man with white hair wearing a tie and sport coat. He had a grocery store cake in his hand.

"Who the hell are you?" Andre shouted.

"Who the hell are you?" Bill mimicked.

"You came," Annie responded with a smile.

"I brought a cake. It seemed like the proper gesture." He scanned the apartment. "Neat place. Where should I put the cake?"

"I'll take it," Annie grabbed the grocery-store brand cake placing it on the counter.

"Whose grandpa is this?"

Bill held out his hand. "I'm Denise, Marty, Natalie and Kara's grandpa."

Andre instinctively shook his hand and asked confused, "Are you lost?"

"Annie invited me."

There was another knock at the door which had been left open. "Piz-za?" The teenage girl shyly announced. She held one heated bag in her left hand and there was a second on the floor in the hallway.

Three of Andre's friends approached the open door from the hallway and excused themselves around the pizza delivery gal.

"Finally, someone arrives that I know," Andre announced and shook their hands.

"I just need a signature from Andre Deaver."

"Honey, you just sign it for me," Andre ordered Annie.

She did and let the teenager scuttle back to the pizza place.

The guests hovered over the pizza ravenously ransacking the first two boxes like they hadn't had a bite to eat in days.

Annie was able to back away from the madness and stood near the window.

"Is it okay to approach?" Jon asked slowly moving towards Annie.

"Proceed." Annie waved him forward. "My buzz is gone, now I just feel like shit."

"You should drink more."

"No."

"You should eat something."

"Probably."

"Then drink some more." Jon suggested and Annie considered the idea. Jon continued, "Would you like me to get a piece of pineapple pizza for you?"

"Gross. I ordered that?"

"It's going pretty fast. I'm not personally a fan of exotic fruit on my pizza. I prefer vegetables and meats. Fruits?" Jon shook his head.

"Thanks for coming. Nice shirt, by the way."

"You like it?" Jon looked down at his navy blue T-shirt that had the conventional font stating: Red Sox Baseball. "Why isn't anyone else wearing Red Sox paraphernalia?"

"That's a can of worms I don't wish to open."

"Andre seems nice." Jon said sarcastically.

"Be nice." Annie continued as if she were talking to herself, "Jeez, why do I have to regulate? I feel like a kindergarten teacher."

"I'm sorry. I've seen him around the building. I think I rode up in the elevator with him once. He was on his phone, no acknowledgement."

Annie shrugged it off.

Bill walked up to Annie and Jon with a strange smile on his face. "If you take the two oldest people in his room and add their ages together I'm willing to bet they don't equal my age."

"Thanks for coming."

"Jon." Jon held out his hand, Bill shook it.

"Bill."

"Thanks for coming," Annie repeated.

"It was this or watch the *M*A*S*H** marathon."

"Who's the lead character in that show?" Jon asked.

"Hawkeye." Bill responded as if he were asked his own name.

"He wasn't bluffing," Annie said to Jon.

"Who's the lead character in *Hogan's Heroes?*" Jon asked Bill.

Bill was taken aback, as if Jon asked who was buried in Grant's tomb. "Hogan." Annie and Jon chuckled. "It's his heroes."

"Thanks for coming."

"Stop saying that, Annie. This is actually kind of fun. I'm going to try and snatch a beer and a slice." Bill looked at Jon. "You sir, were bogarting the Boston Lager . . ."

"Go nuts." Jon replied.

"Don't be afraid to mingle."

Bill turned away, paused, then turned back. "Hey look, I'm an old man . . ."

"You're not that old."

". . . if anyone is bothering you, point them out and I'll go over there and start doing some old man rambling about the Nixon Administration and 'kids these days'. It's always fun to watch eyes glaze over." Bill winked and then turned back towards the kitchen area. "I think I'm going to stick with the people I know."

"That guy's awesome. Where did you find him?"

"He's a regular." They watched as Bethany and Bill conversed with one another. "He said he wasn't going to show." Annie said to herself.

Bill popped his head up and screamed with amusement to Annie. "Hey!" She looked over to him as he held up the Boston Red Sox ice cube tray. "Neat! I'm afraid to use them."

"Is he putting ice cubes in his beer?" Annie asked trying to view Bill's actions. She sighed and leaned against the wall. She felt a slight cool breeze enter the apartment from the open window. There was a dramatic temperature difference. The more people to arrive the hotter it was getting and it just reached the point of stuffiness.

"He reminds me of my biology teacher in high school. He was this cool old teacher that everyone loved. I got a C in his class."

Bethany approached the two. "Hi." She said flirtatiously to Jon.

"Hello." He held out his hand again. "We met by the door." He acted as if he didn't recognize her advancement.

"Bethany, heel!" Annie said. "He has a girlfriend."

"Sad." Bethany surveyed the crowd.

"We're in the wrong clique," Annie advised her friend. "We're not one of the cool kids."

"Marry up. That's what momma always said." Bethany looked at Jon. "Not flirting. What do you do, Jon?"

"Nothing."

Bill shoved his way into the group. "I thought those ice cube things were great but I didn't want to use them because they would melt." He had a cup filled with the Boston Lager in one hand and a slice of cheese pizza on a plate in the other.

"You don't do anything?" Bethany clarified still speaking to Jon.

"I was laid off. I was a content writer for Boston Public Television. Federally endorsed plus lack of federal funds equals last one in, first one out."

There was an awkward silence for a moment as no one knew how to proceed after the downer statement.

"That sucks," Bethany finally replied.

"Gotta keep moving on." Jon put the beer bottle to his lips and drank a hefty gulp. He bulged his eyes wide. "I'm going to see about that pizza."

"It smells good," Bill started. "I can't eat and drink. I need another hand."

Bethany took Bill's cup and he thanked her finally able to pick up his slice.

"I should mingle, right?" Annie said in a spacey tone looking outwards towards the whole room.

"You are mingling."

Jon finished his beer and popped open another one. He placed it on the counter as he looked at the empty pizza boxes. He decided to take the initiative, stack them and put them aside. He lifted the lids of a whole pizza and found a veggie supreme. "Nice," he said to himself and grabbed two slices from the third and final pizza and placed them on a Red Sox plate. He folded his first pizza slice lengthwise and took a bite.

Andre stood on the opposite side of the counter. He wasn't portraying the friendliest of demeanors but his tone was eerily calm.

"Hello," Jon said with a full mouth.

"Enjoying my pizza?"

"It's . . . good." Jon wasn't sure where the questioning was leading. "Enjoying the party?"

Andre nodded and looked towards Annie. "She puts on a good show, I guess."

"Good show?"

"She wants to be a party planner or something like that."

"Yes she does."

"Who would pay for someone to do this?" Andre chuckled.

"I think she wants to do it on a grander scale than an apartment party."

"How long have you known each other?"

"A week. Maybe."

"This cutsy, innocent boy routine . . . I'm not buying it. What's your girlfriend's name?"

"Jonie."

"Jon and Jonie?"

Jon nodded.

"Where is she?"

"Detroit. That's where we're from." Andre stared down Jon. His discomfort caused him to continue talking. "It's a whole long story. We were looking for jobs and I found one here and she was going to move but I got laid off." Jon looked downwards at his beer and relished taking in a big drink. He thought he heard Andre snort as if he enjoyed Jon's misfortune. "Look, I like Annie." It sounded horrible when he said it and so he backtracked immediately. "No, wait. I mean she's cool and friendly. She's a good friend."

"You've known each other for a week. She can't be that good of a friend."

"I don't have many friends here. Actually, I don't have any friends here."

"Find new friends."

"Do you want to be my friend?"

Andre palmed a slice of pizza. "Fuck off." He turned around changing faces and delighting at the four guests that arrived at the party. They were his friends, non-threatening, and the ones he wanted to speak with.

"Why did you decide to show? You were so adamant about not coming."

Bill shrugged his shoulders. "I don't know. I guess I had nothing better to do."

"Flattering."

"I miss genuine, courteous interaction."

"Not sure you came to the right place." Bethany said with a sinister smirk. She continued, "You don't get that from your friends?"

"I don't have any friends, Bethany."

"Bullshit," she responded.

"You do have friends, Bill. I met some of them." Annie added.

"They're not . . ." he shook his head and took a sip from his beer.

"They were interested in seeing you."

"They were interested in saying that they wanted to see me."

"Call Teddy."

"The widower! No."

"Call Winnie." Annie insisted. "That was his name, right?"

Bill shook his friends. "You're my friends, right?"

"Yeah!" Bethany and Annie said together.

"That's fine by me." Bill looked out of the window. "You need a balcony."

Jon approached the group. "It's been fun guys," he said with a wave. "I think I should leave."

"What happened?" Annie asked shifting her head to spot her boyfriend.

"Nothing."

"You're not leaving," she ordered.

"What an asshole, what did he do?" Bethany demanded.

"Nothing." He raised his hands slightly as a way to stop them from doing anything rash. "It's okay."

"Time for a drink." Annie brushed past Bill and Jon. She stood at the counter looking at the slightly melting Boston Red Sox ice cubes. She popped three of them out and tossed them into her glass.

"One of us should do something," Jon said to Bill and Bethany as they all observed Annie on her mission to supply her stomach with more alcohol.

"You're right. One of us should do something," Bill responded.

Annie continued building her drink pouring cranberry juice inside the glass following it with an unmeasured amount of vodka.

"She needs food," Jon said.

"You're right. She does need food," Bill replied.

Bethany looked at both of them. "What are you, the old guys in the balcony from the *Muppets*? Do something." They looked at one another then at Bethany. "You guys are douche bags. Here, I'm tired of being nice." She handed the cup of beer back to Bill and rushed past them heading straight for Annie.

"How did that word ever come to mean what it means now?" Bill asked. He tilted his gaze towards Jon. "Do you know what a douche bag is?"

"I know what a douche bag is," Jon quickly stated hoping that this particular conversation would cease.

"You know this one time . . ."

"Don't even!" Jon shot back.

"I wasn't going to tell a story," Bill said with a smile. "I just wanted to see your reaction."

Jon shook his head lightly in disbelief trying to hold in his smile at the joke. "I'm sorry," he said sincerely.

"For?"

"I just had this thought that you would be a great friend if you weren't so old. Wow, that was truthful. I'm sorry again."

"Don't worry about it, kid."

"I felt stupid for thinking of it. You're cool. I want to be your friend."

"Who do I remind you of?" Bill asked.

"A biology teacher." Jon replied.

"Just so you know, I'm not a wise old man or anything."

"Quite alright, I'm not a wise, young man."

Bethany patted Annie on the back. "Sweetie. Pizza. Have a piece." She blocked the glass from touching Annie's lips. "I forbid."

"Hi. I'm Jessica!" Jessica held out her hand and Bethany shook it supplying her name. "Nice." She exclaimed pointing her finger upwards at the hanging Red Sox flags.

"*Grazie.*" Annie responded trying to retrieve control of the glass.

"I'm jealous, Annie, I want to be in your state of mind."

"Allow me." Annie grabbed Jessica's plastic cup of melting, rattling ice cubes and tilted the cranberry juice inside. She then took the vodka and began pouring. Jessica eyed the cup with a sense of gloom. Annie was making it very strong.

Bethany reached for the bottle and stopped Annie from filling it further.

"Wow that looks pretty strong."

"Here you go. Drink this and we should be on par. Did you have pizza?"

"I had a slice. I'm watching my weight with the summer coming up."

Annie eyed Jessica's stomach. "Bitch, you're like a buck-ten."

Jessica's eyes bulged at the statement. She took a sip of the drink and her face squinted like she bit down on a sour lemon. "Maybe I'll have a second slice."

"We have breadsticks too!" Annie snatched a breadstick and shoved half of it in her mouth aggressively, comically.

Andre was watching thanks to Raj's spying on the scene at the kitchen counter. He sighed disappointingly and walked over to Annie. "Everything okay?"

"Everything's fine," Bethany answered.

"I don't recall asking you." Andre stared directly at Bethany and flared his nostrils with each heavy breath showing his dominance. He averted his eyes back to Annie. "You're not allowed alcohol until you sober up a little."

"Mean." Annie pouted like a five-year-old.

"It's for your own good. Can we all agree?" He wanted to bring the others into his corner.

Jessica took another sip then stirred her drink with her index finger avoiding the question.

Bethany remained defiant with silence.

"Fine. Drink yourself into a coma." Andre turned and went back to Raj.

"What's up?" One of the guests, a young man in a Celtics hat shook Bill's hand. "This party isn't too wild, I hope." The man, maybe twenty-five but had a face of a fifteen-year-old with tiny dark eyes and the flecks of stubble on the edge of his chin was his attempt at a goatee, held a full bottle of microbrew at his side.

"You're intoxicated young man."

"Little bit." He placed his thumb and index finger within an inch of one another. "Are you catching up?"

"Your company only encourages me to do just that."

"Sweet."

"I have a friend you can acknowledge. His name is Jon."

Jon held out his hand and the man shook it. "Travis."

"And I'm Bill."

"Pleasure." Travis shook Bill's hand. "So, not to sound um, rude, but were you alive during prohibition 'cause that would be so gay."

"I don't quite see how being alive during prohibition would be homosexual."

"It's an expression," Jon said leaning towards Bill.

"I'm aware of that. I think it's rude."

"Are you two gay or something?" Travis asked and studied their faces.

"Now are you asking if we are gay as in homosexuals or gay as in the expression of not cool that you were mentioning?"

"Um," Travis scratched his hair lifting his hat up and down with each motion. He was too drunk to have a semantics conversation. "Homo gay."

"I'm not," Bill responded. "Jon?"

Jon shook his head.

"Oh, okay." Travis responded.

"Do you know when prohibition was?" Bill asked.

"19-something?"

"Jon?"

He drew a blank. "I like his answer."

"Do they teach history in school anymore? It was repealed in 1932. That was eighty years ago."

"Oh." Travis nodded and took another drink.

"I'm seventy-one."

"Cool."

"Who's winning?" Bill nodded towards the television giving up on logic with the inebriated hipster.

Travis smiled and looked back at the television content with having a question placed before him that he could answer. "It's tied. Two each."

"Still? I'm going to use the restroom," Bill stated and placed his empty cup onto a side table and walked towards the bathroom.

Travis leaned in to Jon. "That guy is the shit!"

"He is the shit."

"Do you have some weed?"

Jessica continued talking taking only a break to suck back the melted ice mixed with the light remains of the watered-down vodka in the cup. Bethany continued pouring herself drinks in order to cope with Jessica's banal topics. Jessica was fixated on Bethany's hair and the fact that she didn't go regularly to a salon floored her.

They talked reality television and Bethany exaggerated each statement popping her "Wow" and "Really? That's unbelievable!" when she sincerely meant the opposite. Even Annie was becoming annoyed with Jessica's constant talking and, even though she could get behind the reality TV topic, she still couldn't get much of a word in edgewise.

When the subject turned to shoes Annie made her getaway.

"I need to mingle with others," Annie spouted when her patience was up. "You two continue."

Annie slipped away quickly before Bethany could rush away. Behind a false smile and being too kind to ditch Jessica, Bethany clenched her teeth hard.

"My neck is killing me!" Annie told Jon and Bill. "All I've been doing is this," Annie nodded her head up and down, "for the past twenty minutes. How are you?"

"Do you have a deck of cards?"

"Of course, I couldn't create a drinking game though. I really wanted to with Sox deck I bought."

"Where's the deck?" Bill inquired.

"Over there." Annie pointed towards the kitchen counter. "Be forewarned, Bethany is going to try to pawn the blonde chick onto you."

Bill strolled to the counter and found the deck. He smiled. "This one?" He shouted across the room holding the deck up. Annie nodded. "Fantastic! Who's up for some strip poker?" Bill held out his arms.

"It was fucking gross!" Andre shouted. The party had died down to a pair of guests unwilling to move from the couch. It seemed that they were going to be planted there for the night but Andre would kick them out prior to his departure into the bedroom.

Saturday Night Live was concluding and Annie was roaming around the apartment tossing empty cups and plates into the plastic garbage bag.

"He was kidding. Jeez! Get over it."

"It put the idea of a naked old man into people's heads."

"Gross!" One of the guys on the couch shouted. "Old man balls." He chuckled at the term and the other one on the couch giggled.

Andre tilted his head acknowledging the proof that his complaint was legitimate. He grabbed a pair of beer bottles and spilled the trace amounts of booze into the sink. "Jon doesn't have a girlfriend."

"Yes he does."

"Where's Bethany?"

"She's over at Jon's," Annie coyly responded.

"Uh huh. I don't want you spending time with a cheater."

"She's sleeping on the couch, I assure you of that. Jon's crazy about his girlfriend and Bethany was too drunk to do anything. Raj even helped her across the hallway." Annie paused in the middle of the living room and hiccupped following it with a tiny burp. She clutched her chest. "Oh, that hurt."

"I don't want the image projected upon us that we have some sort of open relationship or that we have weird friends. In my line of work image is everything, you know that, and I don't want people like Jon or Bill or Bethany tainting what I've built."

Annie chuckled. "You said taint."

Andre dismissed Annie's idea of humor. "Seriously, Annie!"

"Everyone knows you. You have nothing to worry about." Annie picked up the last plate and one of Andre's friends lifted his empty beer bottle and she placed it in the garbage. "Thanks for helping." She sarcastically responded.

"Come here," Andre ordered and she complied. They huddled in the kitchen and he started on a mini tirade about her attitude. He said that she drank too much and couldn't control herself. He was upset by her manner and that he felt her guests were invited out of spite. "I hate feeling like you don't respect me." He allowed his statement to sink in and concluded by saying, "It's like you're out to ruin me."

Andre huffed to the bedroom door and looked back at the couch.

"Guys, party's over." They didn't move. "Guys!" Both men on the couch slowly shifted their heads around. "You don't have to go home but you can't stay here."

They rose from the couch with the same groans that are let out at six in the morning when their alarms were set to start beeping. They said their quick goodbyes and thanked both of them.

The door closed and Annie noticed the quiet that blanketed the apartment.

She felt a pang of guilt having thought her actions had truly humiliated Andre.

Annie wiped down the counter and took the trash to the chute in the hallway. Standing in the empty hall with no sounds other than the lights above her she began questioning her life. She knew better than to do it at one in the morning after having drank a hefty amount of alcohol but the reflection made her want to cry.

She was frozen in the hallway and stared down to the end, past her door, past Jon's door, to the door that faced her. It seemed so far away.

Annie sat down in the hallway and crossed her legs. One might think that she was meditating but she hardly expected any tenants to cross her path at this hour.

She didn't want to be a thirty-one year old single waitress living with her parents which seemed to be the reality she would face if her relationship with Andre ended.

This is what being trapped felt like, she thought.

15

"I still feel it. Watch out, Bethany, when it strikes it strikes hard."
Annie popped an aspirin and took a drink of water. "One day you're
twenty-three and drinking like a fish, the next day you're thirty and
muscles you didn't even know you had are aching thanks to the
lovely sport of binge drinking."

"I felt fine by noon. I was going to come by and see how you
were doing. I figured a text message sufficed."

"I appreciate your concern." Annie grabbed the coffee pot and
started towards one of her tables. "You have about five years left.
Five years of easily getting over a hangover."

"Drinking last night?" Annie's customer asked when she
approached the table. He was an old man wearing a light blue
sweater and a plaid shirt underneath. His eyebrows were wild and
bushy, brown like the few flecks of hair still remaining amid the gray
atop his head. He was reading the paper and had pushed his empty
plate to the side of the table.

"Saturday night."

The man shook his head. "Damn two day hangovers. I can get
about three drinks in me."

"Then what?"

The man looked over his reading glasses at Annie and with a smile said, "Last time I was so dehydrated and ill the next morning I spent two days at Mass General."

"Yikes."

"Needless to say my daughter-in-law wasn't too thrilled about my actions on her wedding day."

"The open bar will get you every time."

The man placed his hand upon Annie's. "Every time."

The diner door swung open and Annie instinctively turned to shout her "anywhere you'd like" statement instead she delightfully said, "Good morning, Bill."

Annie's customer looked upwards. "Mornin', Bill."

"Ladies. Blueberry pancakes. Butter, whip cream and syrup." Bill unhinged the newspaper from under his arm and tossed it onto the table. He removed his beige spring jacket and hung it on the coat rack on the dividing booth partitions. He looked at Annie's customer and nodded. "Franklin, good morning."

Annie placed a cup of coffee on the table and poured Bill a mug full from the pot.

"How are you feeling?"

"Everyone is asking me that. No one says 'Great party. Had a great time.' It's concerning me."

"Everyone had a good time and it was a great party. How are you feeling?"

She shrugged her shoulders.

Bill started, "I enjoyed myself. It was a nice distraction."

"From?"

"Things I needed to be distracted from."

"You are a vague, mysterious individual, Bill." Annie studied Bill's profile as he turned and began reading from the front page of the paper. Annie observed that he was too concentrated in his own thoughts to comprehend the words he was skimming. "Every thing okay?" She asked.

"Difficult day."

"It just started. It could always get better."

"The difficulty has yet to present itself."

"Shall I press?"

"How about those blueberry pancakes. Butter . . ."

Annie finished, "whip creamed and syrup. Got it. Working on a heart attack?"

"Heart's going to stop at some point. I like to make things easier."

Annie shook her head and with a smile stepped into the kitchen and put the order up for Omar.

"I'm sorry I missed your party on Saturday," Omar sneered. "I would've totally been there if you invited me."

"Omar," Annie responded almost begging for his pity.

"Just saying it hurt."

"Will you accept my sincerest apologies?"

"Will you give me a handy in the bathroom?"

"Oh God, Omar!" Annie took the sexual harassment in stride and shook her head in disbelief. "Is that all you really think about?"

"Sometimes I think about going back to school and getting my Master's."

"You have a Bachelor's?"

"In English."

"What are you doing here?"

"I got a Bachelor's degree in English." Omar lifted his arm as if that was proof enough. "What are you doing here?"

"I wanted to be a party planner."

There was a moment of silence as both reflected on their life choices and where they were currently situated.

"How about that handy?" Omar said.

Annie smirked, "No. How about you go fuck your own self?" She retorted as she started through the kitchen door.

When Annie passed through the threshold she was taken aback. Sitting on the opposite side of Bill's booth dressed in a T-shirt and workout shorts was Jon. He smiled.

"Hey! Coffee?" Annie asked.

"Coffee sounds brilliant."

"I'll make sure the brew is of highest intelligence."

"I've heard the coffee here is good."

"Who's your source?" Bill asked looking up from his paper.

"Common courtesy."

"You lied for the sake of lying?"

Jon's eyes rolled upwards as he contemplated the question. "Jeez. Why did I say that?"

"You like the sound of your voice," Annie stated.

"I do. It's a good voice. Not too low, not too squeaky. My father has a squeaky voice."

"Say something of value or listen to your own voice in your head," Bill advised and Jon's lips tightened up as he looked at Annie as if he were pushed down a peg by his own father.

"I'll be right back," Annie said and turned away.

"What kind of job are you looking for?" Bill asked as he turned to the second page of the front page of the paper.

"Media. Development. I'm a creative writer by trade." Bill didn't respond but he scanned the second page before moving to the third. "Why? Do you know someone who might be able to help me out?"

"No."

"You're odd."

Bill placed his hands on the table looking right into Jon's eyes as if he were studying his demeanor. "I don't think you really know how to read or talk to people. Not you specifically, people you're age. You have lost the art of communication via social media and cell phones. Silence is fine and simple questions are often meant to garner simple answers. I think your generation is scared of not being relevant."

"Isn't everyone's?"

"The answer isn't copycatting, the answer is creativity and opportunity and riding the wave of circumstance. World War II defined the generation; the 1960's defined that generation through civil rights marches and calls for peace. Ever since 1972 there hasn't been anything new. I challenge you to think of something new that you, again your generation, have created." Bill smiled. "That, my new friend, is the opening of a discussion where simple answers are not expected but rather opinions." Bill closed the newspaper and placed it aside. "Slow news day. Entertain me, monkey."

Jon belted out a hardy guffaw. "You're either an asshole or a button presser."

"Can't think of anything?" Bill pushed.

"Okay then, I'll stay un-insulted and seated. In regards to your question, you want me to give an answer like Apple's iPod or the Internet only to be refuted by your insistence that an iPod is just like a CD Player or Walk Man or the Internet is a vast form of communication."

"Continue."

"I think your generation is trying to insist that it is still relevant and you're making claims of our lack of creativity by defining our generation as a carbon copy of the previous ones. You're generation is the one concerned about its relevance."

"You're putting words in my mouth."

"Are they the right words?"

Annie approached and placed the coffee mug down on the table.

"They aren't the wrong ones," Bill replied.

"Annie," Jon started. "Name something innovative that our generation has created."

"Cloned sheep. What will you have to eat?"

Jon looked at Bill with a raised eyebrow. "That wasn't there during your generation."

"We had copy machines," Bill mumbled and looked down at his newspaper.

"I haven't had the chance to look at the menu."

"Just order something. What do you want?"

"Can you recommend something?"

"Breakfast or lunch?" Annie asked.

"Hmm, not really sure."

"You're getting a turkey club," Annie stated and turned around.

"Wait!"

Annie turned back around and faced Jon. "Do you not want a turkey club?"

Jon bit his lip. "Actually that sounds all right. Fries?"

"Included."

Annie started towards the kitchen. "Wait!" Bill shouted.

Annie spun around. "I'm getting dizzy, if you two want something don't wait until I turn all the way around."

"I think I want to talk about something."

"About what?"

"About my difficulty."

"Is it difficulty urinating?" Jon asked. Both Annie and Bill snidely looked at Jon who cowered back into the booth with his hands raised apologetically.

"I have to call my granddaughter today. It's her birthday," Bill said and then didn't continue further. Hesitancy hung in the air as both Annie and Jon waited for Bill to continue. "I have difficulty talking about my children; to my children. It was all about decisions and fights and lingering animosities and misunderstandings. I'm a private guy." Bill concluded.

"We know," Annie said. "And I appreciate your comfort-ability in sharing." Annie looked at Jon for validation. "Jon?"

"Me too . . . even though comfort-ability isn't really a word."

Annie rolled her eyes and knelt next to Bill's side of the booth. "Bill, why can't you call your granddaughter and wish her a happy birthday?"

"I'm afraid I will have to talk to my daughter."

"You're afraid to talk to your daughter," Annie confirmed.

Bill nodded. His blue eyes were moist and soft. He struggled to continue but pushed through his timidity, "They have caller-ID so they wouldn't answer anyway, but still, what if they do. I wouldn't know what to say."

"Why don't you talk to them?" Jon cautiously asked.

Bill squished in his lips as if he had to hold in his words for fear that if his mouth opened they would spill outwards. He shook his head and finally took a breath. "That's irrelevant for this particular discussion."

"Just call," Annie answered patting Bill's hand twice as she stood up. "You have nothing to fear but fear itself."

"Do you know who said that?" Bill asked.

"Roosevelt." Annie replied.

"Which one?"

"Teddy!" Jon shouted. "Wait, was he the one in the wheelchair?"

"That was Franklin." Annie replied to Jon and looked at Bill. "The answer is FDR."

"Very good." He smiled. "I know I will call because she is my granddaughter, it's just getting to that point." Bill reached across the table to his napkin and placed it in his lap. "That's the difficulty."

"How long has this 'difficulty' been going on for?"

"Years. Every birthday, every Christmas. I always call and they don't answer. I'm used to it now, I suppose, but some days it's easier than others."

"When was the last time you saw any of them?"

Bill sighed heavily and rubbed his hands together trying to recall that last time, counting the years, the ages.

"Long time."

"When was the last time you talked to them?"

He repeated, "Long time."

Annie went back towards the kitchen to place Jon's order. She retrieved Bill's pancakes before they got cold and delivered them to the table. She then went back for Jon's turkey club. Upon returning found the conversation between the young man and the older man had tilted toward life and ambitions.

As they ate, Bill shared stories of his youth and offered his advice on where Jon should take his career. Towards the end of the meal and conversations, Bill looked over his shoulder to ensure that Annie was in the kitchen, or at least out of earshot. He asked, "What's your story with her?"

"What do you mean?" He asked innocently.

"I mean, what's your story? What's the connection? What's your angle?"

Jon looked out the window at nothing in particular. "Everyone assumes. They just assume that I want to sleep with her or date her or something." He reconnected eye contact with Bill. "I like her. Plain and simple and platonically. I like the way she makes me feel and I like that we can offer each other unbiased advice. All the people I met while at the television station were arrogant jerks or parents uninterested in going out and grabbing a beer. They lived in the outskirts of the city and weren't on the prowl for new friends." Jon crossed his arms and lowered his head contemplating his new found relationship with Annie then considered his growing friendship with Bill. "I like Annie as my friend."

Bill looked over towards the kitchen door which opened on cue. Annie approached Aldo and leaned over to ask him a question.

Bill smiled and looked back at Jon. "I like her as a friend too." Both turned their heads and looked at Annie as she stood over Aldo and pointed down to the crossword puzzle he was stuck on. He nodded and she smiled as he filled in letters. They were consumed by the unquestioned friendliness she offered to everyone. Jon and Bill both noticed they had been staring.

"Jon. I need you to do me a favor."

"Sure."

"Leave."

"Are you going to ask her out?"

"Seriously."

"Sure thing." Jon dug into his wallet but Bill held up his hand.

"My pleasure. Save your pennies."

"Come on, Bill."

"If it makes you feel any better about it I'll be paying with the social security that my generation is using to bankrupt your generation."

"Leave her a good tip." Jon said standing up.

"Always do." Jon held out his hand and Bill shook it. "Let's not wait too long to do this again."

Jon walked to the front door of the restaurant and waved to Annie and wished her a good day. She smiled and reciprocated.

Annie approached the table with a coffee pot that Bill waved off.

"Have a seat, will you?" Bill requested and Annie took a seat on the opposite side of the booth and moved Jon's empty plate towards the window.

"What's on your mind?" She leaned forward crossing her arms in front of her body as they rested on the table.

"Are you busy this afternoon after work?"

"I usually stick around until one or one-thirty. I'm free after that. Why?"

Bill hesitated a brief moment averting his eyes downward as if ashamed to make his request. After a succession of a few small breaths he said, "I would like to invite you over to my apartment." He looked up at Annie. "I'd like you there when I make that telephone call."

Annie was stunned and leaned back. "Okay." She nodded. "Okay."

16

Before she had the opportunity to be bored she felt the monotony of the long afternoon start to encompass her. Even after she jogged to the bay and back and showered, she would still have hours to kill before the evening. Bill was going to make his phone call at seven-thirty that night. He was originally going to call in the middle of the afternoon because he believed it would have been easier on everyone but Annie convinced him to make the call in the evening.

"What about Andre?" Bill asked.

"This is more important than an evening with the man I spend every evening with," she responded.

When Andre came home Annie was moments away from exiting the apartment.

"I need to head out for a bit," she said. He inquired and she advised him of her plans with Bill. "I'll probably be back by nine."

"What do you care about this guy?"

"He's my friend."

"Friend? He's eighty. What could you two possibly have in common?"

"Seventy-one," she corrected. "You know friends don't have to share the same likes and dislikes."

"Of course they do, that's why they're friends."

"What do you care anyway who my friends are?" She pointed towards the oven. "Dinner's in there."

She headed towards the door but Andre grasped her in arm squeezing his frustration. She winced a moment and their eyes met.

"You're going to some old guy's apartment so he can call his granddaughter? Why am I not one-hundred percent convinced of this?"

"You don't believe me?" Annie whipped her arm away. "Join me." It was a challenge that she prayed for him to accept. She pushed him further. "Come on," Annie grabbed onto his arm and walked towards the door spinning him around. He motioned his arm loose. "Well then? Either you trust me or you don't. I'm not going to defend my plans or who I want to hang out with every single day. If it's Bill or Bethany, they're my friends, my choice. So, come on. If you don't trust me, then you better come along to make sure I'm doing exactly what I told you I would be doing."

"Jesus Christ," Andre rolled his eyes with disinterest in hearing her droll on. "Just fucking go."

Annie stormed out of the apartment and walked down the hallway. Her arms were crossed in front of her. She was halfway between the apartment door and the elevator when she realized she was out of breath. She stopped.

There was something about the ease with which Andre let her go. It caused a drop in her self-esteem as she contemplated the reasons he kept her around, or why she stayed. They were questions she wished to avoid as the fear of the answers were too much to bring to the surface, as if the thought would bring it into reality.

Where would I be then? Annie asked herself and turned back towards the door. A part of her wanted to rush back in and hold on to her security blanket but that wouldn't have been fair to Bill.

Annie anticipated a fight and ultimately decided that if one were to happen she would rather it happen later rather than sooner. She might as well hold the hand of her friend rather than fight about the idea with Andre.

So Annie turned back down the hallway and hugged herself tightly until she reached the elevator. She uncrossed her arms and pressed the down button illuminating it and hoping the car would arrive quickly before she changed her mind.

The bell chimed and the elevator doors opened. She stepped inside and pressed the button for the lobby as she kept her eye down the hallway.

The doors closed and she leaned against the back wall breathing a sigh of relief.

The mist hung in the Boston air. She could taste it and it felt like her face was in front of those misters that blew moisture into a crowd in line at an amusement park waiting in the summer heat to board the rollercoaster. Annie wasn't aware how wet she was getting until she entered the lobby of Bill's apartment complex and saw her appearance in a mirror. Despite the horror, she ascended upwards to Bill's apartment.

"Is it raining out there?" Bill asked with the scent of scotch on his breath.

"Misting."

"Let me take your coat," Bill offered and Annie handed it over. Bill tossed it onto his recliner. "So."

"Let's do this." Annie rushed to the kitchen telephone and stood looking back at Bill.

Bill stood his ground. "I, um . . ."

"Come on, it will be okay."

"What if they're eating dinner? I don't want to call while they are eating dinner. They'll think that it's bad enough that they have to listen to my voice for thirty seconds after I interrupted their dinner. We should wait. Let's wait."

"What if you're granddaughter is going to sleep soon. You should call. You should call. Now."

"You're right, she's probably asleep. Maybe I should call tomorrow and apologize for not calling today."

"Bill."

"Come on!" He squeaked back.

"What happened?" She let her guard down.

Bill felt dizzy and placed his hand upon the recliner. He dropped his butt down onto the chair, onto Annie's wet jacket, and placed his head on his hands. "You want a drink?" He looked upwards. "I'm sorry I should have offered you a drink."

Annie inched her way towards Bill. She had empathy in her eyes and desire to help.

Bill buried his head back into his hands and finally stated: "I killed my wife."

Annie stopped in the middle of the living room half way between the kitchen and the recliner. She was frozen. Was this a confession? Would she have to serve this man every morning knowing that he was a murderer? And why wasn't he in jail?

Bill recognized the stagnancy in the room and he shifted his head towards Annie.

"Oh no!" He lifted upwards and Annie jolted backwards. "I didn't kill her kill her." He held his hands upwards pleading for her to listen, afraid she was going to bolt for the door. "I chose to remove her feeding tube. It was a mutual decision."

Annie let out a heavy sigh. She had been holding her breath for what seemed like an hour rather than seconds. "Yeah, I think I'll have that drink."

Bill poured her a shot and a half's worth of scotch into a rock's glass. He poured a second one for himself. Holding it up, he announced, "To . . ." He groaned worrisomely and drank it back.

"To that," Annie said and sipped. "Oh, good heavens." Her face puckered up and she coughed. "It's lighter fluid."

"It's an acquired taste."

"Who the hell would want to acquire that taste?"

"Try it again."

"Eh." She took another sip. "Uch, still bad."

"But getting better." Bill smirked as he took another drink from his glass.

Annie plopped her butt down on a kitchen chair and placed the glass on top of the table. "Sit, Bill. Don't alter the conversation into lightheartedness. If I'm going to drink this rubbing alcohol then you're talking. Welcome to therapy." She smiled and brought the glass to her lips. She sniffed upwards before taking the drink and it was enough to cause her to cough and make the same silly, sour face as if she had actually drank it.

Bill chuckled and took a seat. His slight smile faded though as he looked across the table to Annie.

"I'm sure they don't have very favorable things to say about me, if they talk about me, if they keep my messages on the voicemail for their children to hear." Bill stopped in hopes of hearing Annie say something that would pull the spotlight from him. It didn't so he reluctantly continued but as he opened his mouth to speak he found trouble getting the words out. His throat had closed up and he was being overcome with emotion. "Okay." He said aloud trying to persuade himself to push forward.

Bill had never been to therapy. Even after his wife passed away he refused to seek an emotional outlet by talking with a professional. His friends had slowly begun to disappear. They stopped calling and inviting him to play cards until one day Bill spent the day in his apartment, in his pajamas and wondering how he could continue onward in life with zero interaction. His lack of movement came so easily.

He took to bed that night and lay with his hands on his chest staring at the ceiling. The next morning he would wake early and walk to the small diner he passed on several occasions but rarely entered. He would stick with this tradition as a way to interact with people, both strangers and those familiar. Waitresses would know him by name and Aldo, the owner, would invite him out for a drink, for a dinner with his family or a beer and a ball game. He vowed to play his cards close to the chest and avoid any real emotional connection. He would hint but never reveal.

Now Annie sat across from him. She pierced his armor and wanted to tear down the wall. It wasn't the first time since his wife's death that someone had tried to get through the door but it was the first time he was interested in actually opening it.

"When you get old you start to have conversations that are bizarre. It's like when you're a teenager and you talk about movies and gossip about friends, then you're in your thirties and you talk about ways to cut down your energy bills and the best doctor to take your children to when they have an ear infection. You talk about back problems and minor medical issues. One day you talk about death."

Bill continued, "My wife and I talked about death. We talked about cemeteries and coffins and funeral services. We bought plots. We talked about feeding tubes and DNR bracelets and legal issues."

Bill took a drink, a big gulp that was hard to swallow. Annie noticed the tears forming in his eyes. "We talked about it. We. We agreed that if either one of us were in a vegetative state then the other should pull the plug if it was medical opinion that we would never recover. We even legalized our decision. We both believed that living like that is not a life worth living. There is no joy that could be brought upon the family that has to spend time seeing an unresponsive person. It wasn't fair for the person; it wasn't fair to the family. One of my wife's cousins went through that and it wrecked her emotionally and physically. We decided to make our decisions soon thereafter."

Bill looked downwards. "That decision is never easy because you are placing the responsibility of your death into the hands of the person you love the most in hopes that they would never have to act on it." He looked up at Annie as a tear drop fell from his eye down his cheek. "She had a stroke six months later while in a movie theater. She liked to go to matinees by herself when she had the day off and I was at work. The theater workers came in at the end of the movie to clean up and found her. They thought she might have fallen asleep. By the time the ambulance was called though and by the time she got to the hospital it was too late. She was alive but she was too far gone. The doctors thought it was a miracle that she was even alive.

"I believe her soul had left her body," Bill stated with a degree of certainty. "She was unresponsive, on a breathing tube, a feeding tube, had a faint heartbeat."

Bill shook his head and sniffled. "My wife was . . . too far gone. She was just sixty years old."

Annie leaned in and took hold of Bill's hand. She squeezed it with love. She stood up and excused herself. In the bathroom she grabbed a box of tissues and brought it back into the kitchen. She took the first few sheets and wiped her eyes and nose.

She could only think of one thing to say, "Bill, I'm so sorry."

He waved his hand as if he had heard that phrase too many times for it to mean anything anymore. "You see the problem now, Annie, is not the decision to pull the plug. It was the lack of opinions I gathered from our children. She was alive for two weeks after that stroke and they had ample time to see her. Every time they did I told them to say goodbye as if they would never see her again and they assured me they did because the reality was that she was fragile and could go at any moment. I refused to fulfill the promise we made to one another for two whole weeks because I wanted everyone to say their goodbyes. I didn't consult my children because, truthfully, it didn't matter what they had to say. The only opinion that mattered was my wife's and she made up her mind six months prior. The plug was pulled and," Bill wagged his finger, "they were saddened that she passed away but they were angry when they found out how. No legal paper that I presented to them swayed their hostility towards me."

Bill clasped his hands together and placed them on the table. Annie could see that he didn't regret the decision. Deep within his body she could see that he knew it was the right choice. He continued, "They yelled, they shouted, 'Dad, how could you? Without even talking to us about it!' I pleaded my case. At the funeral they didn't speak with me. The last thing any of them ever said to me was said by Bill Junior. 'Dad, as far as any of us is concerned, when mom died, you died too.'

Annie's mouth fell open.

"No birthday cards. No Christmas cards. The only voice I ever hear of theirs is the one on their answering machine when I call them. And I don't even know if their children hear the messages I leave for them." Bill finished off his drink and placed the glass back onto the table with a thud. He stood up and groaned as his legs stretched.

He walked to the telephone that was attached to the wall and pulled down the receiver. On the counter was his address book and he moved his finger to find the phone number. Bill dialed the number and let it ring.

There was silence as Annie watched Bill stand with the telephone in hand. He sighed listening and then said cheerily, "Hello Denise, it's your grandpa. I wanted to wish you a very, very happy birthday. I hope you had a great birthday and I love you very much." He paused a moment then ended the call with, "Goodbye," and hung up the telephone.

"How old is Denise?"

"She's fourteen."

"And the last time you saw her . . ."

"She was seven."

"I'm so sorry. What would your wife think about this?"

Bill had the answer at his fingertips as if he were waiting such a question to be asked, as if he pondered his response for the last seven years. "She would be disappointed in our children. She would be disappointed in me for not pursuing solace more aggressively."

"Aggressive solace. That's like fighting for peace."

Bill let out a joyous breath through his nose. "I think she would be disappointed that we are no longer a family. I don't know how any of them feel about any of this anymore. They might be so used to ignoring me that they don't know any better and there might be too much awkwardness if that silence is broken. Or they might just be afraid to talk to me, afraid of peeling back the old scars." Bill looked at the clock on the stove then turned to Annie. "I think it's time for you to leave."

"Okay," she whispered and stood up. Her hand went back to her glass of scotch on the table and she took the rest down.

"Sometimes gasoline is the best relaxant," Bill joked about her reaction to his scotch.

Annie nodded while trying to unhinge her soured face.

She exited the kitchen and walked across the living room towards the door. Bill rushed up to her and grabbed her jacket. "Don't forget this." He held it open for her and she slipped her arms inside. She could still feel the dampness resonating on the exterior of the jacket.

Annie turned and looked at Bill. He looked back. She placed her arms around him and he hugged back.

"Thank you, Annie. Thank you."

17

It was a combination of a small meal and a scotch that made the walk home fill her head with cloudy thoughts. The mist had lightened but it still blanketed the city with its film of wetness.

Annie wanted to call her mother and father just to say that she loved them. She was thrown from her own thoughts when a man with Celtics hat about her age shouted in a thick Bostonian accent, "Hey sweetheart, you look beautiful. Join me for a drink."

"I highly doubt I do," Annie responded to the man refusing to leave the patio of the bar. She could feel her hair being matted down further by the moisture.

"Yar gorgeous! Let me warm ya up!"

"Thank you but I have to get home." She continued walking past the bar and the man holding his glass of dark beer.

"You think you're too good for me?" The man yelled out.

Annie shook her head and picked up her pace creating as much of a distance between her self and the bar as possible.

"How were things at the retirement home?" Andre asked with a snicker when Annie entered the apartment.

She rolled her eyes. "They were fine."

He turned from the couch to look at the door. "You look like shit. Is it raining?"

"Not exactly; and thank you," Annie responded sarcastically.

"Hey, chicks dig honesty, right?" He said smugly.

"We do dig honesty but we don't dig blatant, irrelevant comments that just happen to be truthful. I may look like shit, Andre, but I didn't need you to tell me that if I'm just going to dry my hair and put on pajamas."

"Whatever." He turned back to the television.

Annie glanced at the clock as she entered the bedroom and decided she could make a quick call to her parents once she was done drying off and changing. She stripped down and put on a pair of flannel pajama bottoms and an old Bruins T-shirt. She ran a brush through her hair muscling through a pair of knots.

She locked the bathroom door for privacy and sat down on the closed toilet Annie scrolled to her parent's home phone number and sent the call.

"Hello mom," she started. "How's it going?"

A freak cold snap had brought light flurries over the western side of Michigan. Her mother refused to leave the house to go run a few errands due to the possibility of unfavorable road conditions. Her father ended up driving her and sitting in the car the whole time reading a magazine while she was in the store. "We got home about ten minutes ago. The road was fine. I could have driven it myself. Don't tell him I said this but your father was right. It's way too warm for the flurries to even stick. You don't expect these things the last day of April. What's on your mind, honey?"

Annie was staring at the shower curtain lost in her own thought. She quietly replied. "I just wanted to call and tell you that I love you."

"Well I love you too. You know what . . ."

Annie recognized the hesitation in her mother's words. "What was that?"

"Nothing, Annie. I was going to make some crack about marriage and grandkids but I know that is irking you these days so I stopped myself."

Annie let a smile creep across her lips.

There was a loud sigh as her mother prepared to offer advice that went against the very grain of her desire to have a married child with a grandchild on the way. "You know the term 'shit or get off the pot'?"

Annie instinctively looked down at the toilet and wondered if her mother knew she was sitting on the toilet seat lid. She cautiously replied. "Yeah. Why?"

"Just want to make sure you know that term."

A tear fell down Annie's cheek. It was teardrop representing happiness recognizing that her mother was finally easing back and maybe even subtly insisting that Annie walk away from what was becoming a dead end relationship. There was also sadness in that tear as she realized the difficulties in walking away. She struggled with what she deemed worthwhile nowadays.

"Thanks, mom."

"You're welcome. Dare I inquire about the sudden call professing your love for your mother?"

"Just something I wanted to do. Is dad around?"

"He's in the bathroom and you know how he likes his time in the bathroom. Let me see if he plans on being in there a while."

There was a loud scream on the opposite end of the phone as Annie's mother buried the phone into her shoulder and hollered for her father. Silence followed before a second round of yelling took hold.

"I hear the toilet flushing. It will just be another minute."

"Make sure he washes his hands before picking up the phone."

Moments later the phone clicked and Annie's father was on the line. "I'm hanging up," Annie's mother said. "Good night."

"Good night, mom."

"What's going on?" Her dad jumped in. "Everything okay?"

"Yes, dad, everything is fine. I just wanted to let you know that I love you."

There was a knock on the bathroom door.

"What's that?" Her father asked.

"I'm in here, Andre!" Annie shouted then lowered her voice to her father. "I'm in the bathroom, dad. It's just Andre."

"Who are you talking to?" Andre shouted from the other side of the door.

"Is everything okay? Why did you lock yourself in the bathroom?" Her father's voice was etched with concern.

"Privacy." Annie covered the speaker on the phone. "I'm talking to my parents!"

"In the bathroom?"

"Yes, in the bathroom."

"Why?"

"Because I didn't want to be bothered!"

Annie's father asked, "What's going on?"

There was another knock at the door, harder and slightly hostile.

"Nothing, dad. Andre wants to use the bathroom. Hold on a sec."

She hopped off the toilet lid and unlocked the door. She swung it open piercing Andre's eyes with her own. She began walking past him but he clutched onto her wrist and grabbed the cell phone.

"Hello? Who is this?"

"It's Richard Ferguson," Annie's father replied. "How are you doing, Andre?"

Andre shoved the phone back into Annie's hand without answering and walked away.

"Really?" Annie announced. She grunted her frustration and burned her livid glare unto Andre. She backed into the bathroom slamming the door closed. She heard a picture frame fall on the opposite side of the door.

"Genius!" She heard Andre sarcastically faintly yell from the living room.

"Dad," Annie started.

"Honey, what's wrong?"

Annie shook her head and fought off the whirlwind of emotional. "Is there a manual on life?"

"No."

"I suspected not. What about all those self-help books?"

"Those are designed to make the author money. The good ones are for those with bigger problems than yours."

"How do you know what my problems are?"

"Are you bi-polar?"

"No."

"Problem child?"

"Am I one or do I have one?"

"Do you have one?"

"No."

"What about going through a divorce?"

Annie hesitated considering the question. "Not exactly."

"Then I highly believe those books are of no relevance to you. What do you mean 'not exactly'?"

"Rough patch."

"It happens." With no reply back her father inquired further. "How rough?"

Annie looked at the bathroom door with unease. "I don't know."

"Well, your mother and I knew each other for one year before we were married and we had our first rough patch three years thereafter. So, if this is the first one you're having after, um . . ."

"Five years."

"Right, five years, you're ahead of the curve, I suppose."

"Should I stay with him, dad?" Her monotonous tone was frightening in that she recognized how she had all but given up but still had no place to turn. A knot formed in her stomach and she placed a hand on her belly wincing with the gastric pain.

"Is he cheating on you?"

The question was asked seriously and Annie hesitated responding. "No," she said definitively believing any evidence to the contrary was mere coincidence.

"Does he make you happy?"

"He did."

"Can he again?"

18

Bethany had the morning off so Annie had to deal with the rush with two waitresses she was friendly with but not exactly friends with.

Janice was a local, born and raised, but it was apparent that she made a wrong turn in life. She chain-smoked and talked of her independence constantly. "I don't have to listen to nobody." Her tar-stained fingertips and ghastly oral hygiene indicated that she had more troubles than Annie would care to have. Janice's voice was rough like sandpaper and an inflection of superiority like she thought her opinions were more correct than yours. She had a very different thirty years than Annie had.

Home for the summer was Simone, friendly and awkward, she just completed her third year at the University of New Hampshire. She often pulled in a few hours on a long weekend here or there and through winter breaks. Although she had been employed at Aldo's for five years her skills were never up to par. Her saving grace though was her warm smile that she shined upon every customer. She often shied away from general conversation with the employees and Omar didn't even expel his remarks in her presence.

"Simone!" Bill shouted as he entered and gave her a monstrous hug. "Welcome home."

"Thanks, Bill."

"Coffee and a half-stack, please."

Bill took a seat and flipped open the front page of the newspaper.

Simone returned with a filled coffee mug and placed it on the table. "What are you going to do when newspapers are replaced with the tablets?"

"I reckon I'll be too old to care. I'll just reread these antiques and reminisce about when the president visited a small town factory in western Massachusetts," he replied tapping the newspaper.

Simone fled to the kitchen to place the order.

Annie approached Bill. "I think I'm jealous," she started jokingly, although a hint of truth was hidden underneath. "How did you sleep?"

"I slept well, Annie. Thank you again."

"Of course."

Bill smiled and then slowly moved his head downward towards the newspaper.

Annie coyly stepped away and attended to her other tables.

"Annie!" Aldo shouted and she stepped over.

"What's up, Aldo?"

"There might be a vacancy. Do you know any girls interested in waitressing?"

"Is there a reason you don't hire men to serve food?"

"No." Aldo paused to let his next point hint home. "Do you know of any that ever applied?"

"You never had a man apply to be a waiter here?"

"Never. My son waited tables but he didn't fill out an application or anything."

"I'll keep my ears open for you." Annie motioned backwards and then leaned close to Aldo. "Is someone quitting?"

"I hope so."

Annie lowered her voice to a near whisper. "Who?"

"It's against company policy to reveal such information."

"It is?"

"It is now." Aldo smiled. The door chimed open but Aldo kept his suspicious smile on Annie. "You have customers."

Annie rolled her eyes and lifted up to make her announcement that anywhere the diners wished to sit was fine but she choked on her own breath when she saw it was Raj and Jessica.

"Well hey there!" Jessica stated cheerily waving.

Annie's barely audible response was, "Shit."

"There she is! Can't believe this is my first time seeing the lovely Annie at work," Raj remarked loudly.

"Sit anywhere you'd like, guys."

"This one!" Raj responded pointing to an empty booth two seats in from the door. Jessica tossed her spring jacket into the inside of the booth and sat down. She wore black workout pants and a tight pink shirt. Raj was donning shorts and Harvard hoodie. He meant to dress down but his attire probably exceeded a hundred bucks. They were instantly garnering the attention of the other patrons, the true working class who drank coffee that was unflavored.

"How are you two doing? What brings you out here?"

"We're doing well," Jessica started. "We were looking to get some cool fresh air and decided to walk up this way."

"You walked all the way up here to visit me?"

"We needed a destination. This way we get to harass you and get in a nice long walk," Raj said.

"I'm honored."

"This place is quite a sty though," Raj said. "What do you recommend that doesn't have cockroaches?" His tone was louder but the comment, even at a whisper, would have made Annie uncomfortable. She felt judged and now had the sudden fear that the supposed dump that Andre's girlfriend worked at would put an unflattering mark on how he was perceived.

"Nothing has cockroaches, I assure you, and everything tastes remarkable."

Jessica flipped the page in the menu with a disgusted look on her face. "This is weird."

"Want to go to Zaftigs?" Raj asked. "There's probably a wait though."

"And they're three times the price," Annie added.

Jessica looked up at Annie skeptically. "What's good?"

"Breakfast is good. Do you like pancakes?"

"No carbo-overload."

"The omelets are tasty."

"Can you do egg whites?"

"We can."

"Veggie egg white omelet then?"

"Are you asking me or ordering?"

"Ordering."

"Okay." Annie looked over to Raj. "For you, sir?"

"How about a coffee and the chance to peruse the menu." He looked over to Jessica. "Thanks for making sure I was ready to order."

She slowly closed the menu ignoring his remark. "Coffee too."

"I'll be right back."

Annie left the table. Jessica leaned in close to Raj. "I feel like I need to wash my hands but I'm afraid to go near that bathroom. I wish I brought my hand sanitizer."

"Hey is that the old guy from the party?"

Jessica turned her entire body and not-so-subtly looked at the opposite side of the restaurant. She turned right back around. "It is! Ewww."

Raj shook his head in humored disbelief. "Why is that 'ewww'?"

"It just is."

"A pair of coffees." Annie said dropping the two mugs on the table. "Cream and sugar's over there." She pointed at the edge of the table. Looking at Raj, she asked, "You ready?"

"Another minute," he said holding up his index finger.

"You can have two if you'd like."

"Let's compromise, minute-thirty."

"Annie," Jessica started, "Do you have any flavored creams?"

"Sorry. Just good ole half-and-half."

"Oh." Jessica's disappointment couldn't be hidden.

Annie nodded and headed to Bill's table. "How are you doing?"

"Just fine."

"Half-stack," Simone announced placing the plate in front of him.

"Thank you," he replied and grabbed the small syrup bowl on the edge of the plate and drowned his half-stack of pancakes.

"Anything else I can get for you?"

"No, thank you, Simone." She smiled and he reciprocated. Feeling awkward standing between Annie and Bill, Simone motioned away to drop a check down at one of her tables.

"Aldo mentioned that someone might be quitting soon, do you know anything about that?"

"Maybe he's talking about you?"

"Maybe? Or he is?"

Bill stuffed a forkful of pancakes into his mouth and talked with his mouth full. "He didn't reveal anything to me. We're watching the Celtics game tonight though. I can ask him."

Annie shook her head. "Why would he even want me to leave?"

"I think you should."

"Oh yeah? Am I not up to par?"

"Oh coffee wench!" Raj shouted from across the restaurant in a high-pitched voice and clapping his hands twice. "I'm ready." He rolled his R purposely, snobbishly for fun.

"Excuse me," Annie stated but Bill made a quick move for her hand and ended up grabbing onto her wrist.

"You're way above par." Bill tilted his head, thinking. "Or way below par." He let go of her wrist. "Whichever one means you're better than a waitress, so whether or not Aldo is hoping you quit or not, he probably hopes that you won't be here as long as Janice for fear that you might turn into a Janice."

Annie felt accomplished somehow like her attitude was shining. "Thank you."

Bill waved her off. "Go now, coffee wench."

She did and bee-lined to Raj and Jessica's table.

"French toast," he ordered.

"That's it?"

"Should I get more?"

"The bacon is good when crispy," Annie advised her acquaintance although she wasn't telling the full truth. She hadn't really cared if he ordered bacon or not and she hadn't had a piece in months. She simply said it for no other reason than because.

Raj looked over to Jessica with a smile that asked her permission.

"Order what you want. It's going to be greasy."

"And crispy."

"Really greasy," Jessica said with her permanent look of disgust hanging off of her face.

"Really crispy?" Raj looked at Annie for confirmation.

"Wicked crispy."

"You got my sale."

"I'll put that order in right away."

Within ten minutes Raj and Jessica had their food. She poked at the egg white omelet and was hesitant on putting fork to mouth. Raj dove into French toast and complimented the nearly burnt bacon. At the end of the meal there were only scraps on Raj's plate and three-quarters of an omelet on Jessica's

"It's okay if you want something else. We can make whatever you want."

"No, I'm okay. Thank you."

"You want a to-go box or something?"

"No."

"I enjoyed it, Annie. Compliments to the chef."

They paid for their meal and left a mediocre tip. She wasn't sure if they were bad tippers in general or only thought ten percent was a decent tip for someone they knew. Either way she was insulted by their discourtesy and hoped that they would keep the downtrodden appearance of the restaurant to themselves. Annie could only imagine the conversation she would have with Andre if Jessica blabbed about her unfavorable opinion of her workplace.

Andre rarely stepped foot inside the restaurant and he would be hard-pressed to eat a single item. Curse the day Annie considered bringing the food the restaurant served into the apartment. "If you're a waitress it might as well be at a place that no one we know goes to," he once told her.

Annie spent the afternoon starting her search on the Internet for a different job; one more along the lines of the career she wanted to pursue. She wasn't sure where to begin. She typed in event planning, party planning and caterers but found that with each search, all the positions were looking for candidates far more qualified than she.

It was frustrating.

The next afternoon when Annie arrived home from work she saw Andre standing near the kitchen counter.

"Holy shit!" Annie shouted at seeing someone inside the apartment.

Andre laughed and clapped his hands. "That was the best face I've ever seen you make."

"What are you doing home?" Annie asked catching her breath and holding on to her chest.

"The company got us tickets to the Sox game today against the Angels. So, change and get ready, we have to start heading down there like five minutes ago."

The landline phone began to ring and both instinctively grabbed for their cell phones.

"I'll get it," Andre offered. "Get ready."

Annie rushed into the bedroom and Andre leaned over the counter towards the telephone. He saw a phone number he didn't recognize and a company name that meant nothing to him. He let it ring suspecting it was a telemarketer. It was the only kind of call they got on their landline unless it was his grandmother.

"Are you going to get that?" Annie shouted.

"No! It's a telemarketer."

He tapped his foot waiting to see if the telemarketer would leave a message. The red light started flashing and he lifted the phone off of the cradle and dialed for the message.

"Hello, this message is for Annie Ferguson, I received your number and information from Aldo. He mentioned that you were interested in event and party planning. We have an opening and I'm willing to give you a shot off of Aldo's recommendation. It's comparable pay and right now it would only be part time working at some evening events and helping out in the background so you can still hold on to your serving gig in case this doesn't work out. I'm talking too much as it is. Let's chat. My name is Steven Howard of . . . ."

Andre pressed the number two button and erased the message without listening further. He scrolled through the call log on the telephone and deleted the record indicating the company and phone number. Something about the act pleased him.

"Sweetie!" Andre hollered impatiently.

"Five minutes!" Annie responded.

"Three minutes." He offered back.

Four minutes later Annie exited the bedroom dressed in her short sleeve, gray Red Sox jersey and ball cap. "Who called?"

"It was one of those machines that ask if you need lawn care service."

"Oh jeez."

"Yeah, I think we're the wrong market."

Annie and Andre walked to the door and exited the apartment. They reached the elevator and Andre leaned against the wall.

"I still think we should call the lawn care company and request a quote." Annie tilted her gaze towards Andre with a smile. "We have plants that need tending to."

Andre chuckled and looked towards the elevator. "Are you happy with your job?"

"It's fine. Why?"

"Just wondering."

Annie didn't quite believe him and opted against inquiring further about his odd question.

The elevator chimed and the doors opened.

"Good seats?" Annie asked as they entered.

"Lower deck. Third base line."

Andre tapped the lobby button and the doors closed.

When the doors opened moments later they exited into the lobby. Jon was standing waiting for the elevator.

"Oh hey," he said with a smile. "How are you two doing?"

"We're good. How are you?"

Andre passed by Jon and looked back at Annie. "Honey?"

"I'm good. Let's grab a coffee sometime soon. I have some exciting news."

"Honey!" Andre held the outside door open and nodded towards the exit.

"Okay," Annie said in a hurried tone. "We're off to the game."

"Oh, by all means . . ." Jon held out his arm towards Andre and Annie smiled walking away. "I'll look for you." Jon stepped inside the elevator. "Good seeing you, Andre!" He shouted as the elevator doors began to close.

"Whatever," Andre mumbled rushing Annie out.

They began walking down Beacon Street towards Fenway Park. The temperature hovered in the upper sixties and the dark blue sky was parted by puffy dark clouds. The T to Kenmore would've been too busy the closer they got to the park and Andre wasn't one for being crammed into a compartment if the occasion didn't allow it. Riding with the businesspeople to and from work was one thing, drunken fans filled with beer from across the city was a whole other matter.

The game started promptly at 2:05pm. Andre's coworkers filtered in throughout the first and second innings. Raj and Jessica hadn't arrived yet and Andre was speaking with colleagues that Annie recognized but couldn't quite place.

A hot dog vendor was making his way up the stairs and Annie's ears perked up at the call for a Fenway Frank. She held her hand up and Andre looked over.

"What are you doing?"

"I'm starving."

"No." Andre waved the vendor on.

"Andre, I'm hungry."

"You're not going to eat one of those things. Do you even know what's in a hot dog?"

"I can conjure up a few guesses."

"No one knows what's in a hot dog."

"It's a baseball game," she replied through grit teeth. She decided it wasn't an opportune time to start a shouting match. "I want a hot dog."

Andre leaned in, his eyes were threatening and his body was tense. His response was whispered but he enunciated with anger. "We will get something in a little bit."

With a blank stare and in a monotonous tone she asked, "With your permission I would like to go get something to eat now. I promise not to eat in front of any of your friends so that they won't know what a disgusting person your girlfriend is."

Annie stood up and Andre rolled his eyes and turned his head to face the field. "Just trying to look out for your health," he muttered.

The Sox manager was walking to the pitcher's mound to have a discussion with the pitcher. He had given up two runs and now two runners were in scoring position. It was not turning out to be an ideal first few innings for the Boston Red Sox. The pitcher was able to persuade the manager to give him a little more time.

Annie huffed her way up the stairs into the concourse to grab something to eat. She sifted through her wallet and found just five dollars. It would cover just one hot dog and no drinks but Annie wanted a drink.

She approached an empty counter to order. She heard the groans of the stadium as the Angel up-to-bat knocked a line drive into center field allowing the man on third an easy way home. The pitcher was being replaced and an influx of fans found this the ideal time to get a snack or empty their bladders.

But by the time the fans filtered in she had a Fenway Frank and an overpriced beer on the counter as she swiped her credit card. She put the card back in her wallet and shoved the wallet into her front pocket. It bulged outward but she would rather have an unsightly and slightly uncomfortable wallet and cell phone in her pocket than to lug around a purse through the park.

Annie fixed up the dog and took a massive bite resting her beer on a dirty high-top table. It tasted like a summer afternoon.

"Beautiful day, at least," a man said to his friend as they passed by. Both were older men, diehard Sox fans; the kind that have bad days when the Red Sox have bad days.

"I hope for rain on game days, it's the only way they seem to do anything," the grumpy friend responded. They stood at the end of a ten-deep line at the counter.

Mustard dribbled down Annie's chin and fell to the table. She wiped her mouth and took in a sip of the beer. She people-watched and kept an eye on the monitor as the game restarted with a new pitcher throwing out his first fastball garnering a much needed strike. The crowd cheered. It was followed by a foul ball and then a third strike that caught the batter looking. The crowd went nuts and the inning was over.

Annie stuffed the remainder of the hot dog and bun into her mouth, grabbed her beer and started walking around the stadium. She didn't want to go back to her seat. Each time she habitually felt for the ticket in her pocket her heart would sink like it was a chain on her leg pulling her back. She chugged the last half of her beer and tossed the plastic cup inside the garbage and pulled out her phone. No messages.

She expected one.

She continued meandering around the stadium letting her mind wander. She took in different views of the field walking by the third base line, then back behind home.

She felt a buzzing sensation in her pocket and pulled out her phone.

Where r u!

She almost responded but decided against it. He will feel how I feel when he doesn't respond, she thought, and then realized that he wouldn't make the connection. It still wasn't enough for her to message him back.

Annie's bottom lip quivered and she begged herself not to start in a fit of tears. She was trapped. She couldn't go anywhere. She literally felt that he held all the cards in the relationship and she had no option but to be by his side unless he no longer desired it.

Even when she swiped her credit card for another beer she thought of the Visa bill she would receive and how it would further subtract from her financial gains from serving.

She sipped her beer and tried to convince herself how lucky she truly was. She lived in a great city without the necessity of paying overpriced rent. Perhaps I'm lucky I'm not married, she thought, at least I still have an easy out if I wanted it.

Bottom of the fifth and the Red Sox knock in a two-run homer. Thank god for left-handed batters forcing the ball to the opposite side of the outfield from the Big Green Monster.

They were still down by three runs though.

Annie's phone buzzed again.

Where the fuck are you!!!@!

Annie walked through the underground system that was Fenway Park. She had been in a handful of ballparks but this one was always one she felt strange in. As she bee-lined between beer drinkers and face-painted kids she couldn't help feel that she was in a surreal underground parking lot, minus the cars. It was a closed concrete jungle until she appeared at the opening to the stands.

There was no roar of the crowd, it was between innings and idle chatter created an ambiance of murmurs while the occasional "Ice cold beer!" was shouted in the distance.

The row stood up as Annie made her way towards her empty seat and plopped down next to Andre. He took one look at her and turned away in disdain.

"I needed some air."

"You left the wide open park to get fresh air?" His response was scornful.

Raj turned around in his seat. "You two need to get laid," he stated.

"Oh hey, Raj. Didn't see you there. Hi Jessica."

"Hi." She didn't turn around or lift her head from her smart phone.

"You two have been at each other's throats forever. You've gotta stop that."

Annie and Andre avoided eye contact with one another and felt called out, naked in the reality of the situation.

Raj changed subjects but didn't keep the topic any less sore. "Jess and I saw Annie the other day."

"That so?" Andre raised an eyebrow. "She neglected to tell me."

"Yeah, we stopped in at the high-class establishment called Aldo's. Ever hear of it?" Raj asked with a giggle.

"Oh. You visited her at work."

Jessica commented, "I don't know how you eat there and keep the figure you do, Annie."

"She doesn't eat there. If she actually ate that crap do you think I would be able to tolerate her?"

"Bill eats there every day and he's still ticking."

"And he's going to drop dead of a massive coronary any day now."

"He's my friend, Andre. Please be more sensitive."

"Yeah, Andre. Be more sensitive," Raj joked mimicking a high, female voice. "Adopt kittens and wear ladies undergarments."

Andre took a friendly swipe at Raj but it was blocked. Raj pointed to Andre threateningly but that didn't stop Andre from taking another swipe and missing once again.

"You'll have to turn around eventually," Andre said leaning back.

"Shit," Raj said realizing his predicament.

Andre smiled and turned his eyes to the first row where a beer vendor was starting his way up the stairs. "You buy me a beer and you buy my lady a beer and you can turn around without fear of harassment."

Raj reached for his wallet. "I want to let you know that I'm doing this as a friendly gesture and not at all out of the possibility of continuing harassment."

"Call it what you want."

"I want a beer too, Raj," Jessica said.

Raj raised his hand and ordered four beers total, he muttered at having to pay almost thirty-dollars for alcohol.

"Cheers!" Andre lifted his plastic cup and took a drink.

They had talked through a slow top-of-the-sixth and Raj finally turned around to watch the Angel's batter knock his third foul ball down the third base line.

"Renege." Andre smacked Raj in the back of the head.

"You dick!" Raj turned around and Andre held up both hands innocently.

"It was Annie," Andre said chuckling. "I'll get the next round."

"You bet your ass you will."

The stadium groaned as a solo home run barely edged over the centerfield wall.

Jessica finally turned around and looked at Annie. "Not to be insulting or anything, well, I guess since you didn't make the food it wouldn't matter, but after I ate at the restaurant I got the worst stomach cramps in the world. I was doubled over feeling like I was going to puke every five minutes on the walk home."

"She refuses to quit that shit hole," Andre responded. "I keep telling her that if she wants to be a career waitress then she should get a job some place actually nice."

"Yeah, like a hotel downtown!" Jessica exclaimed.

"Nah," Raj chimed in. "Every businessman that walks in there will be drunker than shit and try to nail her."

"Getting nailed by a businessman would be more respectful than getting eye-fucked by dirty, unkempt creeps." Andre chuckled along with Raj. "She's too smart to fall for one of those douche bags, aren't you, sweetie?"

He put an arm around her. It was an attempt to subtly claim his dominance in the discussion, to prove that she belonged to him and that she knew it too.

"I don't know," Jessica said and Annie knew that the next sentence was apt to boil Andre's blood, "a hot man in a suit working his way through a powerful deal . . . it's hard to resist."

"That's how I got her," Raj announced.

"You were drunk and high," Jessica confirmed.

"Right, but I shared the joint with you and you were so grateful that you accepted my request for lunch and we met at the Commons and what was I wearing?"

Jessica admitted he was right. "A suit."

"And wasn't I a strapping young gent?"

"You were."

"Irresistible even?" Jessica's phone buzzed and she became too distracted to answer the question. Raj turned all the way around to see both Andre and Annie. "I was irresistible."

"I don't doubt it," Annie replied.

"In all seriousness though," Raj looked Annie directly in the eyes, "I personally thought the bacon was tasty as shit but get the hell out of that dive. Andre here can't have his girl stinking of grease and having paychecks signed by the owner of that dump."

"That's what I've been telling her."

Annie replied with a submissive, unenthusiastic tone. "I'm looking for something."

"You have to think up something better than just 'something'." Raj turned around to view the easy third out at first.

"What's up?"

Andre stood at the bathroom door wearing a pair of black pajama shorts. He struggled to maintain the abs he had years ago but he still had a physique that most in their mid-thirties would die for.

Annie looked at him but had long ago lost the thrill of seeing such a strong man in her midst. The blindness of love had faded and she saw a different man. His humor was endearing at the beginning and she remembered telling her father of this boy Andre's sense of humor. Every crack though was deprecating her sense of self or her friends. Maybe it wasn't the case, maybe she no longer heard the jokes towards actors in movies he was watching or athletes missing the easiest catches.

She had taken the comment at the game hard and she took his inquiry to broach the subject.

"Annie, a waitress at a place like that has three kids, they're chain smokers and they live in run-down apartment complexes. I know why you didn't tell me Raj and Jessica came in but you understand what that does to how I'm perceived . . . on how we are."

Annie understood. "It's not like I want to do this the rest of my life. I want bigger things, you know?"

Andre made his way to the bed and fell onto his stomach.

Annie continued, "I really want to do this party planning thing but I don't know where to begin."

Andre took his finger and slid it up and down Annie's bare leg. He moved his body up towards her and leaned in to kiss her. They began making out but Annie felt that he was lazy about it. There was one thing he wanted and he knew this was the way to get it. She could feel him get hard and knew she had to pull back.

"We can't," she advised him.

"Oh." He crept back and fell onto his side of the bed. He was erect and he looked at her with a sinister smile then down at his shorts as if he preferred an alternative to sex if only because it was quicker and he wouldn't have to worry about her satisfaction. He hardly did nowadays anyway. "In that case . . ."

She didn't want to show her disinterest so she sighed and moved towards his boxers. She slid them off and placed them at her side. She looked at his member for a moment before hoping that he would be quick. She wished for silence instead of the over-exaggerated grunting and statements of pleasure that he would usually expel.

When he was finished she raced to the bathroom to wash her mouth out with mouth wash.

By the time Annie exited the bathroom Andre was on his side, the sheets and comforter nestled up to his armpit and his eyes were closed.

She crawled onto the opposite side of the bed.

"That explains why you've been so moody these last few days. You women and your hormones," he muttered and followed it with a yawn. She didn't respond.

I think we should break up, she thought about whispering to see if he would even answer back. Instead, she grabbed a magazine from the nightstand and started flipping through the pages.

19

The difference in appearance of cars from when Annie hopped from the green line onto the blue line was noticeable. The cars weren't as kept and they were considerably aged more than the green line. Even the tracks screeched louder as the subway car swayed through the tunnels.

She tried to read her novel but found the track too shaky. She looked around the near empty car and refused to make eye contact. There was only one other person with a similar predicament of temporary boredom and she stared blankly ahead. A large man sat reading the newspaper and another skinny man in a jumpsuit and orange vest worked the Sudoku puzzle found in the thin, free paper available in the subway terminals.

Annie glanced at the front page of the paper indicating that poverty was on the rise. It made her think of her self. She was technically middle class with Andre but on her own she was well into the lower class. Working class, she thought, it doesn't matter if you call it lower or working, the figures on the paycheck were still far from ideal.

She was afraid that she was becoming a disappointment to her parents. Each generation is supposed to find greater success than the previous, she thought, and wondered where she had gone astray.

At just thirty years old she felt she lacked options.

The subway car pulled into the airport. She desperately wished she didn't need to travel home.

Fifty-eight-year-olds shouldn't have heart attacks. They were still young and they seemed to have so much time in front of them. The eerily calm phone call from her mother freaked her out though and she booked a flight to Grand Rapids; two flights actually, there was never a direct one. Her mother paid for the flight.

The man that used to carry her on his shoulders when she was young and danced with her at daddy-daughter dances in middle school had suffered a minor heart attack. When one of your parents have a heart attack, she thought, there's nothing minor about it.

Her father made a complete career change at forty-five and thrived. He was a doctor, a general practitioner with a solid business. One bothersome patient too many, one too many insurance claims unpaid, one conflict over his partner's constant useless desire to have tests done on patients for the money and he upped and left. His partner's practice ultimately suffered greatly for it. Annie's father provided everyone with plenty of notice of his intent to leave and started writing a book on the Great Depression in Grand Rapids. He researched feverishly and eventually completed a 362 page piece of history. Published locally, he had sold seven-thousand copies which was a far cry from a bestseller but quite well nonetheless. He accomplished his dream of writing a book.

He then found an investment banker with the same lack of enthusiasm for his career and they opened up a restaurant/bar at the Gerald Ford International Airport in Grand Rapids called the 44th Street Public House. Every time Annie would fly home she would step into the restaurant and have a meal with her dad. It became tradition and she loved seeing how busy the restaurant was. He accomplished his dream of opening a restaurant.

After a two-hour layover in Milwaukee, she hated having to backtrack on flights, she deplaned in Grand Rapids and passed by her father's restaurant. She felt a pang of anxiety in the pit of her stomach. He wouldn't be there.

* * *

Aunt Edna was waiting in her ten-year-old pickup once Annie stepped out of the terminal. It was a cool afternoon with drizzle tickling the end of her nose. They waved and Annie popped open the door tossing her carry-on bag between the seats.

Annie's first realization was how dirty the inside of the truck had been. A McDonald's bag was shoved in the backseat along with empty pop cans and energy drink cans. The floor mats had permanent flecks of dirt and mud. There were brown spots on the seat and the smell of cigarette smoke lingered though Edna insisted she hadn't touched a Newport in four years. Annie placed her feet strategically between a CD case and a black hooded sweatshirt.

"Never mind that stuff," Aunt Edna said. Her voice sounded like a gravel pit. She took a quick glance at her niece.

The first thing Annie noticed was how gray Edna's hair was, or how gray the roots were. Her unnatural brunette was being pushed to the ends. She had a small mole on the right side of her chin and the wrinkles in her forehead popped.

"Good flight?" Aunt Edna asked gunning the truck to beat the influx of incoming cars into the passenger pick-up area.

"I got an aisle to myself on the way here from Milwaukee." Annie lied to sound positive. She recalled the snoring man on her left with the breath of a swamp. "How have you been?"

"Lucky enough to still be employed." She laughed; it was more of a phlegm-filled noise from her throat. Annie could almost envision Aunt Edna snorting up something from her lung and hacking it out of the window. "I got a layoff notice though but it was precautionary. They dumped about twenty-percent of the employees but I survived. It was hairy there for a minute."

Annie couldn't recall what her aunt did and before she had the opportunity to politely ask, Aunt Edna tossed out her own line of questions. "How's Beantown? You still with that handsome fella, Andre?"

"It's a cool city but . . . it's okay." She looked outside as the truck turned onto the freeway on-ramp. "Andre's fine."

"Christopher wanted to move somewhere but that idiot can't hold down a drive-thru job at Burger King. He keeps thinking he's going to make it as a deejay." Aunt Edna chuckled, her raspy laugh again tried to bring light to her son.

"Uncle Murray?"

"He's been working overtime a lot. I think he doesn't want to come home."

Annie smiled but wouldn't doubt it. Uncle Murray married into the family but he was an incredibly nice guy who seemed to have made many mistakes in life. Potential never met reality. He met the wrong woman who insisted he take the wrong job.

Aunt Edna continued, "He's going to work as hard as your father and have himself a heart attack. Why waste all that time just workin', ya know? We all die so you might as well put in your forty hours and spend the rest of the week enjoying life."

"I think my dad enjoys what he does."

"Hm." She grunted not believing that one could love their job. She wasn't one to appreciate good news. She thought Annie's father's work ethic was strange and harbored feelings of jealousy that he had accomplished as much as he did. "I guess my sister fell for the right man."

Twenty minutes of freeway driving led them to the hospital. Aunt Edna leisurely walked from the parking lot inside and Annie's frustration was growing. "Move!" She wanted to order but held her increasing annoyance inside.

She breezed past her aunt when they arrived at the room on the fourth floor of the Spectrum Health-Butterworth Hospital in Grand Rapids. She rushed to her father and he beamed as he hugged his daughter.

"I'm sorry I couldn't meet you for lunch," he lifted his hand where the tubes and wires were connected to monitor his recovery. "I'm a little tied up."

"It's okay," Annie replied and fought tears that she had no control over. She wiped her eyes. "Well?"

"Well it sounds as if I'll be sent home any minute pending a blood test comes back looking good."

"Good."

There was a silence between the two; both glad to see one another but both unsure of what to say. He looked pale, weak even, and it wasn't a look that she ever saw her father in. He was always fairly thin, a gene she had been grateful to have adopted, but he looked especially skinny. She didn't want to comment on it though out of fear of bringing negativity to a situation that required positive thoughts.

"So? Where's mom?"

"At home. She wanted to make sure the house was clean before I arrived. The office gave her the next couple days off." He stated it with confusion and acceptance. He looked at Edna. "Good afternoon, Edna. Good to see you and thanks for bringing my daughter to me."

"My pleasure. My day wasn't filled with errands that desperately needed to be completed."

Neither Annie nor her father could gage the seriousness of the comment.

"If you need to go, by all means, Edna, you can."

She shook off the insistence and moved inside the room unfolding her arms. She tried her best to look as if she hadn't a care in the world when both knew that worries and three-hundred-dollars in the bank was all she had.

"I guess pizza is out of the question for dinner tonight?"

"I'm not interested in knocking on the hornet's nest just yet. I get chicken and salad. A lot of fruits and vegetables."

"Ribs on your birthday?"

Her father shook his head disappointingly. "Too soon."

Annie smiled and hugged her father again.

"Sweetie, I told you when you started down that career path that you were going to be all on your own. I don't know thing one about party planning," Annie's father admitted. He took a forkful of lettuce leaves and munched on them.

"I know, dad. You're so good at everything that it makes me frustrated sometimes."

"I've failed before. I just don't gloat about it. Your mother would be more than happy to vouch for that."

"Where to begin! That's the only trouble I have." Annie's mother responded cheering with a glass of wine at the possibility of joking with her husband. "How about the Thanksgiving turkey?"

"How about we ask about Annie's plans on getting back into party planning?"

"No," Annie began. "I'd really love to hear about the Thanksgiving turkey."

"You've heard the story."

"Have I?" She lifted a fist to her chin and let an exaggerated and sarcastic, "Hmm" slip out.

"It starts out like any other horror story," he said.

Annie's mother chimed in, "It was a dark and stormy Thanksgiving eve . . ."

". . . and I burnt the turkey. End of story."

Both ladies chuckled and Annie's father grinned shaking his head.

When the laughter subsided Annie's mother reminded her father said, "Michael, take your medicine."

Annie's father responded in a whiny, childlike voice. "But I don't wanna!"

He stood up and went to the kitchen counter popping off the lid of the orange pill bottle. He tipped the bottle and got one to spill into his palm. With a glass of water he swallowed the pill and pursed his lips as if he enjoyed the regiment.

Annie's father plopped back into his chair with a weak groan. "Sometimes it's hard to imagine someone like me having a heart attack."

"It wasn't a massive heart attack," Annie's mother interrupted reassuringly.

"No, but I like to think I take care of myself, I try to work out regularly, never smoked with the exception of some time in college. Drank moderately. Ate healthy. Yet here I am at fifty-eight clutching my arm at work wondering why I had trouble breathing meanwhile Scott weighing in near three bills doesn't even has high blood pressure."

"You don't have high blood pressure," Annie's mother said.

"I just wonder if decades of skipping the chocolate cake was worth it. So, there's my fatherly advice for the day, don't always skip the dessert." He stabbed some lettuce with the tings of his fork and ate some more of the salad. "It means a lot that you're here, Annie. I'm glad at least one of my children could come in."

"Have you heard from Noah?"

When the younger child, Noah, crossed the threshold of being closer to thirty than he was twenty, he had a mini-quarter-life crisis. He was an assistant manager at the 44th Street Public House and stepped into their father's office stating that he was quitting. Noah stood tall and stared his father directly in the eye. It seemed that he went off the rails once he hit twenty-six. He dabbled in a mystic-theology class offered at a nearby storefront spiritual bookstore and grew bored immediately unable to sit and stew in his own thoughts "meditating". He was upset that he kept falling asleep so he would chug a Red Bull then try to sit still for an hour of meditation. He then sold his car for eight-grand to travel to Africa. It stunned the family and Annie's mother pleaded for him to sit back, relax and not make any rash decisions.

He didn't. The countries that Annie's parents visited outside North America could be counted on three fingers so their son's sudden desire to travel to the African continent floored them. He had been gone two years.

"I emailed him two days ago," Annie's mother replied.

"And?"

"And he gave his best. We are lucky to have the kind of high-speed Internet that we are used to here. It's not like that around the world. He's in Botswana."

"Doing what?"

"Diamond mining? I have no idea. He's making his eight-thousand last."

"I think the dollar goes further there." There was silence a moment and Annie offered up optimism. "He's finding himself."

"I just . . ." Her mom shook her head unsure of how to explain it but she couldn't even wrap her head around it even after two years and vague emails.

"Some people would think leaving a medical practice was crazy," her father said.

"But not talking to your family for weeks or months at a time. Never returning emails or calling us on our birthdays! Come on, Michael." Her mother looked at Annie. "Annie, you really think this is normal? I'm use to the worrying. I don't want to be use to wondering what central-African country my child is in."

She waved her hand as she looked downward at the plate moving her fork along the food.

"Let's talk about something else," Annie insisted; her father nodded in agreement.

Heather sat across the table. The lines on her face were visible under the make-up she applied in order to conceal it. She was one of Annie's good friends since the seventh grade. They had countless sleepovers and movie nights. Cried over boys and laughed over memories. When Annie drank too much at a New Years Eve party at the age of eighteen, it was Heather that held her hair back.

They went to separate colleges and when Annie moved to Boston they only spoke occasionally and saw one another when she was in town. They always enjoyed their time together and always promised to stay in touch more frequently.

Heather had been married for a little under two years after dating for three years. She had met her husband Jay the same weekend Annie met Andre. At the time Annie and Heather were giddy with excitement having met such great men at the same time in their lives.

As they sat in an Applebee's catching up, Annie tried to shine a good light on her life in Boston.

Heather, on the other hand, wasn't so quiet about her unhappiness. "I guess I expected it all to be different," she started. "I expected him to calm down a bit, treat it all like a real marriage."

"What does he do?"

"Everything he did before. He drinks all the time and I usually get called to pick him up at the bar or join him. We fight like once a week. He makes me so angry sometimes and I know I shouldn't blow up at him but I really can't help it. I wanted to spend time with him on the weekends and stuff but he's always making plans with his friends to play video games."

"But Heather, that's who he was when you married him. You can't fault him for wanting to be him self even if you don't really like it. That's who you fell in love with."

"I know and that's the dilemma." Heather's shoulders slumped and she took a big sip of her apple martini. "It would be stupid to say that this was what I was afraid of happening and even expected it change. But I did. I really thought things might be a little different."

"Do you still love him?"

Heather didn't answer and Annie was quick to change the subject. They reminisced about their high school days and gossiped about their mutual friends' lives that they followed on social media. Heather talked about changes and how she would love to move to Boston to be closer to Annie and Annie told her friend that she was considering moving back to Grand Rapids, it was the first hint in their entire conversation that indicated trouble.

They hugged goodbye and Heather gave her best wishes to Annie's father.

"I don't want to go home," Heather said with a chuckle. "Think of the five things you dislike about Andre, think of the things that you wish he would change about himself, if you can put up with those things then you'll be good." She unlocked her car door. "If it's going to drive you crazy then . . ."

Annie smiled as she appreciated the advice. "Thanks."

Annie was in her old bedroom. Not much had changed since she had last held residence at the house. The light green paint was warm, welcoming and the flower patterns she painted herself added a little pop to the room. She always noticed the small mess up she made on the orange petal near her bed. It was a miniscule smudge mark that used to make her sad but then it grew on her. She accepted the imperfection.

Her bed was a twin with a gray/white comforter. Her computer desk had long since held a desktop computer and was stacked with books her mother meant to read. There was an emptiness lingering in her bedroom like it was the skeleton of who she once was. She could trace her roots back to the room, knew every creak in the floorboards beneath the beige carpet and where she could get the best sunlight at the end of the day.

Annie had spent the better part of an hour staring at the ceiling. She was on her back entranced with the spinning fan. She felt that her lack of crying was justified yet she wanted to cry at the lack of being able to cry. Her throat was tight though and her stomach squeezed with nervousness and anxiety.

Being at home in the comforting environment helped her make up her mind.

Five years, she thought. Would Andre convince or beg her to stay? Would he want to stay in communication?

Most importantly, would she actually go through with it?

Would he yell? How would she pack up her belongings?

So many questions ran through her mind and the gravity of the situation to come weighed down heavily on her emotions.

There was a light tapping on the door. She didn't respond so the knob turned as another knock alerted her that someone was entering.

"I just wanted to say goodnight," Annie's father said warmly, quietly. "How's Heather?"

"She's okay."

Annie sat up and looked at her father. He could see the trouble below the surface but before he could inquire she offered her decision.

"Dad, I'm going to break up with Andre." Even though she said those words defiantly they caused the tears to burst outward and she began crying as her father raced to the bed to give his brokenhearted daughter a hug and a shoulder to cry on.

*   *   *

She talked with Jon to inform him of her decision and get his advice.

"I'm sorry. I really am," Jon told her. Word was circulating amongst her few friends in Boston about the impending break-up and she feared that Andre would receive the news before she had a chance to tell him that she wanted to end their relationship.

"I couldn't walk around that city and not think of what I had."

"What did you have?"

Annie opened her mouth to respond but the words didn't expel.

Jon continued, "You still have a job, you still have friends, you're just lacking a nice apartment. And, um, as much as my girlfriend would prefer that I don't allow you to, you do have a place to crash. My place."

"She's okay with that?"

"You're a friend in need," he replied. "Where would you go? Bethany's?"

"She's locked in a place already. I'm sure Bill would let me stay with him or Aldo would let me sleep on a booth."

"People fart on those booths. Old man farts and morning-after-drunk farts. I'll give you my apartment before I allow you to rest your head on the cushion of a booth."

Annie paced her bedroom looking out the window then crossing back to the door. "It's always nice to come home." She said whimsically. "It's a nice place to visit but I wouldn't want to live here." She walked back to the window and looked down onto the backyard and budding trees. "But I kinda do."

"You're coming back tomorrow, right?"

"Yeah." Each statement she made seemed as if she were nonchalantly enlightened by every thought that she made. Her voice sounded dreamy, breathy.

"Are you going to do it tomorrow?"

Annie sighed and closed her eyes fearing that she would back out. Breaking up was a good plan in theory but to go through with it was another matter. "Yeah. Everything is going to change." There was concern in her voice. "I won't have my apartment and I don't have much money. To stay in Boston I would have to get a second, maybe a third job to afford to live there and then I wouldn't even be able to enjoy where I live. How do you do it?"

"Unemployment checks and charitable parents." He paused before continuing his explanation. "Their charity exists because they know it won't last too long because they'll cut me off if I don't come home or find another job."

"How is the job search?"

"Not a whole lot is available in the world of creative writing but you do realize if you move home and I move home we will both be in Michigan."

"We'll be able to reminisce on the great times we shared in Boston. Fine wines at coffee shops and greasy meals served up at Aldo's."

Annie and Jon completed their conversation and she spent the rest of the night attempting to fall asleep. She hugged her pillow on her stomach.

As time crept on she stared at the ceiling as thoughts of drained bank accounts and uncertainty swirled in her head.

This was the price of her freedom.

20

She must have walked ten miles inside the apartment that evening. She paced back-and-forth in the living room and entered the bedroom. Her heart pumped hard and her hands shook with nervousness.

The plan had gone through without a hitch. Her flight landed at 12:30 in the afternoon and she was home by two. Jon had purchased moving boxes and stored them in his apartment until Annie knocked on the door to retrieve them.

"He won't be home until 5:30. God, if he walks in while I'm packing I don't know what I'm going to do."

Annie poured all her belongings into the boxes and moved them across the hall. Every shirt, every book and every DVD that belonged to her was inside Jon's apartment in a matter of ninety minutes. Everything else was Andre's.

He bought the furniture and the cooking utensils. The pots and pans were all purchased on his credit card as was the sheets on the bed.

This is my life, Annie thought as she stared at the five boxes in the corner of Jon's living room.

At 4:30, Annie went back to the apartment and began her pacing.

The door opened just before six. Andre entered with his suit jacket around his arm.

"How was Michigan?" He asked flipping through the pile of mail on the counter. Annie realized that they hadn't talked on the phone during her trip and had only sent each other a handful of text messages initiated by her.

"It was fine," she responded. Her voice was quiet.

Andre looked up and saw the concern in her face and her body language. "What's up?"

I can still back away from this, she thought. I can bring all the boxes back over.

And then she realized that he didn't rush up and give her a hug or a kiss. They were apart for four days and neither had the desire to embrace one another.

"Andre . . ." she choked on the words before they came out. He stood where he was, folding his arms and staring her down. She didn't feel love in his eyes. They barely tolerated one another. She wanted to be free of this relationship. "I think we should separate."

She hated her verbiage. Think? Separate?

"What?" He asked but confusion didn't register in his demeanor.

Annie stood her ground and defiantly said, "I'm breaking up with you."

Andre huffed past her and raced into the bedroom. She heard the closet door open then slam shut. His feet pounded on the floor as he exited the bedroom and walked into the kitchen. "Who has your shit? The queer across the hall? Grandpa? That bitch?" He chuckled at his jabs. He pulled a half-filled bottle of Jack Daniels off the top of the refrigerator. He grabbed a glass and poured himself a drink. He took a sip and looked at Annie. "What do you want from me?" He sneered. "You can leave now." He swallowed a massive gulp of whiskey.

Annie didn't have an answer. She was upset that he just accepted it.

"I'm not going to miss you," he said staring her dead in the eyes. "These last four days were a godsend."

"You don't have to be mean," Annie said feeling the tears start to flow from her eyes.

"What are you still doing here?" He hid his underlying emotions well. Annie could hardly read him and couldn't tell if he was heartbroken or upset or annoyed.

"Do you even care? Do you even want to know why?"

"You've made your decision, Annie. I'm not going to beg for you to stay."

She didn't like how quick this was going. She's had break-ups last for hours but Andre had no interest in talking it out or appeasing her want to talk about where their relationship went sour.

"Goodbye, Andre." Annie walked towards the door and felt his eyes boring holes into her.

"Good riddance," he muttered.

Annie stepped into the hall; the door closing behind her. She waited a moment trying to listen for noise coming from her old apartment. It was no longer her home.

She walked a few feet to Jon's door and tapped lightly.

The door opened within seconds. Annie's eyes were welling up and she shrugged her shoulders to let Jon know that it was done.

He let her in.

On a warm June afternoon two weeks after Annie returned to Boston, she and Jon grabbed some burritos and headed down to the Boston Commons. They brought books and flasks and mixers. Jon stuffed a blanket into a backpack and barely zipped it entirely closed afraid that the strength of the rolled up red, black and white plaid sheet would pop the zipper and he would have to leave the backpack nestled in a garbage can and carry a blanket home.

They sat under the large willows that shaded parts of the Boston Commons. The sun peeked through in spots and the path throughout the park offered a handful of men and women in various forms of leisure. Some jogged, some walked their dogs, some were business-people on their breaks.

"I have a confession to make." Jon poured some contents from the flask into a twenty-ounce Coca-Cola bottle. He closed the flask, screwed the top back on the pop bottle and turned it upside down then right-side up. He unscrewed the bottle and took a drink. "Happiness is rum and Coke."

"That's not so much a confession as it is a fact."

He handed the flask to Annie who proceeded to repeat Jon's actions.

"I bought a Red Sox shirt the day of your party."

"My party?"

"The Red Sox themed party from a month or so ago . . . I didn't have a Sox shirt so I had to run out and buy one."

The confession made her smile. She shyly looked away.

Jon continued sincerely, "I like you, Annie. You're like the girl . . . friend that I never had. Every guy should have one of you."

She looked up. "Thank you."

"No, thank you. Do you know how hard it is to be in a big city with no friends? How the hell are you supposed to make new friends nowadays?"

"I would say through work but that's not really a possibility for you at the moment."

"Everyone here thinks we're two lovers," Jon said as he looked at the people passing by.

"Everyone here is wondering why we don't have jobs." Annie rebutted as she opened the bag from Anna's Taqueria. "I love these burritos."

Jon took hold of the bag and dug for chips. "I love these chips."

The noise of other Bostonians in the area, the birds and the traffic mingled with the chomps on chips and burritos.

"Jonie's coming into town."

"When?"

"End of the week."

"Is this a warning?"

"She knows about you. She'll like you."

"I can't stay in that building."

"She's fine. She's a very confident woman and she knows I love her."

"No, I mean, I can't stay in that building much longer."

A light wind blew a napkin from the picnic blanket and she grasped for it but it got away. It danced across the grass towards the George Washington statue.

"Litterbug." Jon shouted as he instinctively grabbed at anything that might look as if it would blow away with the sudden wind gust.

"There goes my good-karma credits." Annie continued her reasoning for wanting to vacate the apartment complex. "I'm familiar enough with his schedule. I'm just afraid I'm going to step out into the hall one day and find him feeling up some chick with one hand as he fiddles with the keys to get inside the apartment."

"Obvious specific concern."

She breathed a loud sigh and took a big drink out of the Coca-Cola bottle.

Jon took a bite from the burrito as a small bit of sauce tipped over the chewed off part, dripped down the side of the tortilla and onto his jeans. He cursed himself and tried to wipe away the sauce. It left a small dark circle on his pants.

"You have a little less than four months worth of apartment time left. I can sublet it to you if you have $1500 to throw at me per month."

"I don't have that much. How much do you want? We never discussed an amount that I would owe you per month."

"Per month? I thought you'd be out fairly soon." Jon stopped himself and backtracked. "Not that I want you to leave anytime soon but, you know, you were talking about going home. I wasn't going to broach the subject of monetary compensation until the right time. Until . . ."

". . . I was over Andre."

Jon shrugged his shoulders. "Yeah. Are you really thinking of staying in Boston?"

"Jon, I'm not going to be over Andre for a while. And I'm not one-hundred percent ready to give up here. Things have changed a bit. How much do you want?"

"No specific amount comes to mind."

Annie looked off towards the top of the Commons. The lawn seemed expansive and was turning a lush green under a spring season which wrought forth the right amount of sun and rain, warm days and cool nights.

She looked sincerely at her friend. "Jon, how much do you want?"

Annie placed the plate of scrambled eggs, hash browns, bacon and sausage in front of Bill.

"Toast is coming up next," Annie said as Bethany appeared placing the second, smaller plate down.

"Here you go."

"Thanks." Annie and Bill replied at the same time.

Bill stuck a fork into the eggs and placed them in his mouth. "How goes it?"

"One day at a time."

"Not much of a choice." Bill held out his hand. "Have a seat."

Annie took a seat. She leaned in and whispered, "I have a table of women over there that will throw a fit if I ignore them too long."

"Two women, one man."

Annie took a second look. "Three women. Get your prescription lenses updated there, buddy."

"Dick!" Bill shouted over to the table. The man that Annie thought was a woman looked up and nodded.

"Bill, how are you?"

"Very well. Yourself?"

"The same."

They smiled and continued about their business.

"You're shitting me!"

"Language." Bill held up his finger as a stern warning.

"I've waited on that woman, man, a few times and I never even thought he was anything other than a woman. Didn't even cross my mind. How do you know him?"

"Just casually." He continued eating nonchalantly completely uninterested in the bragging rights he rightfully earned.

"I'm appalled. I can't believe I didn't know . . ."

"I can tell."

"He looks just like a . . ."

Bill nodded at the confusion. "Some people don't age well."

"He has breasts and wears bright yellow sweaters!" She kept her voice as down as possible despite her shock.

"Some men grow larger breasts than others," Bill said and looked Annie directly in the eyes. "You grow old. You get on medications. Your testosterone wanes. Anyway, how's single life treating you?"

"It hurts sometimes. Liberating other times." She looked down and pretended to pick at a hangnail that wasn't there. "Afraid."

"Of?"

"What if I'll never find another?"

"You will."

"But . . ."

"But nothing, Annie." Bill placed his hand on top of hers and squeezed with a fatherly gesture of affection. "You will. I guarantee it."

"I'm afraid that in a month or two I'll be living at home. At thirty. With no job."

"Fear justified." Bill took a sip of his coffee.

"And what if this party planning is just a false dream I'm forcing myself to pursue. What if I can't become anything and what if I'm nothing more than a waitress?"

She instinctively looked over to Janice who was giving her and Bill the stink-eye. Her curmudgeon demeanor and deliberate, exaggerated movements were meant to threaten and show hostility. Janice was upset, maybe she needed a cigarette, maybe she looked at the youthful beauty and possibilities that Annie projected, or maybe she was just pissed that Annie was sitting and fraternizing with the customers when she should be on her feet and serving her other tables.

Bill continued, "Everyone fears that the best years are behind them but, you know what? You'll look back on this time and think that these were the best times and that they are now behind you."

"You're telling me to live in the moment?"

"I'm telling you to live. Look, Annie, there's nothing I'd like more than to sit here every morning and have you pour my coffee, bring me breakfast and a smile, but a part of me knows that doing so would make these days the best days for you. You'll look back and see that the best days have passed and, you know what? They would have. I love my kids but when my daughter wanted to go to Los Angeles to be an actress I knew I had to let her because not letting her would kill her. Who cares if she ended up in Minnesota?" Bill shrugged his shoulders. "She tried."

"You should beg your kids to call you back."

"This conversation isn't about me."

"Let's make it about you. Tell me about your wife."

Annie remained silent as Bill looked downward at his newspaper. "Sorry, Annie." She stood up and walked to her other table. She studied the man she thought was a woman trying to see past the feminine exterior. Her eyes deceived her.

"We're okay, honey." One of the ladies said.

"Stay as long as you'd like and don't hesitate to holler if you need anything."

The three didn't respond to Annie's kindness and looked at each other picking up the conversation where they left off prior to Annie's interruption.

She started back towards Bill. "Refill, Bill?"

He held up a hand declining her offer.

Annie took a seat across from Bill once again.

"Ever consider dating again?"

"Are you offering?" Bill asked with a smile.

She avoided the remark. "You've been so adamant about me getting back into the dating world, every day you ask me. Why not you?"

"I've done it all before. I'm comfortable."

There was a moment of silence.

"Was she *the one*?"

He dismissed her question. "There is no such thing as *the one*."

"You don't believe in soul mates?" He didn't answer so she proceeded. "I have to. What's there really in the world besides the one you're supposed to spend the rest of your life with?"

Bill's head popped up as if he were waiting for the right time to strike back. "Oh there's plenty. There are what? Seven billion people in the world? Cut it in half and you're telling me I have to find my one true love in one of 3.5 billion? What if my true love is a man? And all I've been focused on are women. What if you're my true love? Would you see yourself with someone 40 years your senior? The truth is there are at least a million people better than who ever you are with." Bill let the thought sink in before knocking his point him. "But, you see Annie, that very fact is irrelevant. When you first start dating you still have the eye out for something different, right? Something better? Then there's a history and as you build a life with this person it suddenly doesn't matter if your soul mate comes along because . . . it simply does not matter."

Bill paused to gather his thoughts. "So, was my wife *the one?*" Bill shrugged his shoulders. "Maybe, maybe not. I loved her as if she was though and my life with her meant more than the never ending bullshit search for the supposed *one.*"

"That's sweet." Annie had a smile plastered on her face that hurt her cheeks. "You're going to make me cry."

"I try to make at least one woman cry every day," Bill responded jokingly.

She chuckled and successfully held back her tears. "But it's been almost eight years since your wife passed away. Why haven't you sought another woman just to have the company of someone?"

Bill placed his elbows on the table and rested the top of his chin on his hands. "Once I met her she became the only one I ever wanted."

"She's your soul mate. She was *the one,*" Annie said in a whisper with a beaming smile as if Bill's whole point-of-view became irrelevant.

Bill shook his head slightly, barely noticeable, and reiterated. "She's the only *one* I ever wanted."

Annie began rising from the booth and looking off towards counter. "Aldo's giving me the look."

"Hey." Bill blurted out to keep her close. He touched her hand to make his following statement as meaningful as he can. "Most people try to make someone *the one*. If you do that, they're not *the one*."

"I tried to make Andre *the one*," she admitted.

"Don't search for that special someone. They'll find you. There are a lot of special someones out there for you, Annie."

"He hasn't made a move on me. He's not going to make a move on me. I'm not going to make a move on him," Annie said. She was awake and alert at the start of the shift on a morning when the rain was pouring into the streets like buckets from the sky.

"Oh honey, I'm not worried about Johnny Boy, I'm worried about you polishing off a bottle of wine and knocking on the door across the hall in hopes of getting Andre back between your legs. I'm still so joyful that Andre is out of your life." She pointed a finger towards Annie and wagged it lightly. "You may be a little heartbroken but I see the happiness emanating from those sweet cheeks of yours."

Annie looked downward and crossed her arms. "Don't think knocking on that door across the hall hasn't crossed my mind."

"Sweetie, you need to get laid. I need to get laid. Let's go out and find some frat boys wanting something fast!"

"I have considerably more wrinkles then you."

"Knock it off, you're adorable, you're beautiful and probably a tiger in the sack. Don't stand there and tell me you haven't been itching for a rebound."

Bethany replaced the coffee filter and tossed in the grounded up beans. She pressed the on button which lit up and began filtering boiling water through the grounds and into the coffee pot.

The restaurant was minutes away from opening and both women were eagerly awaiting the aroma of brewed coffee to fill the air and replace the scent of cleaning agents.

"How was Florida?"

"Yuck, muggy. Sunny, but muggy." Bethany shrugged. "It was a family reunion so while I wanted to get drunk as a senior on spring break in a tropical environment I was tending to my Aunt Francis who has never been young. I remember her turning eighty like fifteen years ago. I drank the first night then swore off drinking on the second day."

"Why?"

"My uncle was getting a little too flirtatious. I thought he wanted to buy me drinks because he hadn't seen me in years. Then the advances."

"Eww."

"Well, he married into the family so while creepy and gross, at least he wasn't technically a blood relative."

"That makes it better," Annie responded sarcastically.

Janice entered the restaurant bringing in tension towards the morning.

"There's nothing wrong with random acts of sex," Bethany stated.

Annie didn't dismiss the idea.

"Good morning," both Annie and Bethany said at the same time to Janice as she crossed to the opposite side of the counter.

"Hello." She rushed into the kitchen to clock in. She popped out seconds later. "Where's Aldo?"

"The market."

Janice sighed as if his absence was an extreme inconvenience. Five minutes later after three solid minutes of ranting and complaining she decided to slip out for a cigarette. She hugged the building to stay under the canopy and out of the rain.

"Does Jon mind if you bring a sexual deviant back to the apartment?" Bethany asked leaning in suggestively.

The door chimed as a father and son entered.

"What's the matter with you?" Annie was entertained but felt the first hints of annoyance about the constant insistence that she find a man to have fun with.

"That's a long list to sift through." Bethany walked to the table and cheerfully greeted the first two customers of the morning. Both ordered coffee.

21

Jonie could be mistaken for a real bitch. It had nothing to do with her personality because it only took two minutes of being with her that Annie realized how great of a person she could be.

It was how she presented herself. She wore her hair back and it often looked tight, the kind of tight that could cause a headache. Her upper lip had a slight curvature which made her seem prissy as her dark, piercing eyes gazed upon you. She was petite and dressed nicer than one would expect someone to dress in any given situation. She was the kind of girl who may not realize that she was dressing for New York in a city that prided itself on casual. The dark colors she wore matched the dark eyeliner and mascara she applied.

The first impression she emanated was one of manipulation. She would excel as a lawyer but instead received a marketing degree with little idea of the lack of prospects that would be available to her.

"Everyone seems to have a marketing degree," Jonie had complained, frustrated by her constant denial of even a single interview at the places she sent her resume to.

No one ever told her of that first impression she made and surely Jon had felt the same way upon meeting her; a feeling he would never state out loud though.

"Nice to meet you," Jonie said shaking Annie's hand within moments of entering the apartment. She instantly gravitated under the arm of Jon refusing to let go of the man she hadn't seen in months.

"Nice to meet you too." Annie told both Jon and Jonie that she had errands to run. It was a lie she expressed as a way to allow the two lovebirds an afternoon of getting reacquainted.

"Well, we're going out tonight, right?" Jonie asked towards Jon.

"Absolutely. I was thinking Bleacher Bar," Jon responded looking at his girlfriend, then towards Annie.

"I can't wait to learn more about you, Annie." Although it seemed well-intentioned, Annie couldn't help interpret the invitation as a challenge. If Jonie didn't approve of Annie, then she would be evicted minutes after Jonie went back to Michigan.

"Oh." The statement took her aback and she let a smile creep across her lips. "Well, Jon's just crazy about you, Jonie, so I can't wait to learn more about you too."

Annie left the apartment and predicted that by the time she reached the elevator half their clothes would be on the floor lining a path to Jon's bedroom.

Why she was worried that Andre would hear the noises and wrongly believe that it was her and Jon she did not know. Or understand. She ended the relationship but he hardly seemed to care, or fight for it at the time. A part of her didn't want him thinking that she was unfaithful during the tenure of their courtship and she believed that he believed that Jon was a threat.

Annie stepped out onto the sidewalk and paused as a group of joggers raced by her. They were focused on pedestrians in front of them and the music bumping through the ear buds jammed into their ears.

A block from the apartment a homeless man jiggled a cup with change inside asking for a little more. Annie's heart broke for him and she dug out a couple quarters from her purse just before she reached him.

"God bless you, pretty lady," he said.

A conversation played in her head as she continued forward. It was the usual pessimistic attitude that Andre portrayed towards those asking for change. "They're just going to blow it on booze. Don't give them money. Just ignore them." She defended the helpless man or woman when they approached them or asked while sitting upon the ground but he would shrug off her kindness and call her a sucker adding sarcastically and loudly, "I'm sure they're going to use the money to buy something that would advance their social status."

Despite the memory of a callous Andre, Annie found herself missing him. She missed his familiarity and wished that she could lie back in the bed they once shared. It was a miracle, she thought, that in the weeks that has passed since their breakup that she has not seen any evidence that Andre even lived there. In fairness though, she avoided him. She left for work in the morning when she knew it was too early for Andre to leave for work; she arrived back at the apartment too early for his arrival. Many nights she spent inside the apartment for fear that she would run into him. When doors opened and closed out in the hall she held her breath.

Jon ran into him once and all Andre had to say was that he had some mail addressed to Annie. He asked if Jon had still seen her and, if so, if he could leave the mail with him.

Jon responded simply. "Sure. The next time I see her I'll pass it along."

Every few days she would also receive mail that was forwarded from her old address to the new one she registered. Would the mail carrier place her mail with her new address into the old box simply by name recognition? If so, did Andre recognize it? Annie wondered if Andre suspected that she was sleeping on the pull-out couch in the neighbor's apartment.

She felt a sting when she thought that Andre had written her off completely and couldn't care less where she was or with whom. Perhaps it was his way of coping through the break-up, simple avoidance; out-of-sight, out-of-mind.

By instinct Annie arrived at Aldo's. She stepped inside and caught the eye of a waitress she met only once; a high school kid trying to save up some money to go to college, but only had three-hundred-dollars in the bank. She had a weakness for spoiling her boyfriends and they were keen to the idea of her spending her hard earned money on the movies they wanted to see. She paid for more action movies then she cared to see and rarely saw the rom-coms that fought the box office on the same weekend.

"Sit wherever you want," the waitress said and Annie was too considerate to say that she knew the drill. When the waitress approached the table she didn't notice who Annie was at first and asked if it would just be her or if another person was expected.

"Just me. Could I get a water, please? And a coffee?"

"Sure." The waitress nodded towards the edge of the table. "Menu's over there."

Annie looked around the empty restaurant contemplating how it could remain in business with so little business coming in. It was only four in the afternoon though.

It was a different atmosphere than she was used to seeing. The morning sun would beam in from the eastside windows and light the place with bright white that was almost daunting if the light struck at the wrong angles. October was the month that was the worst. Her first October at Aldo's she noticed a major decrease in those with hangovers coming to coat their stomachs with greasy food; the sun shone too brightly for their headaches. The late afternoon light barely broke past the nearby buildings that towered over the restaurant causing the restaurant light bulbs to create an essence of falseness.

She liked mornings.

"Here you go," the waitress said placing the mug of coffee in front of Annie. "Ready to order?"

"I was just going to sit here for a while."

"Oh." The waitress lowered her pad of paper. "Okay. Let me know if you want anything." She moved to a countertop seat where a textbook was opened next to a pad of paper. She buried her nose into the biology text book.

Annie buried her nose into a celebrity magazine she picked up when she purchased Jodi Picoult's new novel. She had reservations about buying the twenty-dollar hardcover but she hadn't the mental clarity at the time to browse for something beyond the bestsellers display.

As she flipped through the magazine pages of celebrities that were celebrities for no reason beyond being the daughter of someone with a lot of money and a publicly leaked sex tape or being on a reality cable television show she felt a sense of despair. It all resonated with their perceived amount success and her lack of it.

"Maybe I should make a sex tape," she mumbled and didn't think she had the youthful looks that these girls had. That added more gloom to her lowering sense of self when she saw the girlfriend/ boyfriend couple presented in the feature story was only twenty-two. It was reported that this supposed star made eight-million-dollars last year being an idiot on TV and making guest appearances at clubs. She suddenly had trouble stomaching a sip of coffee.

She wanted to cry. At what point did the possibilities seem to fall to the wayside?

"Hey!" She called out to the waitress at the countertop. She turned in her seat. "Don't be working here at thirty, okay?"

"Oh . . . kay." She was confused.

"I work here. And I'm thirty."

The familiarity appeared in the waitress' eyes. "I knew I knew you."

"Yeah. Don't be here at thirty."

"Oh trust me. I do not plan on that happening to me," she responded with a chuckle and a tone that demeaned the thought of anyone as old as thirty serving tables at Aldo's Restaurant. She didn't realize the sting of her remark and didn't apologize for it.

Annie faked a smile with a heavy sigh and looked back down at the magazine. "Me neither." She looked at the back of the waitress absorbed in homework and thought how nice it was to be young and optimistic.

Annie continued flipping through the pages of the magazine trying to turn her mood around to something more positive. She tried telling herself that she was still young and still had a whole life ahead of her. Her only problem was the inability to take her own advice to heart.

"Did you always want to be a waitress?" The waitress asked her in a vain attempt to procrastinate studying.

"I went to school for it."

"Really!" The waitress was shocked such a curriculum existed.

"No, not really," Annie replied. "I went to school to be a party-planner.

"Oh that's cool. Why aren't you doing that?"

"I'm not sure."

"I have a cousin who went to school to be a sociologist and barely passed. He graduated though but works at a cell phone kiosk in the mall. He's thinking of going back to school but he's twenty-nine."

"What does one do with a sociology degree?"

The waitress shrugged her shoulders. "I guess you're supposed to use it as a spring board to another degree but he didn't want to get a Master's and my aunt and uncle didn't want to front him the money. He couldn't get a loan or anything because he had like $50,000 in debt. It sucks but, you know, he might go back to school so you can go back to school too."

"That is an option."

"You don't have debt do you?"

Annie shook her head. "Not yet."

"People who have debt are messed up. They're ruining this country. How could so many people owe so much money? I don't ever want to have debt."

"Good luck with that."

"Thanks," the waitress said bubbly.

"Do you want to own a house?"

"Of course! My husband and I will have a beautiful house on a cute tree-lined street like Beacon and we can walk our dogs down to the water. Oh, it will be perfect. I want a house on a lake too, maybe a summer home at the Cape."

"Are you going to have a mortgage for any of these homes?"

"Sure, I guess. I don't know much about that but, like, you need one to buy a house, right?"

"Unless you pay cash. You know, a mortgage is a form of debt. It's borrowed money and so you're in debt to the bank."

The waitress looked confused. Annie wasn't making a lick of sense. "That's not, like, real debt."

Annie opened her mouth to ask a follow-up question but hesitated. She didn't want to listen to another answer from the waitress nor try to correct her naïve view of the world. Let her figure it out on her own, she thought. Annie lifted her coffee and took a sip.

"Maybe I should go back to school," Annie stated, her head facing away from Jonie as she watched the television screens. The roar of the crowd inside Bleacher Bar picked up as the Red Sox centerfielder raced to the warning track to catch a line drive. His grab prevented the runner at second from making it all the way home.

Bleacher Bar was located behind the centerfield wall of Fenway Park with windows looking out onto the field. It was small with the bar lining one wall and a few tables. Most people, including Jonie and Annie, had to stand.

"What would you want to do?" Jonie asked taking a drink of her glass of red wine. There were no tables available so she held Jon's Jack and Coke in the other. He had raced off to the bathroom.

"I don't know." Annie's eyebrows furrowed inward with anxiety and worry. "I don't know what I would do."

"Then don't go back. At least not yet. At least not until you know what you want to do."

Jonie looked upwards towards the men's bathroom. It was situated on the second level up a flight of stairs. A window above the urinals made it possible for the men to look down upon the bar and towards the door that led to the field at Fenway Park. He waved comically, enthusiastically thrilled with the men's room set up. Both Annie and Jonie lifted their glasses to him.

"What a weirdo," Jonie said without moving her lips.

"Hey, you're the one who's dating him." Annie looked at Jonie. "At least we can see him leave the urinal so we should know if he washes his hand before returning."

"Oh, Jon washes his hands."

"Are you certain?"

"He washes his hands after touching a restaurant menu. He's a bit of a germ-a-phobe."

"Really?" Annie looked up towards the window in the bathroom and saw that Jon had finished. Another man replaced him and starred out at the bar. "I never really noticed."

"His obsessive-compulsive behavior is very subtle." There was a brief moment of silence between the two as they watched the pitcher deliver a high pitch that walked the batter. There was moderate groan as the batter took his base. "So, negative on party planning?"

Annie turned back towards Jonie with the same defeated look she projected whenever she was discussing her ambitions. "I just don't know. I used to love it but the lack of prospects is causing me to doubt it. Maybe it's a hobby and not a career, you know, like someone who loves movies but can't write a screenplay to save their life. Maybe I can't plan a party to save my life."

"Jon told me about the one party you threw. He said it was nice."

"It was a handful of decorations. Anyone could do that. No one is going to pay me to throw a house party."

"If you woke up with an infinite amount of money tomorrow morning, what would you want to do?"

"Roll over and go back to sleep," Annie replied.

Jonie acknowledged the statement with a clank against Annie's glass. "I'll drink to that." And they did. "But really, Annie, what would you do after you caught a couple more winks?"

The thought was heart-wrenching. As she shook her head with a lost expression overcoming her face her shoulders slumped downward and she replied, "I really don't know. Do you have any idea how frustrating that is?"

Jon popped up and grabbed his drink from Jonie's hand. "Sad face," he said looking at Annie. He turned to his girlfriend. "Honey, what did you say?"

"Nothing," Annie replied. "We're just talking about career opportunities."

"Or lack thereof," Jon added. He took a big drink and swallowed it hard. "Some tastes you just don't get used to. I'm going to have to return to that bartender for my next one."

"Strong?"

"Very." Jon took an additional sip.

"I'm getting real sick of trying to figure it all out," Annie stated. "I thought I had it all figured out."

"We all had it figured out at twenty-two, didn't we?" Jon said taking another drink.

"Jonie's great." Annie told Bill. "But when she asked me what I wanted to do, I felt lost again. I thought I had it all figured out. Where did it all go wrong?"

"Oh well, no one really has it figured out and if they say they do, they're putting up a false front."

"There's a waitress who serves at night and she's just in high school but she seems to have it all figured out. I wish I could have the optimism of youth; that naivety of youth. All those opportunities ahead of her that she doesn't even know are there. At what point did the possibilities in life fade away?"

Bill plopped downward onto his recliner with an easing groan and popped the foot rest up. Annie looked at the bottom of his socks. They were white with flecks of brown dirt stained on them from the dust accumulated on the hardwood floor and the rug which was worn thin. He wore flannel pajama pants and a gray T-shirt below a raggedy old bathrobe that was comfortably aged to perfection.

"You're looking at what you could've done at eighteen. Focus on what you can do and not the opportunities that were missed. You've missed those opportunities. Instead of repeating those mistakes go find new ones to make." He spoke as if he had this conversation with her a hundred times before. But he hadn't. He wanted this daughter-like figure to succeed.

"That's the problem though. I don't even know what mistakes to make!" She eyeballed the kitchen. Bill took notice.

"Go, of course," he said and Annie headed towards the kitchen to prepare a drink.

She exited with the well-known sour look of whiskey on the rocks. She coughed. "Still haven't acquired that taste."

"How could so many people lack direction?" Bill questioned rhetorically. "I certainly can't remember feeling that way. I can't remember anyone I know feeling that way." He pointed his finger accusingly towards Annie. "You're all like James Dean in *Rebel Without a Cause*! Ever see it?"

"No."

He waved it off. "It's all right. Don't feel obligated to watch it. The kid is all rebelling without a cause."

"Imagine that."

Bill considered the film, "I guess he was lost like you. Everyone seems to be lost."

"Who's everyone?"

"You and . . ."

Annie raised an eyebrow.

". . . Jon."

"That's two."

"Is this about me or about you?" There was no answer. Bill lifted the remote control and turned the television on. "Don't stand. Sit."

Annie did as she was told as Bill started viewing the channel guide. He stopped at *Shawshank Redemption*. Bill commented, "How about the all *Shawshank Redemption*, all the time channel."

"They do seem to play it all the time. I love this movie," Annie stated. It cut right to a commercial. Bill tilted his head towards Annie as she took another big sip of the whiskey. She noticed his gaze. "I'm stressed. Don't judge me."

"I'm always judging you." Bill smiled at his attempt at brevity. "Always."

The telephone rang and both halted their conversation recognizing that this was a very rare occurrence. It rang a second time.

"Are you going to answer that?" Annie asked.

"Do you want to answer that?"

It rang a third time.

"I'm not expecting any calls," Annie replied.

Fourth time.

"Me neither."

Annie lifted off of the couch and raced to the telephone as the phone rang a fifth time. "Do you have an answering machine?"

"Yes."

Annie looked at the caller ID which only indicated a Minnesota call and a phone number she didn't recognize. "Minnesota," she stated looking at Bill.

He didn't respond and Annie lifted the phone and clicked the dial icon. "Hello?"

Bill stared at her curious on the conversation.

"I'm a friend of Bill's. Would you like to speak with him? . . . Just a friend . . . not a girlfriend . . . . okay." Annie put the phone into her shoulder and started walking towards Bill. "It's Chrissy." She held the phone outwards and Bill crossed his arms shaking his head. She insisted and he shook his head again with more dramatics and flare. She held the phone right to his ear but he still refused to grasp it. He heard the conversation his daughter was having. She was telling someone that an unidentified woman had answered. He remained frozen at hearing the voice of a woman he had not heard in years.

Annie put the phone back on her shoulder. She whispered, "Why won't you talk to her?"

His head shook quickly as if he had a debilitating phobia towards the activity. He quietly responded, "Because I can't. Because it's been too long."

Annie could now see the pain in his eyes. She could see the tension in his body and his hands were shaking under the cover of his bathrobe.

"She's your daughter."

"What am I going to say?"

"Start with 'hello, good to hear from you' and go from there."

He finally released his hands and pointed towards Annie's drink that sat upon the coffee table. She offered it to him and he sucked every last drop back. He handed it to Annie and she exchanged it for the cordless phone.

He let out a sigh and closed his eyes bringing the phone to his ear. "Hello? . . . it's good to hear from you . . ."

Annie offered two thumbs up and vacated the room leaving Bill with some privacy to carry on his phone conversation. She entered the bathroom and closed the door slowly turning the knob so the click of the lock didn't sound throughout the room. She wasn't sure why she felt the desire to be so delicate in all her movements. She sat down on the toilet seat cover and allowed a loud breath to spill outward both excited and nervous at the unexpected call.

She took a moment to look around the bathroom. She remembered seeing Bill lying upon the floor. It seemed so long ago. She noticed the frosted shower liner with hints of mold appearing at the corners and a bar of soap and single bottle of shampoo/conditioner mix hanging from a metal shelf hanging off of the shower head. She guessed that most of the toiletries hid behind the mirror that opened to a cabinet and the drawers under the sink. He was lucky he had someone clean this apartment once a week; she could only imagine how much of a disaster it would be if he didn't get the help. She suspected that his wife did the cleaning in their house in the suburbs and having to scrub a bathtub never quite occurred to him until he found himself alone in an apartment.

His towel was a dark blue and it looked super soft when dry. His hand towel was light green and didn't match the décor of the bathroom one bit. There was a small vase with fake fall-like colored flowers popping out; an item that was probably as old as one of his children and one that he never quite noticed until he had to pack it on moving day.

She rose to her feet and opened the bathroom door as cautiously as she had closed it. She poked her head out hearing Bill's conversation with his daughter.

Annie stepped in front of him and pointed towards the door.

Bill nodded and moved the phone to his shoulder and sincerely said to Annie, "Thank you."

She nodded in return with a smile and left the apartment.

As she walked down the hallway towards the elevator she wondered what prompted the call and eagerly awaited the discussion her and Bill would have the next day at the restaurant.

She felt a sense of pride that better days were ahead because Bill was able to speak with one of his children. She hoped the feeling would last beyond the evening.

Annie shoved her hands into her pockets and strolled down to the street.

The walkway to her apartment building was well lit but she couldn't shake the sense of gloom that she felt every time she walked up to the building since the break up. There wasn't a single time that she wondered if she would run into Andre. She was fortunate to have avoided him and, each time she entered Jon's apartment, she thought of her relief. It was odd to think how okay she had been with not talking or seeing the man she saw almost every single day for five years. It was a strange sensation that she couldn't shake.

This time was different. She heard the screams before the elevator doors opened.

Andre stood at Jon's apartment door banging loudly. He didn't hear the elevator doors open and Annie could hear him shouting vile remarks and accusations towards Jon.

"You fucking asshole! Open this fucking door!" Andre held an envelope in his hand. "I have some fucking mail with Annie's name but your address on it!" He pounded again and his voice cracked as he spouted blames of infidelity. "I can hear you two fucking! Open this door so I can kick your fucking ass!"

"Andre!" Annie shouted.

He stopped rapping his fists on the door and looked down the hallway at Annie.

"What the hell are you doing?" She hollered.

A bald-headed resident with thick glasses from the down the hall opened his door and poked his head out.

Andre shifted his body and stood up straight collecting his wits. He looked at the closed door then back at Annie.

"Someone is having sex!" He yelled not realizing that he shouldn't have said the first thing that came to his mind. There were no noises emanating from the other side of the wall.

"And you're surprised by this?" Annie reached the door and Andre held out an envelope.

"This came for you. It was addressed to this address." Andre pointed to the door. "Do you live here?"

Annie pulled out her key and moved towards the lock. Andre backed away from the door but stood close by. "Yes. This is where I currently live." Her tone was harsh, precise and hostile.

Andre responded with denigrating remarks. "Something is the matter with you, Annie. You're sick in the head. Living across the hall from me is both pathetic and borderline creepy."

She grabbed the envelope from his light grasp. "Thanks for bringing my mail. Good night." She opened the door and stepped inside letting the door close behind her without turning to see his reaction. She knew her casual ignoring of his condescending statement would irk him. She had no interest in getting him back and she didn't care what he thought of her living situation.

"I was here first!" Andre screamed from the opposite side of the hallway like a little boy claiming his spot. There was silence until Andre slammed the door to his apartment.

Annie looked up towards the bedroom and saw Jon and Jonie standing half-naked under the door frame. Jon's arm was wrapped around his girlfriend and they were speechless.

Annie was speechless as well and her emotions began to overflow with a combination of missing Andre, being content that he is no longer a main part of her life and life in general.

Tears spilled from her eyes and she was so overwrought with the stress that she could barely audibly display her feelings. She choked up the noises of crying but they came out as mere gasps of air.

She removed herself from the room locking herself inside the bathroom and immediately collapsing to the floor. She buried her head in her folded arms bending her body onto her bent knees.

There was a light tapping on the door.

"Annie? We're here," Jonie said compassionately from the other side of the door. "If you need us, we're here for you. We can drink martinis and watch *Adventures in Babysitting*."

Jon added, "And we won't be having sex anymore or . . . anything. Ow!"

"Sit on the couch," Jonie ordered Jon quietly but Annie still heard her demand.

"I was just . . . okay."

Annie lifted her head. "I'm okay you two. I just . . ."

"Right. Well, we're here for you."

The comment brought a smile to Annie's tear-soaked cheeks. "Thanks."

Annie composed her self. It had been a solid thirty minutes of thinking and swapping between fits of anger and bout of hope before she lifted her body off of the floor and looked in the mirror.

"Holy shit," she muttered after taking in the look of puffiness under her red eyes, disheveled hair and runny nose. She breathed out a sigh of near-horror as she ran the warm water from the sink to wash her face. "I'm stepping out," Annie announced. "Don't judge me. I look like a train wreck."

Annie walked into the living room where Jon and Jonie were sitting on the couch. Jonie took a sip of the merlot in her wine glass. It was an invite for Annie to abide.

"How ya doing?" Jon asked.

"There's a difference between how I'm doing now versus how I will be doing later. I'm fine now."

"And later?"

"TBD."

"You want to go out?" Jonie asked. "Don't feel obligated. I'm here to visit Jon and I'm visiting Jon."

"Thirty minutes ago you said you were here for me," Annie shot back jokingly while still retaining her saddened demeanor. "Not Jon."

"You should be a politician," Jonie responded raising her glass.

"You should be a journalist twisting a politician's words," Jon said.

"I should be drunk. Now."

Jon stood up. "As the only responsible adult in the room, and by responsible I mean the only one without income, I don't think inebriation is the best route when you have to wake up at five in the morning."

Annie started approaching and Jonie stood up as well.

"Voice of reason . . ." Annie directed towards Jon. ". . . shut the hell up."

They all huddled into a group hug.

22

She was fatigued from a late night of wine drinking and her head ached from the dehydration. She could easily conquer both challenges once her mind shifted from idle movements into work mode.

It was six in the morning and the doors to Aldo's were unlocked. He usually kept them unlocked when he let the first waitress who showed up inside. The likelihood of getting slammed was minimal at this hour.

"One time," Aldo had said once, "Just one time and that was because there was a bus of senior citizens meeting two doors down ready to go on a day trip to the casino."

Annie placed the ketchups and mustards on the table, ensured the salts and peppers were full and walked into the kitchen until she was beckoned to duty.

"How's it going, Omar?" She asked the cook as he chopped up green peppers. She filled a cup with water and gulped it down.

He yawned deeply and kept an eye on the knife responding, "Had a date last night."

"Yeah?"

"Don't think there will be another."

"Why do you say that?"

He stopped and looked at Annie. "Because she said I was too nice. It was our third and final date." He looked back down grabbing another green pepper and started hacking away; the first knife strike knocked loudly against the plastic cutting board.

"I'm sorry." Annie responded then followed up with her own question. "She thought you were too nice?"

"I'm a sweetheart. I'm a gentleman."

"Are you sure you have the definition of those too adjectives correct?"

"I'm flirty with you, sugar-breasts," he giggled.

"You're sexually harassing."

"Tomato. Toh-ma-to." He slid the tiny pieces of green pepper into a larger pile of green peppers.

"Why aren't you a gentleman to me?"

"Because you're a friend. You would never sleep with me or date me so we're friends."

"That's not true."

He shot her a look of pessimism.

"Okay, that's not entirely true."

"It's reality. I'd treat you real good though."

"But since you can't sleep with me you harass me."

Omar placed an onion on the cutting board. "Yeah." He started slicing into the onion. "You better leave. I don't want you to see me cry."

Annie walked to the door leading into the restaurant and turned back. "I'm sorry it didn't work out."

"She was a bitch."

She gave him a warm smile. "She was," Annie responded assuredly.

The first patron of the morning stepped inside. He was a tall, heavy-set man in his late forties wearing a trucker hat and, despite the warm temperatures expected for the day, a flannel button-up shirt that seemed to have been in use since the Clinton administration. He had the look of constant filthiness but she could smell strong fresh soap on his body.

"Good morning," Annie said cheerfully. "Coffee?"

"Please." His voice was as rough as the stubble on his chin. She had a mug ready and poured him a cup. "Do you have any of those flavored creams?"

"We don't. I'm sorry."

"I really like those flavored creams. I really like the . . ." He lifted his eyes skyward. "I think it's the brown one. Cinnamon, maybe. Amaretto." He waved his hand as if removing the idea from a dry-erase board and removed his hat tossing it aside. His hair was long and looked greasy but Annie didn't smell the offensive odors of unwashed hair. "It's irrelevant."

"I'll come back in a minute unless you know what you want."

"I'll need a minute, sweetheart."

Annie stepped away and went back in the kitchen. "First customer is here. You've been warned." She popped back out and saw the man's menu was closed.

He ordered a stack of pancakes, eggs, sausage and hash browns. She filled the hearty, heavy order and had it sitting in front of him under ten minutes.

Customers started entering. She recognized the usual faces and Bethany and Simone meandered in by six-thirty.

The constant ebb and flow of customers and a Motrin kept her headache at bay and she was peeing every forty-five minutes thanks to her desire to stay hydrated by pounding back glasses of water.

Aldo was content that there was a brief moment when all the tables were taken up and he had to pull a pad of paper to write names down. "It shouldn't be more than five or ten minutes, folks!" He stated with a smile. "Thank you for your patience."

At ten o'clock the rush was subsiding and the patrons with no places to be were digging their noses into newspapers, discussing politics or gossiping with their booth mates.

Janice entered to help battle the lunch crowd expected by 11:30. The scent of cigarettes clung onto her clothes and her demeanor represented hostility. "This day needs to be over with now," she blurted out as she crossed the counter and slipped into the kitchen.

Bethany passed by her and exchanged a courteous but meaningless greeting.

She all but tore off her apron. "Done!" She announced slamming it onto the counter and burying her head into her arms. Annie was behind the counter wiping down the previous customer's mess. She swore off syrup after she saw how it stuck to the table and how much of a pain it could be to wipe up.

"Tell me your troubles," Annie said to Bethany.

"I want to go home and nap until tomorrow morning." Bethany lifted her head pulling her phone out of her front pants pocket. "Why hasn't that douche bag texted me back?"

"You sure he's awake?"

"Yes. He had to be in the office at 7:30 this morning. I told him it would be okay to text me."

"You should text him," Annie advised.

Bethany looked at her phone longingly, worried. "I did. Twice."

"Did you sleep with him?" Annie asked in a lowered voice leaning in close to her friend.

"No. I . . ." She tilted her head indicating she went down on him. "If we did have sex I highly doubt I'd feel anything," she mumbled. "It was like the size of a baby carrot."

"It's not the size of the dog in the fight. It's the fight in the dog."

Annie surveyed the restaurant checking for customers eagerly awaiting a refill on their beverages or trying to get the attention of one of the waitresses.

"Whatever. If he can deal with my non-existent breasts, I can deal with his non-existent weenie. I can't even call it a penis, weenie is just so much more appropriate of a term."

"That's what you get for going after the rich and powerful."

"He's not rich or powerful. This is just karma for having once sought those assholes that drove BMWs. He's actually a really nice guy." Bethany looked apprehensively at Annie and responded as if pleading her case and justifying her choices. "He's not that small."

Annie giggled at Bethany's about-face. "Neither are your breasts."

Bethany moaned a saddened sigh checking her phone once again.

Annie looked up and saw Bill opening the door to Aldo's. She wanted to rush up to him for a hug the moment he stepped inside but settled for a simple wave as he approached Aldo. Bill placed his hands roughly onto Aldo's shoulders. "Get off your lazy ass and get a job, old man!" Bill stated.

Aldo turned around and they shook hands. "You're the one drilling into my children's Social Security accounts, why don't you get a greeting job at Wal-Mart?"

"Yeah, us old folks," he started walking towards an empty booth, "we're just living too long nowadays."

Aldo followed and took the opposite side of the booth of Bill. "It's been too long, Bill. What's the good word?"

"I see you every day. You can always come over and talk about that Republican schmuck you voted for so he can vote to stop funding schools."

"Oh Bill, how I miss your insistence that your liberal-leaning atheist should tax my payroll more encouraging me to jack up the price of waffles."

"You're not raising the price of waffles are you?"

Aldo comically shrugged his shoulders. "We'll see who gets elected governor this time around."

"Go elephants!" Bill stated and held up his finger when he spotted Annie. "I'm going to need some waffles."

"Charge him double," Aldo responded. "Call it a poll tax." He winked at Bill.

Annie approached the table and asked, "Coffee this morning?"

"Absolutely."

"We have some things to talk about, you and me," Annie told Bill. "You save some time."

"I expected that you would make further inquiries about last night." Bill pulled a tiny pad of paper from his inside jacket pocket. "I wrote down some highlights."

Aldo pointed a finger at Bill. "No dating the wait-staff."

"Oh, Aldo," Annie started in a lovey-dovey tone, "He's my dream boat."

"Don't tease him, Annie, he has heart trouble."

They had a chuckle and Annie stepped away to hand the order to Omar and fill a mug with coffee.

"What are you doing with the rest of your morning?" Annie asked Bethany.

"I should go by where he works," she stated as if it were a good idea.

Annie deflected with sarcasm. "That should do the trick."

Bethany yawned. "Maybe I'll just go for a run."

"Text me later. We'll go out."

"Okay." Bethany rose from her stool and hugged Annie.

Annie opted to lay low allowing Aldo and Bill to have their conversations without her interrupting until the surly Janice broke up their complaining about the rise in monthly Charlie Card rates for public transportation. She wanted to file her own kind of complaint against having to take care of her first customer who notoriously left a less-than-desirable tip. Aldo moved her into the kitchen to discuss the issue further—the same customer who was a poor tipper seemed to get pawned onto her, she protested. She didn't mind the bad tipper as long as she wasn't the one taking care of him. Aldo promised to be more mindful of who gets pawned onto whom and begged her to get back to work. "I will refuse to wait on them and they can just sit there all day for all I care."

"Have a smoke break." Aldo offered and she gladly obliged.

"You know she hasn't even been here five minutes," Annie advised Aldo who responded with the shaking of his head. Beyond Annie's comment, there would be no further discussion.

Annie stood at the edge of the table where Bill was sitting. She placed the coffee pot down at the far end so his hand wouldn't accidentally hit it and crossed her arms. She was cold, not defiant, and she subconsciously leaned inward to allow for a more private, intimate conversation.

"We talked for an hour. Well, fifty-eight minutes, well, probably less if you include the time that you answered to the point of me answering. When I hung up, my telephone indicated fifty-eight minutes." Bill spoke with nervous excitement but that was quickly abandoned as he reminisced further into their conversation. "It was quiet at first. There were a lot of questions that only had one-word answers but then things started to flow. It reminded me of the talks we had when she was younger; like the times she was in college wanting advice on what to do after she graduated, when she would tell daddy everything." Bill held out his hand towards the opposite side of the booth. "Go ahead. Have a seat."

She sat down and moved inward so that she was directly across from Bill.

"What did you talk about? Why did she call?"

Bill looked down at his notepad and slowly flipped to the next page.

"Chrissy got a big dose of reality which brought on a new understanding on how life and relationships work." Bill took a deep breath and continued. "My daughter is married and has two children. Her and her husband updated a legal document indicating that if they were both to pass away that they would live with Rob's sister who also lives in Minnesota. They changed this because apparently there was some falling out between Rob and his brother because my son-in-law's brother is a drunk and they didn't quite realize how bad it was. Chrissy and Rob didn't ask their children who they wanted to stay with. Chrissy brought it up with Rob and," Bill looked down at his pad of paper, "Rob replied that just like me and my wife, the responsibility falls on our shoulders to generate the outcome we desire. He didn't mean anything harsh by it, apparently it just slipped out but that's when the light bulb switched on and Chrissy realized the weight and the consideration of the decision that my self and my wife made . . . and that was our choice we made for ourselves."

Bill rubbed his hands together letting the friction warm them up then he wrapped them around his coffee mug. He continued,

"She actually asked me how I could have gone so long without fulfilling her wishes."

"What did you say?"

"I said I wanted everyone who wanted to say goodbye to say goodbye."

"What did she say?"

"I could hear her crying and she apologized and asked that I forgive her for not talking to me for eight years."

"And you said?" Annie leaned in with hope and happiness.

"I told her to fuck off and that was at the fifty-eight minute mark."

Annie's mouth dropped as her heart nearly stopped. Her hands went straight for her mouth to hold back a scream. It failed. "What!!! You're lying!"

The entire restaurant turned to silence and all looked over at Bill and Annie.

"It's okay," Bill said to everyone. "She just . . . I don't know." Bill looked at Annie. "I'm her father, Annie. What do you think I did? I forgave her in a heartbeat."

"I almost punched you in the eye," she belted out through clenched teeth.

"Don't ask silly questions."

"Well, what happened after all that?"

"Everything just flowed. And, uh . . ." Bill looked down nodding and smiling. ". . . we started planning a weekend for her to visit. Or for me to go visit them." Bill looked at his pad of paper. "I had to write this down, because I thought it was sweet. She told me, 'It's been just too long and the decisions I made eight years ago out of anger and confusion no longer hold their merit. I miss you, dad. I want to rekindle our relationship.'" Bill looked up with a heartwarming smile as if he could feel the pieces of his life shifting back together.

Annie fought tears as she pressed her palms against her chest. "Yea!" She cheered. "What about the others?"

"I don't know about the others yet . . ." His eyes looked wet as if he was holding back his own set of tears. ". . . but I get to see my grandchildren again. I don't even know what they look like anymore."

Bill held his hands outward and Annie grasped onto them.

Annie walked down the street past the store fronts, the small ethnic restaurants and pet shops that lined the sidewalk. There was an extra spring in her step and all had momentarily seemed right with the world. She slowed her pace and shoved her hands into her pocket. The spring left when she began to wonder when it would all go down the drain. Everything seemed too perfect now and too many things were on the right track.

She cautiously entered the elevator feeling that since she had seen Andre the likelihood of running into him once again was more probable. She thought about moving and she questioned what she was still doing in a city where she had only succeeded at being a server, where constant reminders of her ex-boyfriend lay around every corner.

She walked down the hallway and stopped in front of Andre's apartment. She thought about it; Andre's apartment. It wasn't her apartment or their apartment, it was simply and solely his. She turned towards the other door: Jon's apartment. Not her apartment either.

But she had a key so she let herself into the quiet empty space. The sound of the shower running, water dripping against the backup of the drain and the sudden collapse of water from a soaked wash cloth filled the emptiness.

"Hello?" A voice came from the bedroom.

"Okay to proceed?" Annie asked Jonie as she began walking towards the bedroom.

"Proceed."

Annie entered the bedroom and saw Jonie sitting in bed, e-reader in hand.

"What are the chances of Jon stepping out of the bathroom naked?" Annie asked.

"What do you want them to be?"

Annie shook her head. "I'll leave the private parts to you."

"Good answer." Jonie looked towards the bathroom with the shower still running. "Are you joining us?"

"Am I invited? No is a perfectly acceptable answer. I would understand."

"Do you want to be invited?"

"What are you doing?"

Jonie shook her head. "I don't know. What's left to do in this city?"

"I'm going to hang out here, maybe walk down to Starbucks. Job search a little."

Jonie put the e-reader down and leaned forward. "Can I be frank?" She didn't wait for a reply. "Get out of here."

Annie listened to her sympathetic tone and saw the concern in her blue eyes.

Jonie continued, "This is a great town, I've enjoyed my time here but I think you've done all you can here. If you stay here you'll only keep digging yourself into a rut that you can't dig out of."

"I don't know what to do."

"No one knows what to do. Jon came here and that failed. I stayed home and can't find a single thing. Go live with your parents. Find something in Grand Rapids. You can be a waitress anywhere. Be one there where the cost of living is lower and you have a bigger base of support. What are you going to do when Jon leaves?"

"What are you two going to do?"

"I'm going to go back to my parent's house, Jon is going to be at his parent's house and I'm going to work part-time at the mall with a marketing degree."

"That sucks," she said with empathy. "At least you're young."

"Four years younger than you, Jon is just two."

Annie looked away and quietly stated, "I wouldn't mind having those few years back."

"They ain't coming back."

It was a hard, truthful pill to swallow.

23

The temperatures yo-yoed making it hard to tell how high or low the mercury would move from day-to-day. It was the kind of weather that people who fought springtime colds blamed their ailments on.

Annie entered Aldo's Restaurant and felt the soothing warmth of the interior battle back the chill of the outdoors. This late in the season Annie could hardly believe that the low in the evening was dipping into the upper-thirties. It made one emotionally debunk global warming.

It was quiet. Not to say much noise was ever present prior to opening but Annie felt an eerie emptiness throughout the dining area.

Annie stepped into the kitchen and was surprised to find Aldo wearing an apron and chopping onions with a certain art that was mesmerizing to watch.

"Where's Omar?"

"Good morning," Aldo replied. "Omar quit."

"What?" The news struck Annie and she froze in place as she was hanging her jacket up. It took her a moment to process and then continued with her motion. "He quit? Why?"

"Because I can only pay a fry cook salary. He didn't specify."

"He just quit."

"Yes." Aldo's fingers brought a tomato onto the cutting board and in one fluid motion he sliced and diced. "I know what you want to ask and, no, we did not get into a fight. There wasn't a reason on my end for him to leave. He called yesterday evening and said he quit."

"Wow."

"Needless to say I'm going to be in the kitchen today. He apologized."

"You're taking it well."

Aldo paused mid-tomato. "I have no other option at the moment but to take it well."

"I'll get the ketchup on the tables," Annie said plainly as if the wind was taken from her sails.

"Thank you."

She stepped into the dining area and reached for her cell phone in her back pocket. She had worked with Omar for years and when she opened her contacts list she realized that she didn't have his phone number. It saddened her thinking that he was no longer going to be in her life in any capacity. Her solace might come when Bethany arrived and provided a number or sent a text message inquiring further on Omar's abrupt departure.

Annie began going through the motions until she spotted Janice pacing back and forth outside sucking down the last bits of tobacco in her cigarette. She tossed the butt into the street and blew the smoke backwards as she opened the door to the restaurant.

"Good morning," Annie stated.

"Good morning." Janice replied barely acknowledging Annie as she raced towards the kitchen. It had been recently that Janice insisted on the earliest shift to maximize her tips. The morning rush was generous and usually in a hurry clearing booths and allowing room for more customers, more tips. Yet Janice still found room to complain about the early hours she had sought.

The morale dropped and Annie would be more than happy to focus all her attention on either the customers or Bethany, whichever were available. It may be rude to avoid a colleague but Annie opted for being discourteous.

The door to the restaurant opened and Bethany walked in popping off her gloves and shoving them into her black jacket. "There are perverts awake at 5:30 in the morning. Did you know this?"

"I had an inkling," Annie responded placing a bottle of ketchup onto the booth closest to the door.

"Creepy guy on the T. I'll have to tell you about it." Bethany stopped at the door leading into the kitchen. "Oh, and moving out of my parent's place. That might have been a bad choice too!"

"Oh I'm sure we will have plenty to discuss," Annie said. The comment garnered a strange look from Bethany as she snuck into the kitchen.

Moments later she popped back out tying her apron around her waist. Her eyes were wide and her mouth hung open. She was just as shocked as Annie had been. "Text him. See what the deal is."

"I don't have his number."

"Shit, me neither." Annie finished with the ketchup as Bethany tossed scoops of grounded coffee into the machine. "How can we not have his number?"

"We're bad people," Annie stated as she walked by Bethany and picked up a pad of paper for orders and a handful of pens that were left under the counter.

Janice exited the kitchen and sat on the first stool at the counter. She shoved her head into her hands and groaned. "It's too damn early for this."

Despite Annie's non-verbal insistence that she avoid setting off a conversation with Janice, Bethany asked, "For what exactly?"

Janice's head popped up. "For this." Her arms spread out like a bird in flight. "For work. People should be sleeping at this hour."

"I like waking up early."

"That's fucked up."

Bethany and Annie's eyebrows rose simultaneously.

Bethany curtly replied, "I'm sure Aldo can schedule you to come in later if this is too early for you."

Annie wasn't sure if Bethany's reply was a smug way of stating her dislike of the negativity or an attack on the proficiency of Janice to perform her duties at such an early hour. She knew Janice would take it as a deliberate snide remark.

"Yeah, you would probably love that. Well, tough shit," Janice stood up. "I'm staying."

"Let's just all take a minute before continuing this conversation."

"Whatever. Don't tell me what to do, missy." Janice headed back into the kitchen.

"She's complaining about us," Annie told Bethany.

"I'm sure Aldo is taking every word with the utmost seriousness."

"Be nice."

"I always start out nice."

"Stay nice."

Bethany lowered her voice into a grainy, smoky tone and mocked Janice. "Whatever."

"Do you know anyone looking for a roommate?" Annie changed the subject.

"I'll trade you," Bethany responded. "I'm now shacked up with a crazy lady who probably is spying on my every move. I swear she counts the Cheerios in the box before going to bed to make sure I don't steal any of them."

Annie smiled and chuckled at the exaggeration but then quickly noticed Bethany's serious demeanor. "You're kidding."

"Not by that much. She's out of her freakin' mind."

"So, I will pass on the trading offer."

"I can check around," Bethany stated and stirred cream in her own mug of coffee. She grabbed the sugar and poured in a never-ending mound. "What's wrong with Jon?"

"I'm getting a jump on my impending dilemma. Slow down on the sugar!"

Bethany shrugged off the suggestion. "I love you, sweetie, but you decided to leave . . . leave."

"I decided to leave Andre. I'm just not sure about Boston though. I do like it here." Annie smiled at Bethany. "And I have friends here."

"Well, I don't want you to go and I'm locked in for ten months with Lucifer otherwise I'd invite you in," Bethany said shaking her head. "I swear she helps make my dating life non-existent. She won't allow boys over." She looked down at her mug of coffee. "Do you have any Kahlua I can mix in here?" She moved the conversation back towards her roommate. "She's been dating this Nazi-looking poster boy ever since I moved in and he has yet to spend a night. Weird! And she certainly spends every freakin' night in her bed. Anyway, I'd love to have you join this party but she doesn't want another roommate."

"You've asked?"

"I did. After the break up, I asked."

"I was wondering about that."

"Of course I asked, I even said that I was considering breaking the lease if I can find someone else willing to take over my lease with the intention of moving in with you. You and me. Across the hall from Andre." Bethany's smile was mischievous.

"She said?"

"She wrote . . ." Bethany started. Annie's eyebrow rose with curiosity. ". . . a very professional letter clipped to a copy of the lease agreement I signed with her. I'm stuck."

"I'm screwed," Annie thought. Her head began swimming with the outlook of the future. She thought of more address changes, moving boxes and the cost of traveling back home. Home, she thought. Moving back home after all these years away. She thought about friends back home who were married, who had children, who were making something of themselves. Or were they more like Heather? She thought about what it would be like to bring them their drinks, their hamburgers and their bills and the pity dollar or two extra they would leave on the tip.

Poor Annie and her bad life decisions, they would say behind her back.

The door chimed as the first customer of the day entered.

"Hey Stu," Bethany announced. "We have a fresh brew up just for you."

*   *   *

When Annie entered the apartment Jon was cuddled up on the couch with a laptop in an attempt to find a job in hopes of relocating as soon as possible.

"This is ridiculous, Annie, I really should be with her."

She offered to refill his wine glass only to lift the bottle and find it already empty.

"Shall I go to the store to pick up some alcohol? Or do you want to go out?" She was gauging what her solemn friend wanted to do with the evening. Jon dug into his pocket and pulled out a ten, he held it out.

"This is all I have. I'm not interested in hitting the town."

Annie grabbed the bill. "I'll get us some drinks, maybe pick up a burrito and we'll watch some *Dirty Dancing*."

"My favorite." Jon's facetious comment was a sign that an improving mood was imminent.

The man behind the counter at the liquor store never seemed to recognize Annie despite her frequency over the years. She wasn't sure if he was a cold man who minded the store and didn't believe in customer service or if he just had an extremely poor memory.

Nonetheless, she said hello as he looked up from a laptop that he used mostly to watch movies on. He responded with a suspicious nod.

Annie went directly to the white wine section and scanned the labels always thinking of trying something new but always defaulting to her usual chardonnay. She headed for the rum aisle to grab a much needed bottle.

A gentleman in a light spring jacket and khakis approached and pretended to look at the bottles.

"What do you recommend?" He asked.

"Oh, it's all good. Except that stuff," she responded pointing towards the bottom shelf. "If you have no taste buds and you want to vomit the next morning with the worst hangover you've ever experienced than that's a good choice."

"I'll pass on that." He reached for a bottle of Captain Morgan. "Can't go wrong with this, can I?"

"That's what I was going for." She grabbed a fifth of Captain Morgan with her free hand. She noticed the man's smile. His dirty blonde hair was short, cropped close to the head but there was enough to style it. His eyes were blue but not overwhelmingly so. He was clean-shaven and had a baby face with a little pudge that was cute.

They started walking towards the register. "Can I be honest with you?"

"You can be whatever you want, we just met."

He smiled at the remark. "I was going to go for this regardless of what you said."

"Oh yeah? So if I said that tasted worse than a bar mat at the end of a shift you would have still picked up a bottle?"

"Absolutely. It's my brand."

"Really?"

"I may have picked up Bacardi."

He placed his bottle on the counter and the man lifted off his stool as if the two customers were burdensome and began tapping the keys on the register angrily.

"What's your name?"

"Annie."

"Annie. You have a pretty smile." The compliment made her smile. "And you have heartbreaking eyes."

She shook her head not sure how cheesy the line was meant to be. "You say that to all the girls."

"Yeah, but with you I mean it."

"Well played, sir," she responded regarding his save.

They paid for their alcohol and stepped out into the evening air.

"My name is Randy."

Annie held out her hand. "Pleasure to meet you, Randy."

"Now you probably have a boyfriend and a thousand other gentlemen knocking on your door but may I be so bold as to ask you for a phone number?"

"Sure."

Randy liked her playful nature. "May I have your phone number?"

"No."

The quick remark stunned Randy. His mouth dipped open and he lost his breath. His lips shook as he struggled to come up with the right words to say but none were coming.

"I . . . um . . . really?"

Annie giggled. "I only give out my phone number to polite men."

"I'm polite!" He confessed.

"You didn't say please." Annie started walking down the sidewalk.

Randy quickly caught up. "Annie, I apologize for my rudeness. May I please have your phone number, please?"

"Well now you just sound desperate saying please twice. I don't know about this."

"The second one was for the lack of a please the first time. I didn't want that question to be lonely and without its proper please."

Annie stopped and placed her bag on the ground. She proceeded to tear off a piece of the brown paper bag that held Randy's bottle of Captain Morgan. Pulling a pen from her pocket, one of the ones that always found its way into her pocket during her shift, she wrote her phone number and popped it into Randy's bag.

"Thank you," he responded.

"You're welcome. Now don't be a dick and not call me, okay?"

"I won't be a dick."

"How old are you?"

"Thirty."

"Me too," Annie said, "I'm too old for that 'wait five days bullshit', so don't feel obligated to play games."

Randy smiled enjoying their teasing one another. "Yes ma'am."

"I'm too young for ma'am."

"Yes, Annie."

They parted. Randy walked eastward and Annie headed west to make a quick stop at the restaurant before heading back. She beamed with delight having provided a charming man with her phone number. It had been years since such a scenario played out and Annie realized the last charming man that received her phone number was Andre. She hadn't been out on a first date in over half-a-decade.

24

"You guys don't have Wi-Fi!"

"No, we don't."

"You don't have Wi-Fi!" Jon repeated awestruck as he scanned the connection capabilities of his tablet while sitting near the window at Aldo's Restaurant. He had a cup of Coke resting beside the tablet and grunted. "I'm going to have to connect and that's going to murder my battery." He held up a finger. "No wait," he looked out the window and down the street, "there's a bagel place over there that I can just barely get a signal for."

Bethany snapped her fingers. "Wake up a-little Susie!" Jon looked at Bethany. "What do you want to eat?" Bethany dug her fist into her side impatiently.

"A new waitress?"

Her response was a loud, obnoxious sigh.

"Okay, turkey wrap, light on the mayo."

"Turkey it is."

Bethany went to turn in the order. Annie sped by with a pot of coffee and refilled another customer's mug. She dropped a check at the table and walked past Jon. He stopped her placing a hand on her wrist.

"What crawled up Bethany's ass?" He whispered.

"Man troubles. And you're a man, so you're trouble."

"She always has man troubles. She doesn't have to take it out on me."

Annie placed her hand on Jon's shoulder. "Oh she's taking it out on everyone. She ran into the man she likes at a bar last night. He was with another woman."

"He was cheating."

"No. He just didn't commit to either one." Annie's tone turned to sarcasm. "It's okay though, he told her that his not returning her text messages was his way of saying he didn't want to continue seeing her."

"I should tip her big today then."

"Extra dollar wouldn't hurt."

"You guys don't have Wi-Fi."

Annie started walking away. "Don't take it out on the servers."

She entered the kitchen to find Aldo looking at Jon's order. "How is it out there? God I miss this sometimes."

"It's fine. Rush is over."

"I can tell."

"Why don't you spend more time in here if you like it so much?"

"I have to run a business."

"You run your pen through the *Boston Globe* crossword puzzle."

"I'm present with my customers. I talk to them. I schmooze. Then I do payroll and bills in the afternoon."

"Do you have a replacement coming?"

"I'm conducting a couple interviews this afternoon. Jed was interested in mornings so this guy I hire will take on the mid-afternoon/evening shift."

"Guy, huh? I thought a woman's place was in the kitchen."

"Don't be a smart ass, you know what I mean."

"Is this done?" Annie pointed to a plate of waffles sitting under the heater.

Without looking up Aldo responded, "Needs whipped cream." Then he looked up. "Where the hell is Bethany? No one wants cold waffles."

"I'll do it. She's having a rough day."

"She can have a rough day after twelve o'clock. I have a business to run."

The air was filled with tension coming in at all angles.

Annie pulled out the can of whipped cream and sprayed it on the sides. She tossed a pad of butter in the middle of the waffle and left the kitchen.

"Who gets the waffles?" She shouted.

Annie saw a man raising his hand at the far end of the restaurant and took the plate his way while scanning the dining area for Bethany. She placed the plate on the table.

"Anything else I can get for you?"

"Those were sitting up there for a while," the man said.

"Not that long." She made eye contact with the man and he was far from pleased. "I'm sorry. If it's cold or not to your liking I'll have the cook remake it for you."

"And spit in it for sending it back?" He snorted an unhappy chuckle. "No thanks." He cut the edge of his waffle with his fork and shoved the piece into his mouth.

"The cook is the owner. It would be in his best interests to make this waffle to your liking."

The man chewed it for a moment then, with a full mouth, responded, "It will suffice."

"Your waitress is having an off day . . ."

"Not my problem."

". . . if you need something and she's not around, holler at me, okay?"

He nodded as if she were now bugging him and she walked away stopping at Jon's table. He had a wide smile on his face and was reading the screen of his tablet with his arms crossed.

"You were able to download porn?" Annie asked.

"Jonie got a job interview," he said it slowly letting the words sink in with Annie like the first time he reviewed his email. He kept his eyes averted.

"Wow! That's great. Where at?"

"Clifton Advertising. A copywriter. It pays for shit but it's a start."

"Sure is."

"It's in Pittsburgh," he finally said and looked up at Annie.

"Pittsburgh."

"Pennsylvania." He scrolled down in the email. "They have a recruiter in Toledo Tuesday morning and she's going to drive down and meet with them."

The door of the restaurant dinged and Bill stepped inside. "I'm late, but I'm here," he announced. He pointed to Jon and sat on the opposite side of the booth without an invite.

"Good morning," Annie said.

Bill pointed with his thumb out the door. "Bethany is talking at her cell phone."

"At or into?" Jon asked.

"At. I think she's texting someone and she's not being nice about it."

"Shit." Annie started for the door.

"Hey!" Annie spun around at Bill's call. "Let her do whatever she's going to do. She won't learn otherwise."

"She won't learn at all." Annie continued for the door and walked out into the late-morning air.

Bill looked around the restaurant and stretched his neck to scan the entire place.

"There's no waitresses," he commented.

Jon looked around too. "You want some coffee?"

"I'd love some coffee."

Jon hopped out of the booth and bee-lined to the opposite side of the counter, grabbed a mug, and filled it up. He brought it back to the table and placed it on a paper doily next to Bill.

"Thanks."

Jon repeated the news of his girlfriend's interview to Bill.

"I've been there quite a few times."

"Yeah?"

Bill nodded. "You're just going to jump around the world, eh? First Boston, then Pittsburgh. What's next after that?"

"We're a nomadic generation, Bill. We can do it all through email."

"You crazy kids and your gadgets," Bill responded with a hint of sarcasm.

"Do you think it's easier or harder?"

"I don't know. Benefits to both, I suppose. Nothing beats a face-to-face interaction with the customer or client."

"You can get that. There's video."

"It's just not the same."

Annie stepped into the restaurant waving her hands in the air with frustration. "You were right, Bill. She will never learn."

"I always am. Turkey Reuben and fries."

"You got it." She whisked past him and placed the order, hollering back to Aldo, "Turkey Reuben and fries for Bill. Don't forget to spit in it."

"You just revealed the secret sauce, Annie," Bill stated.

"Oh no I didn't," she responded mischievously.

Bill waved his hand over to the table. "Come here a second, will ya?"

Annie headed over and took a seat. The door to the restaurant opened and Bethany walked in. Her teeth were clenched so hard you could see the tension in the muscles of her jaw. Her hands were balled into tight fists and she looked like she was going to throw her hand through a brick wall. She stepped into the ladies room without making eye contact with anyone.

"It's a good thing you're not running a business here in which you need employees to make it operate," Jon said.

Bill smiled. "Guess who I talked with yesterday."

"Bill junior?"

Bill shook his head. "Natalie."

"Ooh, a girl?"

"Who is this lucky broad?" Jon asked snidely.

Bill's smile faded and he burned holes through Jon with an angry. "That broad is my granddaughter."

Jon blew out a breath of air and a mumbled curse towards himself as he realized his mistake. "My order's up. I'm going to go get my order." Jon shoved himself to the edge of the booth and lifted up.

"Yeah, that sounds like a good idea," Bill responded. His smile came back and Annie wasn't entirely sure if his look was facetious or if he had been seriously offended. "I talked to Natalie. She's the younger one, the ten year old. We talked for about twenty minutes . . . I mean she talked for about twenty minutes. As an old man all I could do was simply ask questions. She's as smart and sassy as her mother. I love it. I've turned a new leaf, Annie. Thank you."

"I didn't do anything."

"You did. Don't sell yourself short."

Jon sat back down with his plate. He shoved the tablet aside and grabbed the ketchup. He poured a hefty amount next to his fries drowning about a third of them in the process. "I meant to do that."

Bill continued, "Do you remember Winnie?"

"Yeah," she lifted her eyes skyward trying to put name to face. "Sort of. Remind me."

"Winston Churchill."

"Right! Duh!" Annie looked at Jon. "Named after Churchill and ended up looking like him."

"Yikes," Jon commented.

"He's meeting me for breakfast tomorrow. Here."

"Fantastic."

"Again, thank you," Bill said and then moved his newspaper right in front of him. "You know just how much to push in order to get results."

"My pleasure."

Annie headed towards the kitchen to grab Bill's sandwich. Bethany stepped out of the bathroom motioning her hands in a circle in front of her body. She was breathing in and out as if she were meditating.

"Well?" Annie asked.

"Karma better kick this guy in the nuts."

"So, you're fine?"

"I think I need to become a lesbian."

"I'm sure lesbians have relationship problems too and I don't think you can really choose to be a lesbian," Annie replied.

"Then I'm done with men."

"If I had a dollar every time you said that one, Bethany."

25

Annie always folded the couch up in the morning to make it appear as if she didn't actually sleep at night and hang out during the day on the exact same piece of furniture. She nestled on the couch cushions, her phone rested beside her. She checked it every fifteen to twenty minutes to see if Randy had called and she had somehow missed it.

She cursed her bladder when her brain received the signal that it had to be emptied and she debated taking the phone with her. She didn't want to answer the call while in the bathroom so she left it on the couch.

A half-second after sitting down on the toilet she heard her phone ring.

"Shit!" She yelled with animosity toward the gods. She struggled to pee harder, motioning her hand as if telling a speech giver to wrap it up. "Come on, come on!" She had a piece of toilet paper at the ready. Each ring was one second closer to voice mail.

Once completed, she kept her pants and panties on the floor and made a dash for the phone.

But it was too late. The ringing ceased. She looked at the number and didn't recognize it. Her shoulders dropped and her hands fell to her sides.

The door began to unlock. "Shit!" She yelled again dropping the phone onto the couch which promptly bounced to the floor and sprinted to the bathroom. She slammed the door closed as the front door of the apartment opened.

Annie put her panties and pants back on and looked at the toilet realizing she never flushed it. She flushed the toilet and washed her hands.

Jon tossed the mail in his hands onto the counter.

"I heard a door slam?"

"Really?" Annie replied faking confusion.

"You pee with the door open when you're alone, don't you?"

"Err . . . maybe."

"Maybe. You're out of breath."

Annie realized she was breathing heavy and shrugged her shoulders.

"I never got winded peeing," Jon said. "Pooping. Well, there's been a rough time or two."

"That's just some information no girl ever wants to hear. I'm so glad we have this brother-sister relationship thing going. Please don't hold anything back."

Annie's phone beeped on the floor at the base of the couch. She picked it up and dialed to listen for the voice mail. It was Randy and his mumbling and backtracking were cute. He was nervous and not a very good message-leaver. She wrote down his return number and deleted the message.

"That smile looks like you got a call from a boy."

She couldn't contain it. "Should I call him right back?"

"Sure. Tell him why you couldn't make it to the phone." Jon's head tilted towards the bathroom.

"Genius. Is this how you won Jonie's heart?"

"Close." Jon headed into the kitchen and grabbed a Diet Coke from the refrigerator. "Call him back," he replied taking a sip. "Prince Charming awaits!"

She started to dial the number then looked up at Jon. "Um, are you going to stand there?"

"I wanted to eavesdrop."

"I'll be in your bedroom," Annie said turning and walking towards the door to the bedroom, she closed the door and pressed the SEND button. There were two rings before a woman with a thick accent answered.

"Hello!" The woman screamed.

"Hi. Is Randy there?" Annie reluctantly asked but she was cut off on her last word.

"What? Who is this?"

"My name is Annie. Is Randy available?"

"No. Not interested. Goodbye!" The woman screeched and hung up.

Annie looked at the number again and the number she dialed. They matched. She pulled up the missed call log and redialed the number that Randy had called from hoping this was his cell phone or a direct business line.

A no-nonsense woman answered. How many calls she answered per day could reach well into the hundreds. "Collins, Benli, Schwartz and Gawande."

Annie was taken aback at the sudden influx of last names and the rapid speed at which they were fired. "Um, is there a Randy there?"

"There's four Randalls or Randys at this office. Maybe five, I'm not sure. Four-hundred people work or intern here. Which Randy would you like?" She was strictly business and had other lines ringing.

"I don't know," Annie responded overwhelmed and defeated.

"We don't have a Randy I-Don't-Know here. Call back when you have a last name."

The phone clicked. "Wow! That was unnecessarily rude." Annie stood up from the bed and walked back into the living room. Jon was reviewing the guide on the television in search of suitable mind-numbing programming. Holding the remote straight out at the screen, he looked at Annie.

"Bad news."

Annie told him about her phone call and he winced in over-exaggerated emotional pain. He offered her his deepest sympathy and filled her with hope that they would once again run into each other.

"If I can run into my ex-girlfriend from high school in Minnesota on a layover then anything is possible."

"No," she replied plopping down on the opposite end of the couch and looking forward. "When you want to meet someone again the chances of running into the person are slim whereas not wanting to run into someone will increase that chance tenfold."

"Not true," Jon said. Annie looked his way. "How many times have you run into Andre?"

"That's different. I've avoided him based on knowing his schedule. I know all his moves, where he goes and when he goes. I purposely take myself out of the possibility of running into him and decrease my chances."

"Hence you need to do the same with this guy. What do you know about him?"

"I know he works at a law firm with four-hundred employees."

"And you know where he buys his booze."

"I'm not going to stalk him."

"If Romeo not-ith stalketh Juliet, we have no star-crossed lovers."

"They end up dead at the end, Jon. They're star-crossed."

"It worked in theory."

"Everything works in theory, that's why they're theories."

"You want something to drink?"

Annie faced towards the television but was lost in her own swirling, saddened thoughts. "No." Annie spoke aloud but she didn't direct it to Jon, she merely projected her thoughts. "Day in and day out I work, I try to find something better, I come home, I do nothing. Is there more?"

Jon shoved himself deep into the couch like it was his security blanket. He crossed his arms and took her words into consideration. "We all strive for something."

"We do? What do I strive for?"

"This might be a Bill conversation."

"What do I strive for?" She repeated and closed her eyes in disappointment at herself.

There was silence between the two and that quiet stretched into minutes. Jon thought of his life and thought of his choices. He didn't feel beaten down like Annie. He knew what he wanted and tried to get it. His days were filled with endless job searches on endless websites only to find no pot of gold at the end of the rainbow, just another day of searching.

Annie spent her afternoons fighting the same battle only she didn't know what outcome she wanted.

"Go home," Jon finally said. His voice was low, serious.

Annie looked at him. The hopelessness in her face indicated that she knew that would likely be the case as much as she fought it.

Jon pressed. "There's nothing wrong with it. Press the restart button. You can turn off the street you're driving on and take a different route. This one seems to be leading towards Janice."

"I don't want to be Janice."

"No you don't and I don't want you to end up being some bitter old waitress who fights all the wrong battles, the small ones that at the end of the day don't matter." Jon shrugged his body. "What do I know, I'm just a writer. I just make it all sound pretty."

"Do you really think I should . . ." Annie's cell phone rang and she looked at the display to see who was called, ". . . go home."

"Randy?"

Annie shook her head and answered the call. She stepped into the bedroom and Jon lifted the remote control back up and scrolled through the stations once again.

"Hello?" She answered wearily. It was the first time she heard the voice in a long time. She considered that it was all a dream but nonetheless, Noah Ferguson was calling his sister.

"Hello Annie."

And then silence. There was no right way to continue the conversation because there was no specific reason that Annie should have received such a call.

Finally, Noah mustered the energy to talk but his question was merely a tactic to get Annie speaking. "How are you?"

"I'm fine." Her tone was suspicious as if she believed her brother was going to ask for money that Annie didn't possess. "How are you?"

"I'm good."

Again there was silence until Annie's patience dropped. "Why are you calling me?" She didn't intend for it to sound rude so she backtracked and thought of a way to pose the question nicer; still the same words came out only with emphasis on curiosity rather than the unintended accusatory tone that was heard the first time. "Why are you calling me?"

"I haven't talked to you in a long time." Noah's words were carefully chosen, enunciated slowly as if he used every second to search for the exact right answers. His voice was deeper than Annie remembered but it had been a year, no two years, since she heard from her brother. "I'm back."

Annie closed the bedroom door squeezing the knob and turning it to prevent any noise from it clicking shut.

"From where exactly? Where were you?"

"Um . . ." He hesitated. "I was in Florida?" It was his admitting of the truth. "Don't tell anyone though, okay? I never left the country so I'm not really back from anywhere. I've been in Florida."

"Do mom and dad know?"

"No. They still think I'm . . ."

"Why didn't you tell us you were in Florida? We were worried? It wasn't fair that you made us worry about where you were until we got used to that anxiety. We thought you were in Africa or Southeast Asia, you emailed mom and told her you were there!"

Noah didn't defend his actions. He remained quiet.

"Look," Annie continued, "You're okay, right?"

"Yeah."

She didn't quite believe him. She thought of Bill and the reconnection with his family and, although she found it difficult to hold a conversation, she liked the idea that her brother was reaching out.

"This number was disconnected, you know. We tried it and . . ."

"I put the phone on hold for a month."

"Why?"

"I needed to figure things out and mom was drowning me. I needed something and I wasn't going to get it in Grand Rapids."

"What did you find?" Her motives were selfish, maybe her brother had an answer to a question she had been asking herself.

"I found Florida." He sighed heavily, defeated. "I saw you and how you were carving a life that was ideal." She thought he made ideal sound cynical. "Happy relationship, probably going to get married, thriving opportunities in a big city. You had your shit together and I didn't. Mom and dad kept pushing college, classes, career, career, career, and I just couldn't sit through another bullshit lecture from some high-and-mighty community college teacher in class I didn't want to take in the first place. I wanted to learn something and that wasn't the place I was going to get my education. I wanted to leave and not tell anyone where I was going so they couldn't convince me not to go. I wanted to do something truly on my own. They would have convinced me not to go and they would have said the same crap they always do, did."

Annie listened. If only he knew, she thought. She began pacing throughout the bedroom. She stopped at the closet door, spun around and walked towards the window. She always peeked outside and saw the street. She heard the dings of the T as it approached its stop then hum as it continued east or west.

"Ya know, Noah, I really don't think anyone has it figured out."

"I'm afraid to call them."

"I know."

It wasn't the answer Noah had expected and he didn't know how to follow it up. She wanted to share her stories about Bill but hesitated letting his situation remain private between her and him.

"I feel like I'm the only one like this."

"Oh no, Noah, no no no. What you're feeling is an epidemic we all are facing. I know people our age and I know people in their seventies who struggle with their personal lives and choices. Call mom and dad."

"And say what?"

"Why did you call me?" She asked once again hoping the answer lay in the question.

"You're the only one I know."

"You're their son. They want to hear from you!"

"What if I start feeling the same things I felt that made me want to leave in the first place?"

"Valid question." Annie was looking down at the street. Pedestrians were minding their own businesses, living their lives trying to run errands or get back to work after their late lunch.

"Well?"

Annie stared out the window. "I guess you would be in the same position you are right now. You ran away from familiarity and there's a certain amount of bravery in that. Some people are comfortable there, I suppose. I guess as long as you're comfortable in familiarity and happy in it then everything is fine. If it's not, well . . ."

"Deep but aren't I just running back to that familiarity?

"Can't spell familiarity without family, right?"

"So, how's . . . Andre? Did I miss a wedding?"

"Noah, I'm a single waitress in a big city who can't afford the rent. Andre and I broke up about a month-and-a-half ago?"

"Are you still in Boston?"

"For now. I don't know what I'm going to do. I'm figuring it all out myself."

"So I'm taking advice from someone whose life is just as fucked up as my own." Noah chuckled in disbelief somehow surprised his bad luck had produced this as well.

"We very well could end up fighting for control of the bathroom once again."

Noah sighed dejectedly. "I'm going to feel like such a loser going home. I don't want to feel that way."

There was a subtle knock at the bedroom door and Annie rushed from the window towards the door. She opened it and Jon stood with a note: Pizza?

Annie nodded and gave a thumbs up. Jon reciprocated with a thumbs up and walked away.

Annie watched Jon walk down the small hallway back into the living room.

"This generation has some balls," Annie started. "It's hard to go back home when you never left. We left, right? We tried."

Jon turned around once he reached the living room and looked back with an unconvincing smile. He had overheard the statement and it resonated within him. He kept a good front in spite of his bad luck finding a job and facing the same humiliation of returning home. He disappeared from Annie's view and sat back on the couch. She knew he was reaching for his laptop ready to search website after website in seeking out the careers portion or reading through a laundry list of job opportunities on a job search site.

Annie said. "We just boomerang back home eventually."

"I'd like to think some of us escape that fate," Noah replied.

Annie smiled. "I'd like to think so too." There was a brief moment of silence. "What did you find?"

"What do mean?"

"What did you find in Florida?"

"Oranges and headaches. I found that if I'm going to work my ass off, never travel and be miserable and alone I might as well do it around some people who might float me some money from time to time."

"So you don't have a girlfriend?"

"I met a girl."

"Yeah?"

"Yeah, her boyfriend is a marine and she didn't tell me that until I let her borrow three-hundred dollars."

"Noah," Annie replied disappointed.

"She thought we were friends and didn't want to ruin our friendship. We were friends, we were friends for about four months. We didn't do anything with one another and once she got the money she thought I was coming on too strong and told me her boyfriend was returning soon."

"Are you going to get the money back?"

"Her boyfriend didn't know what money I was talking about when I went to confront this girl and he said he handles all financial affairs. I've seen Marines. This guy wasn't a Marine fresh from the fight."

There was silence on again on both ends until Noah broke it. "Lesson learned, right?"

"Call mom and dad."

Noah sighed heavily knowing that he was out of options. "Maybe." He was afraid of his parents' disapproval.

"What are you doing in Florida anyway?"

Annie could hear the hesitation on the opposite end. "I'm a cashier at Winn-Dixie. It's a grocery store."

Annie was in the middle of telling Jon about her brother as they walked down the street towards the pizza parlor. Their conversation was interrupted when Jon felt his cell phone vibrate.

"When it rains it pours," he started. "Jonie has another job interview."

"Where?"

"Here."

"Boston?"

"I mean there. Detroit."

"Wow. That would be great."

"That would be great." He placed the cell phone back in his pocket.

"Would it?" Annie asked and Jon looked over to her. "Be great?"

"It would be fantastic."

"You're not acting like it."

"I'm acting like someone who has been job searching without a bite who just found out someone got two bites in twenty-four hours."

They entered the pizza place and both pulled their wallets to pay their portion. They both had no more than ten bucks on them and were happy that the total for the large pie came out to a few pennies under fourteen-dollars.

Fifteen minutes later as the glint of the evening sun pierced the windows of the pizza parlor their order was placed on a stand in the center of the table.

They dug into their pizza as if it was the last meal they were going to eat. A television screen above the register was playing the Red Sox game.

"You think they're going to win?" Jon asked casually.

"Against Chicago? It could be tough."

"I wonder if the Tigers are playing tonight."

"Yeah."

There wasn't any talking for the duration of the top of the first inning.

Jon spoke up saying the one thing that had seemed to be on his mind for the past hour. "I want to go home." Annie didn't respond. She opened her mouth but felt choked up. "I miss Jonie."

"Me too." Annie looked in Jon's direction. "I want to go home."

In the bottom of the first inning the Sox pitcher threw his first pitch right down the center and the twenty-two-year-old blasted one into right field for a home run.

"I wonder if he could call a do-over," Jon remarked.

"I want a do-over but I don't think I'm going to get one."

"I don't think he's going to get one either," Jon replied regarding the pitcher.

26

Two Weeks Later

Annie stepped outside of the restaurant to take in a big breath of air. She had just put in her notice and Aldo acknowledged it with nearly teary-eyes.

Now it felt real. Jon had started packing up his boxes and reserved a moving truck to drive them from Boston back to the Detroit area. Annie would hop on a bus and head west from there.

Jonie had two more interviews with two more companies in Detroit and accepted an assistant account director position at an advertising agency. She had hoped to be able to pass Jon freelance work; his current prospects were minimal and his confidence was waning.

Aldo walked outside and put his hands in the air.

"Ahh," he breathed long and hard. "Beautiful day. Lucky you, you're off in a couple hours and can enjoy it."

Annie smiled slightly and nodded. She felt guilty as if she were turning her back on Aldo.

"I'm sorry things didn't work out with my friend."

"Your friend?"

"Yes, Steven Howard. He said he contacted you. I hadn't heard anything from you so I figured, I don't know, maybe it just didn't seem like the right job for you."

Annie was baffled. "What?"

"Maybe you don't remember. It was a couple months ago. I was hoping he would hire you for his catering company and then you'd be able to get out of this shit hole."

"Aldo, I have no idea what you're talking about."

Aldo was concerned and confused. He looked into Annie's eyes but found that she had no recognition of this contact. "I have a friend, an acquaintance really, but he said he was looking for people for his catering company. I knew that interested you and it would've been a great start. Annie, you're saying he never contacted you?"

"No."

"He promised he would."

She shook her head.

"Bah, son-of-a-bitch." Aldo huffed inside. Annie followed.

"Aldo, it's fine, it's okay. I'm leaving town soon. There's no point in pursuing this."

"It's the principle, Annie. A man gave me his word . . ." Aldo walked through the kitchen towards his office, ". . . and when a man gives you his word, he keeps it." Aldo started pilfering through his desk looking over stacks of paper until coming across a scrap piece of paper with names and numbers listed. "I need to add this into my address book." He lifted the telephone off of the cradle and dialed a few numbers. "Not this Steven Howard though." He muttered under his breath. "Asshole."

"Aldo!" Annie pleaded.

"Annie, if this man offers you a job would you stay in Boston? Say no and I'll hang up."

She didn't answer. She was set on moving back home now but an opportunity was springing in Boston. She nodded and saw Aldo's mouth curve upward with joy.

"Steven Howard, please . . . yes Steven, this is Aldo." His voice was borderline hostile like he was defending his own hurt daughter. He wanted answers. "You told me you would call my brilliant, beautiful waitress Annie and she said she never received such a call . . . uh huh . . . oh . . ." Aldo's eyes lifted towards Annie's. She looked at him with hope; maybe Boston was the place she was meant to stay. Aldo's tone had calmed as he looked downward. "I see. My apologies for being unfriendly. Thank you, Steven."

Aldo lowered the telephone back into its cradle. He let out a sigh and finally looked up at Annie.

"He said he called you. He left a message and he explained that he was sure it was you because the voice mail stated such." Aldo looked hurt and desperate for an explanation on her part. "You didn't call him back?"

"Aldo, I never got that message."

"He's hired for the season now." Aldo's shoulders slumped.

Annie looked away and felt the emotion bubble up inside her. This was the first real chance of pursuing a career she might enjoy and that opportunity had fallen. She bit her lip but that didn't prevent the tears from coming into her eyes.

Aldo stayed put. "I'm sorry, Annie."

"It's getting hard to think that the world isn't out to get me somehow." A tear slipped from her eye down her cheek and she instinctively wiped it away but this motion seemed to cause her eyes to well up even more.

"You're making the right decision. I love you, Annie, but I think it is best that you're leaving."

"I could've had something here." She kept her eyes lowered and shook her head in disbelief.

"Well now you'll have something better somewhere else."

The thought made Annie chuckle.

"You're really leaving us, eh?" Bill asked as he poured syrup over his pancakes.

"Yes. Bumming a ride off of Jon to Detroit."

Bill nodded and cut an edge off of his pancake stuffing it into his mouth. He dripped another healthy serving of syrup on top. He lifted his mug of coffee and took a sip while still chomping away on the pancakes. With a full mouth he said, "We're going to miss you."

"I'll miss you too. We can keep in touch, you can call and we can discuss how I can make your life a living nightmare," she quipped.

Bill appreciated the joke but quickly dismissed it. "You never did such a thing."

"I know."

"I hope you know. I could still be lying on the bathroom floor with a thrown-out back if it weren't for you."

"Aldo will keep watch on you. He's the one who sent me to check up on you."

"Any plans when you head back?"

Annie told him of her intent on picking up the waitress gig at her father's restaurant in the airport. "Living out of mommy and daddy's house will cut back on expenses. Christ, every time I think of it I want to pull my hair."

"It's no big deal."

"Yes it is. Let's not pretend otherwise. I should be married with a handful of kids."

"Perception is reality, I suppose," Bill said. "I'm going to read my paper."

Annie nodded and stood up from the booth. She stepped into the kitchen and texted Bethany about her official resignation from Aldo's Restaurant.

She kept refilling Bill's mug and just before putting down his check he stopped her to speak once again. "Remember a while back I asked you to a Sox game with me?"

"I do."

"I can come up with some tickets if you and Jon would be like to accompany me."

"That sounds wonderful."

"Sad, but I realize that it will take a very short amount of time to pack up everything that I have here," Jon said as Annie stepped into the bedroom.

"How's the job search?"

Jon shook his head. He sat in the middle of his bedroom with empty dresser drawers opened. His clothing was in boxes and he laughed as he called the packing his trial run anticipating it would take days to box everything. He didn't answer the job search question; it was irrelevant.

"Do you want something to drink?" Annie inquired.

Jon stood up using the dresser to help him to his feet. "Sure."

Annie stepped out of the bedroom and walked into the kitchen. She heard a door squeak open out in the hallway and it caused her to pause in mid-stride. The door shut and she felt the okay to continue. Her head bobbed to-and-fro shaking off the idea that Andre's presence irked and frightened her.

She opened the refrigerator door and grabbed two Diet Cokes from the shelf and placed them on the counter. She snapped one open hearing the fizz on the inside peak then wane.

She stared at the counter and reminisced briefly of the old apartment. She could smell its smell, visualize the interior and feel each step she had taken. Annie was in a complete daydream as she recalled what her old home had looked like. She remembered the view from the window and, as she looked over the kitchen counter through Jon's apartment, she envisioned the dark-hued couches in front of the wall-mounted high-def television.

"You're not nearly as good of a server in-home as you are at the office," Jon said walking from the bedroom towards the kitchen. He grabbed the unopened can from the counter and popped the tab. "I ordered this an hour ago," he joked. "What's on your mind?"

"I don't know really. Just remembering."

"Remembering what?"

"What the old apartment looked like."

Jon didn't reply and took a sip of his drink.

Annie looked at her roommate and smiled. "Bill's taking us to a Red Sox game."

"He is? That's awesome. I've never actually stepped inside Fenway Park."

* * *

The next day Jon and Bill sat across from one another playing cards in the booth at Aldo's.

"Do you know gin?"

"I know the drink gin," Annie clarified.

Bill studied his card and dropped one. "Different gin."

Jon picked up the discarded Ace and dropped a ten.

"How are you on drinks?" Annie asked and both grunted an answer that signaled they were fine. "Two peas, I swear."

Annie walked away and approached Bethany as she was sitting at the counter.

"I should ditch the bitch and go west with you," Bethany said.

"Why don't you?"

"She has my social security number. I'm sure she would send a collections agency to gather up the seven months of rent that I would be leaving behind."

"Hmm, well I'll let you know how the great western frontier is and you can figure out at the conclusion of your jail sentence if you want to come west."

"How are the men in Grand Rapids?"

"Scarce. It's the Midwest and I'm thirty. The good ones are married and the bad ones . . ."

"Aren't?"

"No, they are. They just cheat on their wives."

"Any good young men?"

"There might be one, maybe two."

"That's double the ones here." Bethany looked around the restaurant and saw a pair of closed menus on one of her tables. She stood up. "I might need to leave my home here and try something new." Bethany headed for her table.

Annie reflected on Bethany's comment and recognized the same feelings. She felt it wise to advise her that change doesn't necessarily mean better.

Annie pulled a used newspaper along the counter and scanned the front page briefly before flipping to the sports pages. The Sox schedule caught her eye.

She shouted to Bill, "When are we going to the game?"

"Thursday," Bill announced.

"We're playing Detroit." Annie chuckled. Jon lifted his head up and she asked him, "What team are you going to represent?"

"Oh no!" Jon grumbled and dropped his head down. He popped it back up. "This is quite a dilemma."

"Let me answer it for you," Bill stated. "The Red Sox."

"Oh yeah? And turn my back on my beloved Tigers?"

"Absolutely. It's always more fun to root for the home team." Bill picked up a card and dropped his hand. "Gin." He shoved his cards forward for Jon to shuffle. "This is Boston, Jon. I'm not going to sit next to someone cheering on the opposing team."

"So, wear my Sox shirt?"

Bill rose from the booth. "Wear what you want but if Manny Gallegos hits one over the big green monster you're standing up and cheering."

Bill turned to head towards the bathroom but Jon cut him off with a question. "What if he strikes out?"

"You groan and make a comment on how the umps call was bullshit." Bill smiled at Annie. "Excuse me." He headed into the men's room.

Annie approached the table. "You heard the man."

"It's a rough call."

"I'm sure Bethany wouldn't have an issue on deciding whom to cheer and Bill would gladly give her your ticket if you wear an old English D."

"Did you use whom? Who uses whom?" Jon started shuffling the cards. "I'll wear my Sox shirt and Tigers socks."

"You have Tigers socks?"

"I do. And they have little tiger heads on them."

"Cute," Annie replied mockingly. She pointed to his half-empty cup. "More?"

"I've drank so much I'm going to pee every half-hour until next Thursday."

"I remember when I took my son, my oldest son, Bill Junior to his first game. We took the T all the way here and he begged me for a hot dog the second we exited the car. As any good father who has his son away from his mother I bought him a dog at a vendor right there. Bill pointed to a spot where a vendor was dishing out dogs. "It was the week after opening day and it was chilly. We stood outside the park watching everyone pass and ate our dogs before heading inside."

"Have you talked to him?" Annie asked as they continued walking towards the stadium. It was a warm evening and the sun was low in the sky shedding its last beams down on the closed-off street where vendors sold hot dogs and kielbasas, t-shirts and hats and over-priced green monster stuffed animals for kids. It was busy with Boston fans heading in all directions entering and exiting stores, eating and chatting.

Bill shook his head and quietly answered, "No."

They continued a few yards in silence. Jon looked at the hot dog cart they were passing and the man behind it barking to the passersby about his goods.

"Bill, you want a Fenway Frank?"

He continued forward. "We'll get one inside."

Jon stopped though. Annie took notice a few feet ahead and stopped looking towards Jon. Bill then realized he was continuing on alone and stopped. He shifted his body around and saw Jon standing with his hands shoved into his pockets.

"Come on." Jon tilted his head towards the cart. "My treat."

Annie looked back in Bill's direction.

Bill moved towards the other two and approached the hot dog vendor. "Three Fenway Franks, my good man. How are you this evening?"

"Splendid. Three dogs it is and the condiments are right there," the vendor replied nodding towards the ketchup, mustard and relish displayed at the edge of the cart.

Jon pulled his wallet out as Bill was reaching for his.

"Put that away, Jon. Save your dough."

"Twelve dollars," the vendor said handing the two dogs to Jon and Annie. Bill paid and took hold of the third.

They loaded up on condiments and ate their hot dogs without talking. Their silence was filled with the thought that within a few weeks they wouldn't be near one another.

Annie looked at the two men wishing that she could bring her friends to Grand Rapids. She tried to enjoy this time but it also saddened her.

Bill took pleasure in this moment but silently wished he could do this with his sons.

They found their seats in the upper deck almost directly behind the plate. The game was minutes from starting but the section was only about half-full. The moment they sat a voice over the loudspeakers asked the fans to stand up for the national anthem. Bill rose to his feet groaning as he extended his old knees. He removed his Red Sox ball cap, old and faded with a traditional Boston B, and placed it on his side. His white hair stuck upwards like he had just crawled out of bed.

Annie surveyed the ballpark as the winner of a statewide girl's singing competition sang the Star-Spangled Banner. She could smell the city air, a combination of urban landscapes, the Charles River and ballpark food. A handful of clouds amid a fading blue sky along with a slight, comfortable breeze made this moment one of near perfection.

The girl finished the national anthem and the stadium roared with applause.

Bill leaned forward and looked past Annie to Jon. "Glad you wore the Sox shirt, right?"

"I guess," He muttered but lifted his pant legs to reveal orange tiger faces on a navy blue backdrop on his socks. "But I still have to represent," he squeezed his thumb and forefinger almost together, "just a little bit."

There wasn't much of a game. A little excitement in the bottom of the third with two men on and a slugger who kept lobbing balls on the wrong side of the foul pole had the crowd cheering. He eventually knocked an easy pop-up to the third baseman to end the inning.

"Jon, tell me about your plans," Bill requested, "when you get back to Michigan."

"Job search."

"I don't envy your generation. Have all the gadgets you want, I'll take our job market."

"You had a pretty good run," Annie said.

"I did. My business hardly suffered the whole time I managed. I took early retirement. They insisted, I didn't complain."

Jon asked, "When did you retire?"

"About six years ago. The quality of my work suffered greatly after the death of my wife."

"I'm sorry."

Bill waved it off. "Nothing to apologize for."

"Did any of your children move back home?" Annie asked.

"After my wife died?"

"No, after . . . at all."

Bill shook his head. "Chrissy stayed home until she decided to move out to California, the other two ran off on their adventures. It wasn't like it is now; children moving back home. It was unheard of and if it was heard of it was very special circumstances. A young widow, a parent that needed taking care of or a dumb kid who got into too much trouble, things like that."

"Well, we're the boomerang children," Annie started. "We throw ourselves out onto the world only to return back to where we started." She stopped speaking for a moment lost in thought. "Maybe there's some solace in knowing that I'm not the only one. Maybe I can find hope in seeing others' plans going awry and then succeeding."

"Yeah," Bill placed his hand onto Annie's arm, comforting her, respecting her vulnerability. "That's the funny thing about a boomerang. It doesn't get thrown just once."

There was a loud cheer as the Boston right fielder knocked a base hit into right field to start the inning.

Bill sipped his beer and, keeping his eyes on the game, he addressed Annie and Jon. "I'm coming with you. I'm going to fly out of Detroit Metro into Minneapolis to see Chrissy." He turned his head and saw the two looking back at him. "If you don't mind, I would like to join you on your road trip back to Michigan."

"That would be awesome!" Jon said excitedly. He looked at Annie for confirmation that she wouldn't mind the additional passenger and saw his answer in the bright, beautiful smile on her face.

They sang *Sweet Caroline* in the middle of the seventh as Bill stayed seated shaking his head reminiscing of the days when a baseball game was just a baseball game with a quick seventh inning stretch rendition of *Take Me Out to the Ball Game*.

At the end, the Boston Red Sox edged past the Detroit Tigers with an 8-7 win.

27

Bethany looked at Annie pathetically. They were trapped in a trendy, over-priced martini bar thanks to a high school friend of Bethany's who insisted they meet up at this establishment. It was very dark with a combination of intimate couches and ottomans around a dance floor. The music played too loudly and the boys eyed the girls with an arrogant confidence. Bethany's friend was fairly drunk upon arrival and her provocative and aggressive dancing with two other friends was nothing short of a mating call. She was recently single and was desperate for a rebound.

"I'm going to miss you," Bethany shouted to Annie. "I won't be able to deal with this when you're gone."

"Why did you agree to this?" Annie asked.

"I haven't seen her in three years and we live four miles from one another. I thought she would want to have some sort of conversation."

Annie chewed on the mini-sword that accompanied her raspberry martini and looked out onto the dance floor. "I'm too old to be here."

"What are you talking about? There are plenty of men here that are your age and older."

"And they're seeking out a twenty-two-year-old, not a thirty-year-old."

"Whatever. They're all eye-fucking you."

Annie shrugged off the comment as if their glances were irrelevant. It could've been a defense mechanism from being with Andre and only wanting to be with him, a past habit that she couldn't break; or she didn't recognize her own beauty because she couldn't see past the things she found wrong on the inside.

Annie looked towards the bar. She saw a familiar face that took a moment to register. It just so happened that the man turned his head and spotted Annie.

She looked away. "Shit," she mouthed.

Bethany looked towards the bar, then back at Annie. "What?"

"Remember the guy I met? The guy at the liquor store."

"Yeah!"

"He's over there."

"Go talk to him!"

"And say what? Say that I'm leaving town in a week, sorry I didn't call you back."

"You called him back."

"I had intent. I didn't have the right numbers."

"What do you have to lose? Have some fun before saying goodbye to this place."

Annie looked at Bethany then back at Randy. She liked the idea of a final casual encounter. It had been way too long and who knew what prospects lay in Grand Rapids. "Okay." She gulped down the rest of her raspberry martini and stood up.

"Go get him, Annie! Woo!" Bethany shouted slapping her hand across Annie's ass.

She only spent a few minutes talking with Randy until his girlfriend quickly approached from the restroom. When Annie returned to Bethany she was met with a sympathetic gaze. "They met a couple days after we met at the liquor store. Boston is against me," she said defeated. "He didn't hear from me so he went for it." She missed the opportunity to get a job with Aldo's friend and now this opportunity to meet a potential good guy had disintegrated.

"I hate to say it but maybe it's meant to be," Bethany responded. "Wanna get out of here and get drunk at some place we can afford?"

"Do I ever!"

On the other side of midnight, Annie returned to the apartment drunk and interested in only in falling onto the couch. If it was folded out into a bed then she figured it a bonus.

Upon exiting the elevator she strolled down the hall barefoot, her shoes in one hand and her small purse nestled under her arm. She stopped in front of Andre's apartment. She stared at the door. She imagined herself putting the key in the lock and stepping inside. She saw the living room, the kitchen, the bedroom, the bathroom.

She could distinctly remember the closet and her clothes hanging loosely off of the hangers, a mix of blues and greens, blacks and reds; casual wear that Andre rejected and now sat in boxes in the apartment across the hall. She wondered how similar the apartment looked now and contemplated momentarily if Andre actually still lived there.

She pictured his charming smile and his body when he had his shirt off. She saw him sitting on the couch watching a Pats game and hollering comments at the television obnoxiously.

She found him grotesque and beautiful at the same time. She missed and loathed him. He was like the family member that you couldn't stand, the one that kept causing you personal trouble, yet you couldn't turn your back on.

She was alone in the hallway and it felt like the times they would be out at a bar or club with his friends, she was always just outside the crowd of people. Excluded from the conversations, she was overwhelmed with boredom and lack of self-worth.

What was Raj and Jessica up to? She asked herself. Were they engaged? Or married? Or broken up?

"Party planning? Really?" Andre mocked her ambitions almost from the first day they met. He did a great job of keeping her down, keeping her dependent of him, keeping her Andre's girlfriend.

She turned her back on the door and went into Jon's apartment.

She heard labored breathing and the occasional snore from the bedroom. She took off her dress, fumbling with it over her head and stumbling around in the living room. Her black dress dropped to the floor and she snapped off her bra and let it fall as well. She went to one of the boxes that held her nighttime clothes and pulled out a pair of shorts and a t-shirt. They felt comfortable against her skin

Annie rested her body upon the couch and put her hands behind her head. Staring at the ceiling she thought about the future. She thought of a new life in an old place.

"You didn't beat me," she muttered.

She was done with this city and the man that brought her here.

28

Her phone buzzed inside her purse. She groaned and slowly opened her eyes to see the light of day burning through the windows. She thanked God she had the day off. The phone continued buzzing as she dug through her purse.

She answered the phone groggily. "Hey, Noah."

"Did I wake you?"

"The vibrating phone woke me. So, indirectly I think you did." She was happy to be witty upon waking up and suffering from a minor bout of dehydration. Her tongue sucked against her lips dryly and she stood up to get a drink of water.

"Want me to let you go back to sleep?"

Annie looked at the clock on the stove and was shocked to see it was ten o'clock. "No, I should be up now anyway. What can I do for you?"

"I haven't called mom and dad . . ."

"I know, I would've heard something from them."

". . . I was going to today. I, um . . ."

Annie gulped down an entire glass of water and refilled it under the faucet. "You want some words of wisdom?"

"Something like that."

"I don't have any. It's going to be quite a shock for both of us coming home at the same time."

"I'd wait longer, I just can't."

"Noah, when it all comes down to it our parents want us safe and happy. I'm sure they worry about you every single day."

"I doubt that." He jumped in.

"I don't," she shot back sure of her self. "Why would you even think otherwise?"

He responded, "Because I think they just feel that way about you. You're the good one. I'm the burden."

It was years of calls home from the principal's office or rebellious teenage years that caused Noah to feel that his bad behavior reciprocated into animosity. He didn't quite know how to turn it off and sometimes the offer of advice from a parent felt like nagging orders.

Annie answered, "I am the good one but that doesn't mean they don't feel that way about you." Annie had a feeling she was going to regret the question she was about to ask. She even bit her lip in an attempt to hold back as long as possible but it finally escaped past her lips. "Do you need any money? Do you need any help getting back?"

There was silence and the longer the silence hung in the air the more she felt she just dug her own grave. He declined the offer and she felt a big sigh of relief.

Annie informed her brother of her impending departure with Jon and Bill. She hoped that by relaying the happenings of their lives it would make Noah feel better about his position. Noah held his cards close to the vest; he wasn't interested in revealing in-depth details of his own life. Curiosity was gaining steam but Annie felt that by pressing she would only start to push him back away.

Their call was short, just ten minutes, but she hoped her words provided Noah with the courage he needed.

Annie went into the bathroom. Upon exiting she felt an inkling of guilt having Jon in the bedroom for such a long time. Was it polite to knock on the door or would he have easily heard her and come out to start his day?

Respecting his privacy, she chose to sit on the couch with a yogurt and start recovering from the martinis she ingested the night before. Reruns of *Step by Step* played in the background offered her solace.

Annie pulled out her laptop and started sifting through her social networks and email. She got caught up in a story about a celebrity marriage dissolving due to infidelity.

At eleven she heard the front door unlock and twisted around as her heart nearly stopped.

Jon entered fully dressed with a *Finagle A Bagel* bag in hand. "Hey! Look who's awake. You were knocked out cold when I left this morning. I almost drew a mustache on your face." Jon waved the bag towards Annie.

"What kind of bagel is it?"

"Cinnamon Raisin."

"Classic! I'll take it. Thank you very much."

Jon tossed Annie the bag and took a seat on the couch as Annie started taking chunks of the bagel, mashing it into the little cup of cream cheese and eating it.

"A week from Monday is when the truck is going to be here. We can break everything down next weekend except the couch, which won't really be broken down, and you can sleep there and I'll sleep on a mattress."

"Okay."

"Do you know anyone who would like to help us move?"

"No one ever likes helping anyone move."

"I know. Anyone nice enough to give us part of their morning?"

"Bethany?"

"Anyone who won't complain the whole time and actually carry boxes down?"

"Andre?" She jested then turned the subject. "How's Jonie doing?"

"Good. She officially started her new job making entry-level money and being overwhelmed with work. I think she's glad she rejected the Pittsburgh offer though. It may have been a thousand dollars more a year but that's really only fifty-cents more per hour of work."

"Well you're close to family and familiar settings."

"Yeah, plus she knows how to navigate the snows in Detroit."

Annie chewed on another bit of the bagel. "Can't let snow control your life and you can't live your life based on fear." She swallowed the piece.

"We'll be gone in a week," Jon stated almost in disbelief.

Annie felt a great sadness. She caught herself staring towards the window. Jon noticed it too and saw a tear roll down her cheek.

"Are you okay?" His voice was low and soothing.

She nodded. "It's real now."

"No, it's real a week from Monday."

"I invested so much time in someone that I felt that I had to continue pouring time in hopes to get the return I wanted. I shouldn't be here now, I shouldn't have been here two years ago but I was too far in to walk away. I was afraid of being old and alone and I kept digging myself into that hole. I was afraid of trying to make it on my own two years ago and now, I'm going back to my parents, and I'm starting over."

"A wise person told me just a few minutes ago that you can't live your life based on fear. I, for one, am glad that you made the decisions you did. I have a new friend. I have three new friends because of you. You made the rest of my time here better and less lonely and helped me keep my sanity. You were the right friend at the right time. And now I get to drive to Detroit with you and Bill. I can't imagine a better way to leave then to leave that way. We're closing the chapter, not the book."

"Hi mom." Annie stepped out of the cool coffee shop into the heat of the early summer. The truly warm air of summer had finally arrived.

"So, you heard from Noah, eh?" She played along but there was no fooling her mother.

"Yes, apparently he wants to come home." Her mother's words were chosen carefully as an attempt to get Annie to provide information. Annie sensed that her mother's knowledge on Noah was minimal. "Have you spoken with him?"

"As a matter of fact I had."

"And you didn't tell me?"

"He asked me not to tell." There was silence on the other end. "I'm not going to compromise his trust in me; it didn't seem like the best move since I haven't talked to him in almost two years."

Her mother's sigh was loud and deliberate. Annie waited for a response. "It hurts when your own son can't confide in his mother."

"I understand." Annie decided to press on what her mother and her brother discussed. "What did you two talk about?"

"Well, he didn't say much. He asked me if it was okay to come home and that he would fill us in from that point. I asked if he needed any money to get home and he said no which I think might be a good sign. He was very short and didn't tell me much."

"I think he was testing the water."

"What water? What does he think I'm going to say or do? Did he think I wouldn't love him even after he refused to talk to us?" Annie could hear the trouble in her mother's voice. The extra breath and the hard swallow that followed every sentence like she was fighting an overwhelming emotional outburst that would be fully released at the end of this call hadn't been stifled as much as her mother had hoped it could be. Annie knew it would be a short call. "For the last two years all I've known about him were the emails he occasionally sent about his adventures in lord-knows-where and it was all a lie!" Big sniffle. "Now that I know he wants to come home, I just want him to come home." She was on the brink of crying when she said, "I just want to hug my son again."

Annie had nearly lost it at that point. She felt the lump in her throat slide up and down as she heard the pain in her mother's voice.

"I need to go, Annie. I'll talk to you later."

Before Annie's mother could release the call Annie stopped her. "Mom?"

"Yes?"

"I love you."

"I love you too, sweetheart."

The call ended. Annie gathered her composure with a big breath of air and stepped back into the living room.

29

Annie left Aldo's Restaurant.

She couldn't believe that she would never walk back into an establishment she had spent so much of her past five years in.

Aldo had hugged her tightly like she was one of his children heading off to college. He fought tears and said that it was a pleasure to have had her in his life.

"You are too good for this place." He pointed his forefinger right at Annie as he stood within her personal space. "Don't you ever sell yourself short and don't you ever end up in a place like this again."

They hugged one last time. "I love this place," she told him.

Annie crossed her arms, hugging herself as she turned around in the empty street to take one last look at Aldo's Restaurant. A part of her wanted to run back in and shout that she had just been kidding and force Aldo to put her name back on the schedule. She liked working there and she would miss it.

Annie turned back around and walked away fighting the tears that wanted to roll down her cheek.

Annie opened the door to the apartment and stepped in noticing how vacant and empty the room looked. Boxes were placed on the side filled with everything that had been stored in the kitchen. The counters were empty, the table that was supposed to be used for dinner had its legs removed and sat idly against the wall as did the coffee table that had once sat next to the couch.

She heard talking from the bedroom and slowly made her way down the hallway. As she approached she could tell by the frustration in his voice that he was talking to his parents. "Yes, mom . . . Fine, I'll go the extra one-hundred miles for your comfort . . . they don't extort people in Canada . . ." He sighed loudly. "Okay, I'll see you in a couple days."

Jon ended the call and dropped his hands to his side.

"Hundred miles?" Annie inquired.

"My mom doesn't want us driving through Canada because . . . I don't know. So, whatever it's like an extra hundred-plus miles more but only an extra hour. Not worth the fight, right? Considering they're the ones fronting this little excursion."

"Nope," Annie replied.

Jon closed up one of the boxes maneuvering the flaps of the top so its contents wouldn't spill out. "I figure we can probably get in ten hours of driving the first day, maybe that will get us six-hundred miles, and then do the final two on the next day."

"Why did I think it would take more than two days?"

"Well, my primary concern is that I'm traveling with a woman and a senior citizen. I don't want to make any judgments but, stereotypically speaking, both demographics aren't exactly known for the ability to want to hold their bladders."

"I'll attest to that from a woman's point-of-view."

"Why do women have to pee so much more than men?" Jon asked.

"The mysteries of the female anatomy are a wondrous, confusing thing." She looked at the boxes on the floor. "Need any help?"

"I need a break." Jon walked from the bedroom towards the kitchen. He swung open the refrigerator door and peered inside in hopes of finding a cold beverage, any cold beverage. There was one Diet Coke remaining and a microbrew. He grabbed the beer thinking that he was doing Annie a favor if she were thirsty. He cracked open the bottle and took a drink holding the refrigerator door ajar. Jon pointed to the Diet Coke. "Want it?"

Annie declined and grabbed a plastic cup for water. Jon wished he had taken the soda instead. He took a sip from the beer and placed it on the counter.

"Last night. What are we going to do?" Annie asked.

"Red Sox game? What's Bethany up to?"

"Do you care this much about baseball in Detroit?"

"Not really. But there is a certain kind of energy here about the game," Jon defended.

"I have no problems heading down to the park and watching one last game," Annie began, "Bethany wanted to do something tonight."

"Bethany can join us. Text her."

"It's our last night," Annie stated with a smile nodding her head. "Let's go watch the Red Sox."

"One more!" Bethany slurred holding up her finger then pointing to her near-empty glass.

"Okay, Bethany, let's take it easy."

"My best buddies are leaving tomorrow," she said sadly to Jon and Annie. "What am I supposed to do? Life is going to suuuuuuuuck!"

"You'll survive," Jon replied. "I have faith." His eyes gravitated towards the screen above the bar as the pitcher threw a ball just above the outside corner of the strike zone.

"I'm telling you, Michigan is the happening place. You outta come," Annie said.

"Where's my drink?"

Jon took the now empty glass away from Bethany. "You ordered fifteen seconds ago. Maybe it should be your last."

"No." She pouted.

"It's the middle of the sixth," Annie told Bethany. "If you keep this up you'll be vomiting all over the bathroom floor by the top of the eighth and who knows what's on that bathroom floor after eight innings of Red Sox baseball."

"I don't wanna throw up," Bethany replied with a worried gesture placing her hands on Annie's arms.

"It's okay," Annie replied in a comforting motherly tone. "Let's get you some water when the waitress returns."

"Water's gonna make me throw up!" Bethany looked away and noticed a gentleman leaning against the bar talking with some of his buddies. All kept an eye on the screens while maintaining conversations. "He's cute."

Annie turned and saw the group of guys.

"Which one?"

"The tall one."

Annie looked back and saw a man with his ball cap hanging low over his face. A sobered Bethany might notice the large spare tire around his waist or the scrunched up nose or the puffy red cheeks. Annie could almost make out a string of acne on the side of his face. His eyes would bulge outwards every few moments as he nodded with the conversation amongst his friends. His collared shirt was too tight and too small, a hint of his belly appeared at the base of fabric.

Annie looked back at Bethany. "The tall one with the hat tilted downwards?"

"Mmhmm," she said seductively.

Jon finally took notice; an eyebrow rose with curiosity and he wanted to confirm this with Annie.

"You're cut off," Annie ordered.

"Noooo."

"Trust me, sweetie, you're hammered beyond reasoning."

"Hi," Bethany mouthed and waved to the man at the bar.

"Jon. Do something!" Annie pleaded.

"Those guys look like douche bags, Bethany." Jon pointed his thumbs upwards. "Raise your expectations, that whole group of guys are off limits."

The drink arrived at the table and Bethany grabbed it sipping a healthy amount through the straw.

"Waters!" Annie told the waitress and she responded affirmatively and walked away.

"I think I should go talk to him."

Jon sarcastically commented, "Nothing like a single girl walking up to a group of guys to get a good night going. I'm all for it."

"Yeah!" Bethany lifted a fist in the air.

"No!" Annie grabbed Bethany's hand and shoved it downwards. "Jon, I swear, I'm going to stab you if you don't do something."

"Empty threats," Jon muttered. "Plus this is too good to not see through."

Jon saw the desperate, defeated look in Annie's face and he decided to stop joking around, at least for the moment.

"Bethany, forget about that guy."

"No. You two are mean."

"We're mean because we love you," Annie confessed.

The waitress returned with the waters placing them down on the table and immediately headed off.

"Drink this, now!" Annie ordered and switched her alcoholic drink with the water. Bethany playfully pouted and started to suck up the water. She took big gulps and Jon knew that she was moments away from the hiccups.

"Maybe we should go," Jon said to Annie like a parent not wanting to alert their child of their plan.

The voice and the overwhelming man stepped in out of nowhere. "Hello." He smiled at Bethany and made no eye contact towards Jon or Annie.

"Hi," she bubbly responded.

"What's your name?"

"Bethany."

He held out his hand and Bethany shook it. "Ralph."

"Ralph?" Bethany responded taken aback by the name. It was uncommon and she responded with a snorted chuckle from her throat.

He smiled like a smug salesman trying to remain calm amid a dispute between a bickering couple in his office. "Ralph is my name." He placed his beer bottle on the table and leaned in. A toothpick was locked between his teeth.

Bethany's uncertainty seemed to wash away. "Well have a seat, Ralph."

"Hello there," Jon said and held out his hand. Ralph's hand was slimy as if they constantly oozed perspiration. Ralph remained leaning over the table, his hulking body resting against his arms that he kept crossed and situated in front of him. The lighting from above beamed down on his baseball cap and caused a harsh shadow to cut across his face.

"So, Bethany, the Red Sox are playing Seattle but with you being here I would have to believe there are Angels in town."

She giggled.

Jon looked away and his eyes bugged wide trying to comprehend what was going on. He stood up and moved to Annie who was all but ignored thus far. He whispered into his ear, "You okay if I go to the bathroom?"

"Please don't leave us," she responded half-joking, half-serious.

"I'll be back. I promise. Just concentrate on the game."

As Jon started to walk away he felt Annie's hand clutch onto his arm. He turned back around and was met with a big kiss from Annie. He was in shock and stood still as he felt the warmth of Annie's lips against his. Her free hand moved up to his neck and, when she released her lip-lock, she moved her cheek close to Jon's and they both whispered to one another centimeters from each other's ears.

"Hopefully that kept his goons from thinking I'm available. Hurry. The fuck. Back."

"Okay."

"Do you actually kiss like that?" Annie asked.

"No."

"That was a really horrible kiss."

"It was awkward."

"Very. Go to the bathroom."

"Thank you."

He took off towards the men's room desperately hoping he wouldn't have to save both Bethany and Annie from a group of drunk boys reliving their frat days when he returned.

Fortunately, upon returning, there were still just Ralph, Bethany and Annie at the table. Ralph awkwardly nestled his cheek on his fist and was facing Bethany, almost posed, as he flirted.

Jon shuffled his chair closer to Annie so they could discuss the play-by-play of the scene playing out in front of them.

"I have a plan," Jon started but his attention was taken away by a ball that was edging close to the outfield wall. It seemed to sail in slow motion and the bar erupted in chants of "Go! Go!" and it did. The place blew up in a flurry of cheers and hollers as the Red Sox knocked in a two-run homer to even things up. Annie and Jon had their eyes on the game as did Ralph and Bethany. The next batter up hit a single into left field which kept the momentum of cheers going. Seattle decided to change pitchers and Jon advised Annie of his plan. "Okay, all we have to do is say it's our last night in town, get this guy's number for Bethany and then we leave and just toss it out somewhere on Beacon Street."

"I like your plan."

"There's one fallacy to this plan. It's the sixth, it's tied and we could have to suffer through this display for another hour."

"That's quite the kerfuffle. Time is our enemy." Annie and Jon looked at their friend who seemed to soak up every cheesy line that Ralph was spewing. When the waitress came around he ordered a Crown Royal and Coca-Cola.

"If I ordered nachos would you eat them?" He pointed to Annie and Jon.

"Sure," Jon replied then received an elbow in the ribs by Annie. "Or, maybe. No?"

"We're good," Annie said.

He ordered nonetheless.

"Ralph?" Annie said and the man turned to face her.

"Yes, sweetheart."

"This is Jon's and my last night in town and we were hoping to spend it with our dear friend here."

"Well, you are, aren't you?" Ralph looked back at Bethany. "Bethany, my dear, are you not spending time with your friends?"

"I am . . . am not?" She wasn't sure how to answer the question appropriately so she replied with a full answer. "I am spending time with my friends." She reached across the table and grabbed Annie's hand. "My Annie is leaving town. It's so sad." She released her grip and Ralph took her hand jumping at the opportunity for physical contact.

"Bethany, we all face these hardships but I am here to comfort you through this tough time." He tried his best at sincerity but his eyes gravitated towards the screen as the relief pitcher took his first throw into the strike zone of the Red Sox second baseman.

"Aw, thank you."

Annie was upset that she felt insulted that Ralph didn't even inquire on where she and Jon were moving to. She imagined his reaction would've been unpleasant and uncaring. Just the thought made this man crawl under her skin more.

The inning was played out with no additional runs as Ralph continued to butter Bethany up more. Sweat marks were beginning to show on the armpits of his shirt but Bethany didn't seem to notice. When the nachos arrived, he started stuffing one after another into his mouth. He continued talking though, and occasionally spitting out a piece of the chewed chip forward.

"Does she not see this?" Annie asked as the bottom of the seventh turned into the top of the eighth.

"She smells of desperation and he's playing her like a Julliard-trained cellist."

Annie continued to watch trying to take her mind away from the man sleazing his way towards her friend who opted to buy her yet another drink. Bethany's speech was slurring more and her head kept bobbing.

When the waitress came back around Annie asked for the check emphasizing that anything Ralph had ordered shouldn't be on their bill.

"Oh shit!" Jon gasped when he saw the bill and how much Bethany had drank in combination with their orders. "This is almost a hundred bucks!" He saw all three of their drinks listed under the dinner they consumed in the first few innings.

"Let's just pay it and get the out of here."

They split the bill in half and Annie jumped into the middle of the conversation between Bethany and Ralph.

"Ralph, we have to get going."

"No, it's the bottom of the eighth and it's tied!" Bethany responded like a child whose toy was being taken away.

"No, we really must." Annie stared threateningly into Bethany's eyes. "Bethany, come on."

Ralph replied in a tone of self-assurance knowing that he should get a return on his time-investment. "Oh, that's not fair."

Annie had little trust for this man who kept eyeing his friends for confirmation that this was a sure thing and to leave him be. He was a former frat boy that grew out of the look years ago but kept his confidence in spite of his ill-fitting clothes.

Annie looked at Ralph, "Let's program your number in her phone. She'll call you, I promise."

"Look, sweetheart, how about you go leave town and let her stay out and have some fun. I can show her a good time 'cause I'll be here tomorrow and you won't be."

Annie took a good long look at Bethany who was watching this play out uncertain of whether she wanted to go with her friends or stay with Ralph. He seemed to be the first guy in a while to pay attention to her and the amount of alcohol ingested didn't make her realize was the kind of jerk that she always seemed to gravitate towards.

With no more patience left in her body, Annie replied, "Thanks for your time here, Ralph. Go fuck yourself."

He leaned in close to her and eyeballed Jon. "You gonna say anything, little man?"

"I'm a little man. If I jump into this then I have your fat ass and five of your dickhead friends kicking my skinny ass. I'm fine with her showing how small of a person you really are."

"Pussy," he snarled back.

"Good one," Jon replied with thick sarcasm.

"Let's go." Bethany finally said shyly.

"What?" Ralph turned towards her. "After the drinks I bought you?"

"You didn't buy her anything! We just paid the bill and all her drinks were on it." Annie shouted taking hold of Bethany's hand and looked directly into Ralph's eyes. "It's been a pleasure."

"I'm going to hang out with my friends," she responded as if her inebriation had worn off and she saw the scumbag for who he really was.

They walked towards the door leaving Ralph alone at the table, humiliated.

Jon, Bethany and Annie stepped outside the bar and stood close to the bouncer. A massive brick house of a man checking driver's licenses at the door. Bethany was leaning against Jon mumbling incoherently.

"Great evening, I would say," Jon said sucking in the night air.

"Should we get in a cab?" Annie asked.

"Oh yeah, she would barely make it across the street."

They waved an eager taxi driver looking for a fare over to the curb. Ralph and a couple of his buds stepped outside as Jon and Bethany entered the cab.

"Hey!" Ralph yelled pointing to Bethany.

Annie looked at the bouncer then at Ralph. "Stay away. I don't want you groping me again, you pig!"

The bouncer looked at the men. Ralph plastered on a smile and chuckled as if it were a joke.

Annie smirked and entered the cab.

"Is she going to throw up?" The taxi driver asked.

"I hope not," Annie said looking over to Bethany who was resting her head on Jon's shoulder.

The driver slammed on the gas weaving into traffic and responded. "You and me both."

Bethany looked directly at Annie. She understood the predicament she got them all in. "You guys are the best."

*   *   *

Bethany was in a fit of tears by the time they arrived at the apartment. She apologized insistently about the mess she made of their last evening together. Jon and Annie told her not to worry about it.

"Wow, you have a lot of boxes!" Bethany remarked when they entered. "It's still light out, let's do something."

"No!" Both replied and led her to the couch. She plopped down, her feet wide apart and her knees touching. She placed her elbows on her legs and tilted her head into her hands. She took in a huge breath of air and faintly stated, "The room is spinning. I think."

Jon opened the refrigerator and took the final item out: the Diet Coke. He snapped the tab and put the can to his lips. He saw Annie staring at him with a look telling him to freeze where he's at. She tilted her head towards Bethany.

No, Jon mouthed and took a sip.

Annie offered a stern scowl that would scare any man into doing what she asked.

He sighed and slowly walked towards Bethany. "We're not dating, I don't have to do what you say," he said towards Annie. Standing above Bethany he took one last spiteful sip then held it downward. "Here," he said to his highly intoxicated friend.

"Oh, thanks." Bethany grabbed the can and tilted her head back drinking every last bit. It was her water after spending days in a desert. "I'm so worried that things aren't going to turn out like I want them to, you know? You ever feel that way?" She was thinking aloud as if she was in therapy. "Here I wanted freedom and I feel like I ended up in jail with the devil as the warden." Bethany leaned back on the couch and belted a loud sigh. "I don't want to be a waitress at thirty."

All Annie could do was listen and understand. She wasn't a role model, in fact, she was the person that Bethany should be afraid of becoming.

"Uh oh." Bethany belched, it wasn't dry, in fact, it gurgled outward and she put her hand in front of her mouth. "Oh shit." Bethany lifted off the couch and raced for the bathroom. Seconds later Jon and Annie heard the delightful sounds of regurgitation in a toilet bowl. They winced as the toilet flushed.

"I'm so glad my drink was put to such good use."

"I didn't think she would slam it."

There was another round of vomiting and the toilet flushed again.

"I don't think I got it anywhere!" Bethany yelled.

Jon replied to Annie, "Good, I didn't want to re-clean the bathroom."

Annie couldn't help but smile and laugh at the situation.

"Don't laugh," Jon said trying to hold back on the infectious laughter.

"Ew, it's in my hair!" Bethany screamed.

Jon was entertained by the turn of events. He sided up to Annie and wrapped his arm around her and brought her close to his side.

"Are you okay?" He asked regarding Bethany's remark.

"Yeah. For a moment in my life I was the person she was afraid of becoming. I'm not that person anymore."

30

The buzzer sounded.

Annie's eyes opened slowly. Adjusting to the light she squinted as she lifted herself up from the couch with a groan. She had a light headache. Her mouth was dry and she could taste the icky bile between her teeth increasing her desire to desperately gargle mouthwash.

The buzzer sounded again proving that it was not a dream.

Jon hopped out of the bedroom and raced to the door. He pressed the open button on the buzzer display.

"We should have been awake an hour ago. That's probably Bill."

"Or a serial killer."

"I have to get the truck. And I have to pee."

Jon rushed back to the bathroom door. Swinging it open he saw Bethany lying on the floor with no evidence that she puked again. Her head was resting uncomfortably against the bathtub porcelain.

"Bethany," he whispered hoping she would stir awake. "Bethany!" Only a slight movement as she hugged her arms around her body tighter.

Jon grabbed her arms and dragged her out of the bathroom laying her down in the hall.

"Classy move," Annie commented.

"I'll drag her back in when I'm done." Jon closed the door and began peeing.

A knock at the door signaled Bill's arrival. Annie opened it up.

"Good morning!" Bill shouted. He leaned in and whispered to Annie. "I almost knocked on the other door."

Annie backed away putting her hand over her mouth to avoid the odor from going further than her palm.

"Good morning, Bill. I'm glad you didn't."

Bill entered wearing a loose fitting ball cap as if it was a fashion statement by the elderly. His sunglasses hung over his chest strapped to a lanyard. He wheeled in a small suitcase.

"I didn't see a moving truck down there." Bill looked down the hall spotting Bethany. "You kids must have had quite a going away party. We're running late, aren't we?"

Jon exited the bathroom and grabbed Bethany's hands. "Hey Bill," he said bent over Bethany.

"Don't do that!" Annie shouted.

"I was going to put her back where I found her."

Annie walked past both Jon and Bethany and entered the bathroom. "Just leave her there."

Jon approached Bill. "Good morning, we're running late."

"I figured."

They both watched Bethany groan and turn on her side nestling her body into a fetal position.

Bill asked facetiously, "Do you have a pen? I think it would be fun to draw something on her face."

"I think that would be fun too."

Neither one had the will to go through with the comedic gesture.

Within two hours the apartment was vacant. Everything was settled in the back of a moving truck ready to head west. Jon, Annie, Bill and Bethany stood near the door. Bethany was wearing a fresh shirt provided by Annie and sunglasses. Her hair was pulled tightly back hiding its dishevelment. She was fighting an angry hangover that she wouldn't shake until late in the evening and a neck strain from laying on the bathroom floor all night.

"So long, apartment," Jon said, his voice echoed off the walls and the floor.

Bill was the first to leave followed by Bethany.

"Thanks for letting me stay here."

Jon put an arm around Annie and she wrapped her arm around his waist. They leaned in close sharing a sideways hug.

"My pleasure."

They stepped out of the apartment. Jon locked the door behind them and started down the hallway. The elevator doors opened and Bill and Bethany entered.

Jon continued towards the elevator but Annie stopped in front of Andre's apartment door. She sighed once again.

All three looked back at her in silence.

"Goodbye, Andre," she whispered. It was her final farewell.

Bethany popped up along side her, moved forward and knocked on the door.

"Come on!" Bethany grabbed Annie's hand and they ran to the elevator in a fit of giggles.

Bill let the doors start to close but, with a smile, pressed the 'open door' button at the last moment. They all stood in the elevator staring anxiously down the hall.

The doors weren't closing.

Each second felt like a lifetime as Annie shifted her eyes from the elevator panel towards Andre's apartment.

"Close," she whispered, praying.

"This isn't good," Jon responded.

Bill pressed the 'close door' button with no luck.

They heard the unlocking of the door down the hallway and all four people in the elevator held their breath. The elevator doors slid closed and all breathed a collective sigh of relief.

Andre opened his apartment door and popped his head out. He looked both ways down the hallway and saw no evidence that anyone was there. He shrugged it off and closed the door.

"I don't wanna cry. I don't wanna cry. I don't wanna cry," Bethany said however with each sentence the urge was becoming too great. "I'm going to cry." She sniffled and reached into her purse for a tissue.

"Damn it," Annie replied, her lip starting to quiver. "Now, I'm going to cry." Bethany and Annie wrapped their arms around each other and hugged while tears flowed down their cheek.

Bill and Jon looked at one another content at their ability to suppress their emotions during these occasions. Bill lifted his wrist to view the time.

When Bethany released her embrace she went right for Jon. He hugged her not as tightly as Annie had.

"You'll be fine."

"Bye." Bill waved hoping that he didn't need a long, drawn-out hug.

"Well I'll still see you at the restaurant. Have a good time though."

"I intend to." Bill walked to the passenger side of the truck and lifted himself inside.

"I'm going to miss you." Annie looked at Bethany saddened to leave one of her best friends behind. She would have liked her to come along but that simply wasn't an option. Instead, she could only hope to remain long distance friends.

"We'll see each other." Bethany assured her.

"We will."

They hugged one last time and Annie wiped her eyes as she stepped up into the cab of the truck.

Jon placed the keys in the ignition and started it up. The engine roared to life and they felt the vibrations under the seat.

Sitting three across in the rental truck Jon checked his mirror then tapped the horn twice. "Here we go."

Annie was astounded by how quickly the urban landscape could turn into miles and miles of rural country. They drove on the freeways through small suburban cities and wide open country.

The radio played top forty and Bill had the luxury of being able to tilt his head forward, cross his arms and doze off for an hour at a time. There wasn't much discussion and the time dragged on, boring.

"Did you drive out here?" Annie asked Jon.

Jon shook his head. "Flew. I spent two nights in a hotel and signed the lease on the third day. Then bought a bed and from there . . ." He looked across the cab to Annie. "What's the longest road trip you've ever been on?"

"My parents took us to one of my dad's cousin's cabins in Houghton. It was nine hours not including stops."

"With stops?"

"Eleven-and-a-half."

"Jeez."

"No one was thrilled to come home either. We convinced my father to stop for the night on the way back. I told him to use my allowance money to pay for the hotel."

Bill's head shot upwards and his eyes popped open. "I have to pee," he announced.

"On a scale of one-to-ten . . ."

"Jon, I'm seventy-one, it's always a nine or a ten plus I drank a coffee before we got on the road." Bill squinted at the clock display in the center of the dash. "Two hours?"

"Just about."

Annie chimed in. "I could use a bathroom break and please bear in mind I'm a girl and not a fan of squatting over sludge in a dim-lit gas station bathroom."

"I'll keep that in mind." There was a billboard on the north side of the freeway reflecting fast food restaurants four miles ahead.

"Hey, how about there?" Bill nodded towards a second billboard. "Four miles ahead!"

"Dunkin' Donuts?" Annie said looking at the billboards. "You can take the man out of Boston but you can't take Boston out of the man, eh?"

"How about lunch?" Jon asked.

"Let's start with Dunkin' Donuts and go from there," Bill stated with finality.

They pulled off the freeway within a few minutes and were struck with a plethora of eating choices but Bill was insistent on his first choice so they pulled into the parking lot and allowed Bill to go to the bathroom inside the Dunkin' Donuts. Annie was inside and out before Bill returned and stood with Jon who was stretching his legs outside of the moving truck.

Jon grunted loudly as he bent over at the waist and tried to touch his toes. "I think we're doing okay."

"Ever wonder who lives out in this area?" Annie asked looking around and only seeing fast food restaurants and gas stations.

"Well, the town has to have a lawyer and a doctor and a school so teachers live here too." Jon pointed out to a small hill in the distance. "You could have a whole metropolis on the other side of that hill."

They turned their heads to see Bill exiting with a small paper bag in hand. He waved it in the air. "I bought a little road trip snack."

"Let me guess. Donuts?"

Bill walked right by Jon and muttered, "Asshole."

Jon grinned at the remark. "Our choices are various kinds of burgers and chicken sandwiches or tacos."

"It's all gonna slide out with a vengeance four-to-eight hours after consumption so it's all good to me," Bill commented as he stepped into the cab of the truck.

"We're getting different hotel rooms based on that information," Annie replied and hopped in.

They settled at night about fifty miles from the Pennsylvania border; about eighty miles from the Ohio border, and the next day would be an easier four-to-five hour drive.

It was a simple three story hotel with about one-hundred rooms. It was clean and ideal for the weary traveler or the parents coming to visit their son or daughter who attended college at the nearby university. There was a handful of the same fast food restaurants they were accustomed to stopping at throughout they day lining the road.

"I just want a salad," Annie said grabbing her stomach and thinking what another greasy burger and fries might do to possibly upset it.

The front desk clerk, a cheery woman told the trio of an American-style restaurant a mile away.

"Is it good?"

The clerk snickered. "Good enough. I've been guilty of getting the Super Brownie Sundae on more than one occasion." She reached under the desk and pulled out a slip of paper. "And we have coupons!"

Bill, Jon and Annie headed to Charlie's All-American Restaurant which was decked out in license plates from across the country, road signs and goofy pictures of the Statue of Liberty donning sunglasses or the Mount Rushmore heads with smiling white teeth.

Annie stabbed a handful of lettuce and shoveled it into her mouth. The healthy greens made her feel better about the double cheeseburger she consumed in the middle of the afternoon.

She asked Bill, "If you could do it all over again, would you?"

"Absolutely," Bill responded without taking a minute to consider the question.

"Even knowing what you know now?"

He looked upward recalling a memory or a thought he wanted to share. "Mark Twain said something like, 'I have known a great many troubles, but most of them never happened'. How many problems do you have that don't really exist?" He took a bite out of his cheeseburger and continued. "It's a little silly to consider the alternative. Not silly, I guess, unwise."

"You don't want to consider the 'what ifs' in life?" Jon asked.

Bill shook his head. "Not anymore. You can't help but think that way sometimes but there isn't anything you can do about it and you don't know how the alternative would play out anyway. I believe we make the best decisions."

"I've made plenty of bad decisions," Jon claimed.

"Me too," Annie added.

"So have I," Bill said. "But you could have made worse. You make the best decisions you can and let fate sort out the bodies. Other decisions may not have brought us all together. You can't take things back and I'm grateful for you two for coming into my life." Bill looked directly at Annie. "Just a simple smile on a bad day or giving me the confidence to chase after the things I've lost can mean the world. I'm very happy with my life." Bill took a massive bite from his burger and, with a mouth full of food, he said, "And I'm very happy that I've gotten to share a piece of it with you two."

Annie placed a forkful of lettuce leaves in her mouth and smiled at Bill's sentimentality with a mouth stuffed with a bite of his burger.

She said, "We're destined to make decisions. We can ponder and consider until we're blue in the face but that only means that we were going to ponder and consider until we were blue in the face anyway and still make the decision we were destined to make."

"Just live life." Bill took a few fries and swirled them around in ketchup. When he looked up he eyed both Annie and Jon, studying their demeanor and the way they looked towards him but not at him. "You'll both be just fine." He reassured them.

31

"You'll be okay?"

Bill looked at his watch. "I can entertain myself for three hours."

"I'd be happy to take you to a restaurant. You can come home with me for a bit."

"No bother." Bill lifted the telescoping handle of his luggage bag and looked both ways down the drop-off area of Detroit Metropolitan Airport. It was overcast, rain was imminent. "I'd hate to kick you two out of here but a moving truck sitting outside an airport terminal . . . you're begging to get arrested."

Jon couldn't argue the observation. They started out with a strong handshake and quickly moved to a hug, patting each other on the back. When they parted Bill tapped Jon on the shoulder and turned his attention to Annie.

They smiled at one another and Annie quickly moved into his open arms. She hugged her friend tightly fighting back tears.

"I cherish our friendship," Bill whispered.

"I'm so glad I got to know you."

When they unlocked their embrace all they could do was stare at one another. He would smile thinking of her like one of his own daughters, happy to have had the relationship that he was long seeking, and having her insistence that he find a path to his own children.

Annie saw in him a man, a grandfather, who offered his wisdom and expertise and encouraged her to find out who she was, if she really wanted to. He rarely pressed.

"You let me know how it goes, okay?"

"Of course. We'll be in touch."

Bill backed up closer to the sliding glass doors but kept Annie and Jon in sight.

"Until we meet again, my friends." He offered a circular, slow-motion wave then turned around and walked into the airport.

Jon and Annie hopped into the truck and looked at one another.

"I'm going to miss him," Annie said.

"Me too."

Jon pulled into his parent's driveway and fumbled with his keys nervously as they went to the front door.

Both of his parents were awaiting his arrival and it was only seconds after shaking Annie's hand that Jon's father insisted they start unloading the truck. "We've cleared a spot in the garage for the big stuff." His voice was high-pitched yet rough, piercing to the ears and not very subtle.

"You boys have fun," Jon's mother shouted then took hold of Annie's arm. "Come on, honey, let's have a drink," she said grasping onto Annie's arm and looked out towards the street. "Oh hey." She began waving at the car that parked on the side of the road putting the passenger tire inches onto the obsessively manicured grass.

"Damn it," Jon's father muttered. He spoke to his son, "You have to tell her to not run over my lawn." He ignored his father and waved at Jonie as she exited her sedan. "Hi Jonie!"

Jonie raced up the driveway and jumped onto her boyfriend wrapping herself around his body. They hugged tightly and she slowly lowered her legs back to the ground. Their kiss was long and passionate.

She gave a polite hug to Jon's father and ran up towards Annie and Jon's mother. She hugged the mother first then provided Annie with a big embrace.

"How are you?" She asked looking Annie up and down.

"I'm doing just fine. How's the corporate life?"

"I thought it would be more exciting and more . . . creative, but . . ."

"No?"

Jonie shook her head.

Jon's mother butted in, "We're going in for some cocktails. You don't have to go back to the office, I hope."

"I brought a change of clothes. I'll be in in a second." Jonie walked back to her car as Jon and his father were lifting the door to the back of the truck.

Annie, Jon's mother and Jonie chatted over daiquiris. Jonie explained her new job in greater detail and Annie felt a sense of panic and fear when she realized how little of a plan she had created for herself. Here was Jonie, who was once struggling to find a bite in the job market just a few weeks prior, now employed fulltime with a decent benefits package. Annie felt a greater sense of hopelessness as opposed to the solace that she should have taken from the success story.

Annie enjoyed the company but her thoughts drifted home—a place where she could temporarily have her own bathroom. She chuckled at the gleeful thought that she would have access to her own private bathroom; a luxury she hadn't had for over five years.

"What are you planning once you get to Grand Rapids?"

Annie bit her bottom lip. "I'm just going to work for my dad until I find something more permanent, I suppose."

"What does he do?" Jon's mother asked.

"He runs a restaurant at the Gerald Ford Airport. The 44th Street Public House."

"Sounds lovely. Are you going to be a manager?"

"Just a server. For now."

"Oh. Well, that's cute." Jon's mother tapped Annie on the leg and stood up. "Who wants more?" She grabbed her empty glass and pointed to Jonie and Annie's still half-filled drinks.

They declined the offer.

Jonie leaned in towards Annie and whispered, "She can be tough in her own way. You're doing just fine. She's very smart and when she's drunk she's quite blatant." Jonie took a sip from her drink before continuing. "You know, I was so worried I was going to lose Jon."

"Why would you be afraid of that?"

"Because of you. I was afraid of you and when I found out he was insisting you live with him after the break up I went crazy. I screamed at him and I don't yell."

"Why did you let me?"

"I trusted him more than I feared you. Then I met you and I saw that he needed you. He needed a friend."

Annie heard the front door swing open and Jon and his father were lugging in two boxes. She turned her attention towards them.

"Hey," Jonie whispered to get Annie's attention and while remaining quiet she said, "I'm glad . . . I don't know, I guess I'm glad you made the decision that you did to come back. I think it's the best for you."

"I'm afraid coming back is not going to lead to anything."

"Annie. Stop being afraid."

32

Annie held on to Jon tightly. She didn't want to let go of her best friend.

"I'm going to miss you," Jon told her releasing his embrace. "You were the friend I needed at the time I needed one."

"With leaving Bethany, then Bill, then you and Jonie, I don't feel as if I have anyone I can confide in who knows me like you all did."

"Don't discount your family."

"I don't but I can't go drink wine out of a coffee cup in public with my dad, now can I?"

Jon smiled and they hugged once again as the bus destined for the west side of the state pulled up.

There were only six others waiting to hop on board and half the bus was filled with those picked up on previous stops.

The driver jumped down and loaded the luggage of the other passengers on board.

Annie sighed as the driver bent down to pick up her bag. "Miss, is this going under?"

"Yes. Thank you."

Jon said, "I'll ship your boxes tomorrow."

She started backing towards the bus. "Thanks."

"Goodbye, Annie."

"I've said goodbye too many times. I'm just going to say thank you."

"For what?"

"For coming into my life."

They both smiled at one another.

Annie climbed onto the bus and was fortunate to find two empty seats near the back. She took her seat placing her purse on her lap. She looked out the window and saw Jon standing outside looking back at her. His hands were shoved into his pockets and he stood confidently with a smile.

Annie waved, and he waved back.

ONE YEAR LATER

"Cheeseburger with bacon, no pickles. Fries and a Jack and Coke."

Annie turned around recognizing the familiar voice. She had to see him to believe he was there.

Bill waved from the entrance of the 44th Street Public House and walked inside pointing to an empty four-top.

"Of course!" Annie ran to him from the opposite side of the bar and placed her arms around Bill's neck.

"Thank god you're working. Do you have any idea what it took to get a layover through Gerald Ford Airport?"

He rolled his suitcase to the side of the table and tossed his carry-on bag onto an empty seat. He tossed a newspaper onto the table and took a seat.

"It's good to see you." Annie beamed.

"It's always good to see you, Annie."

Annie placed his order and brought over a Jack and Coke. At two in the afternoon on an idle summer weekday Annie was able to have a seat adjacent to her friend.

Bill explained that he was, once again, heading out to Minnesota to see his daughter and grandchildren. His sons still remained silent but Chrissy was slowly working on bringing them over to her side. He had spent Christmas with her and the children and they even spent a week in Boston enjoying the Commons and baseball games at Fenway Park.

"Boston is in town in Minneapolis," Bill said as he dug into his suitcase and pulled out a stuffed Wally the Green Monster doll. It was the Boston Red Sox mascot. "I got this for Natalie. I'm going to try to make her a Sox fan instead of a Twins fan." There was so much delight beaming from his face.

Annie encouraged him to never quit reaching out to his family.

They caught up. She told him about her brother. She explained that one month inside the house had caused him to leave once again. "He's in Chicago now. Living with a friend and trying to do something with his life there."

He told Annie that Bethany was "the same as always." Annie spoke with her occasionally and they stayed current with one another on social networking sites. Bethany was in search of a change. The problem was she didn't know where she wanted to go or what she wanted to do. ". . . but we seem to talk about that every day," Bill said.

"Jon?" Annie started when Bill inquired, "He lives with Jonie. They got an apartment together and he's working at a coffee shop."

"Still wants to be a writer?"

"He's working on it. It's a tough place to be a writer though. Jonie tosses him some freelance work every once in a while."

"And how are you?"

Annie explained that she was still living with her parents and how the more she applied to catering companies and party planning companies the more she felt the desire to work in such a field wane. "I like it here though," she defended her situation. "My dad isn't getting on my nerves; in fact, he's giving me more responsibility and he's enjoying a more time off. There's talk of him expanding to Detroit Metro Airport."

"And you would run it?"

"I think I'm at the top of the list." Annie looked around the restaurant, at the décor and atmosphere. "He says this is the legacy he can pass on to his children."

"He found his passion at . . ."

"Forty-five. Quit his job, wrote a book, and opened up a restaurant." Annie shook her head in disbelief as she thought about all her father had accomplished. It brought hope.

"It's never too late until it's too late." Bill sipped the ice-melt of his drink. "Do you like it here?"

"I do. I really do."

"Most importantly, are you happy?"

"I'm getting there."

"Are you happier than you were a year ago?"

Annie smiled.